LITHEGOL
The Prophecy

"A young Master Knight will enter the Order of Lithegol, bring forth Excalibur and take his place as the High Sentinel, thus ushering in the End of Days."

LITHEGOL

The Prophecy

Josh Oelrich

A special thanks to Jared, Preston, Beth, my early readers and Scottie for your editing, insights and help.

For Amy, Parker, Tyler and Steven.

LITHEGOL

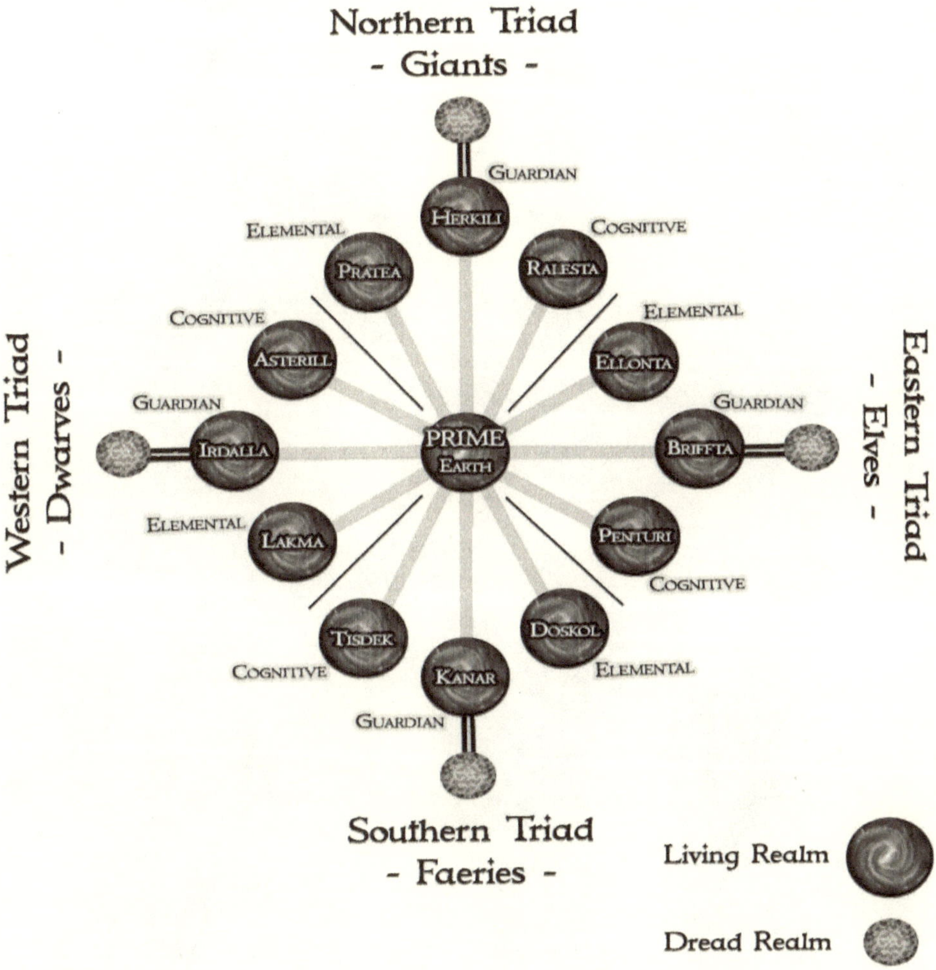

Northern Triad
- Giants -

GUARDIAN

HERKILI

ELEMENTAL

PRATEA

COGNITIVE

RALESTA

COGNITIVE

ASTERILL

ELEMENTAL

ELLONTA

Western Triad
- Dwarves -

GUARDIAN

IRDALL'A

PRIME
EARTH

GUARDIAN

BRIFFTA

Eastern Triad
- Elves -

ELEMENTAL

LAKMA

PENTURI

COGNITIVE

TISDEK

COGNITIVE

KANAR

DOSKOL

ELEMENTAL

GUARDIAN

Southern Triad
- Faeries -

Living Realm

Dread Realm

Chapter 1

The Escape

Michael Brenlan rushed through his bedroom door, slamming it behind him unintentionally from the nervous energy in his body. He thought of his situation and a combination of anger and helplessness welled up inside. He couldn't believe that his mom had told him to leave if she didn't come up to his room within five minutes. He instinctively glanced at his watch. It was 1:05. He thought about the crazy events of the day that had led up to that moment.

He had awoken thinking it was going to be just another Saturday on their Linkston, Indiana farm. Once he finished his chores, his mother had driven him to Jeff's house. Michael thought of all the good times he had had with his goofy friend and the pit in his stomach returned. He wondered if he would ever be able to play basketball, visit the hilarious rapid barking dog at Jeff's neighbor's house or hang out playing video games with him again. Since meeting him three years ago, Jeff had been part of what helped Michael feel normal and allowed him an escape from his intense training regimen at home.

On the way to Jeff's house, his mother had acted nervous and distant and had shared that they would be leaving on an extended trip that night. Then the strangeness had begun. The first unsettling event happened while he was playing Jeff's new fully immersive virtual reality game, "Epic Combat." Michael's evil sensor had gone off and he had watched through the window in horror as the United Legion soldiers dragged Jeff's neighbor, Nick and his father into their SUV.

Michael had always had this special ability to detect evil and it had been going off like crazy since the United Legion soldiers arrived. When he was three, his parents had invited some friends and acquaintances over for dinner. Michael had cried and cringed every time a certain man from the group was around him. His parents hadn't known what was going on and then a few weeks later the man had been caught and it was discovered that he was a violent criminal.

When Michael's dad arrived to pick him up from Jeff's, Michael had awkwardly said goodbye to his best friend, not knowing if he would ever see him again. On the way to his dad's old Camaro, a squawking crow with a gray patch had flown over from Nick's house and circled over his head. When Michael mentioned the crow to his dad, a look of panic had flared in his dad's stern blue eyes.

Michael wondered what his dad knew about the crows. They were obviously significant since later that day their screeching was the precursor to the most terrifying door knock Michael had ever heard. He stared out at his room, trying not to think about the decision he would have to make in five minutes if neither of his parents came. He felt an ominous chill as he thought about what may keep them from coming. He remembered the paper his mom had mentioned and stumbled forward, his gaze falling on the Imagine Dragons band poster above his bed. He could visualize him and Jeff rocking out at that concert. How could he possibly leave his quirky friend behind? This all seemed like a bad dream. He wished he could just wake up and find everything back the way it was three months prior before the United Legion arrived in Linkston.

To the right of his bed was the United Legion deployment map, the push pins scattered in thick clusters throughout the eastern United States. They were much sparser in the western half of the country. He remembered putting up the map shortly after the newly elected President of the United States, David Sampson had deployed the United Legion troops at the start of 2025. Michael still couldn't believe that the President and his leaders had manipulated the voters and leaders of America into electing him. The Freedom Alliance group had formed shortly after the first deployment, in direct opposition to the fascist governing body but there were way more citizens still loyal to the President and the United Legion than Michael would've ever guessed possible.

A glimmer caught his eye, and he watched as the slideshow of 3D projected images from a HoloFrame danced across his dresser. The first video showed his stocky father steadying the four-year-old Michael on his tiny bike. The next was he and Jeff cheering as they raised up a basketball trophy, followed by a short clip of Michael receiving his black belt in Taekwondo, his dad standing proudly next to him.

Michael's childhood had basically been an immersive academic and combat training program and his parents had always told him that a mysterious visitor had appeared and instructed them that he would become a powerful leader someday. He had often wondered if he was destined to join the Freedom Alliance. The prospect of fighting the evil United Legion soldiers invigorated him and had helped him get through the escalating rigors of his training.

Michael leaned in and lifted his pillow. There was a paper there, as his mom had said there would be, and it had a bold heading that read: "Destination 1." He examined it and noticed a note scribbled on the back. He recognized her tiny handwriting: "When it's time, take the hidden escape route. Just pull down on the candlestick on your wall and lift up the trap door near the back of your closet. Be sure to pull the door down and latch it before you leave. There is a secret box and more instructions in the hidden compartment of your suitcase. You must open the box tomorrow, on your actual 16th birthday. You must fulfill your destiny, with or without us. We love you and believe in you, Michael. With love, Mom and Dad."

He read the words again, unable to believe what he was seeing. So, his real birthday was tomorrow, March 21st? They had always celebrated it on May 25th. But why had his parents lied to him? And what was this box he was supposed to open? What did it all mean?

Michael pushed his emotions down and glanced around the room. He stopped on his antique desk, the shimmering castle screensaver on his laptop catching his eye. He had always been fascinated by castles. Something about them just made them seem otherworldly. Sometimes he felt like his only connection with the outside world was his computer, even though it was a bit old school.

Most people had the latest full 3D projected wrist computer, called the WriProc or WriP for short. Not many people still owned a laptop. But his dad had set him up with a good one, with all the latest processors and enhancements. His dad had been a Special Forces soldier and some kind of a government agent that also specialized in computers.

Michael was sure that his parents saw the laptop and the Internet chiefly as a mechanism for him to do his homework or his special assignments. But his dad had been very clear from the beginning— allowing him access to the Internet had come with one condition: he wasn't to disclose his name or location to anyone through the web, ever. Sometimes their paranoid stranglehold drove him crazy and his parents would never really say why they did it other than to say it was to protect him from the world.

He grabbed his laptop and packed it in his suitcase on the bed and looked at his watch again, his heart dropping into his stomach. It was 1:09. He only had one more minute before he was supposed to take off... by himself. He sat on the bed and gazed longingly at the old faded door to his room, hoping one or both of his parents would knock. Then he had a scary thought—*what if a knock came but instead of his parents, it was a behemoth United Legion soldier from downstairs?*

He heard a familiar soft five knock pattern on his door, and he rushed to open it. He was overjoyed to see his mom standing there, in her warm jacket, with a scarf and a stocking hat. She had her usual warm smile and was breathing heavily. Before he realized he was doing it he pulled her head into his chest for a hug. Part of him was afraid that if he let her go she might leave for good.

She squeezed him tight and whispered in his ear, "Let's get back in your room. We don't have much time. Luckily for us, I was already packed for our extended trip." Michael noticed that his mom's gloved hand was holding her brown suitcase and she had what he recognized as their 72-hour kit backpack over her shoulder. She came in, locked the door behind her, and said, "Ok, let's go! We need to get out of here."

Michael thought of the United Legion and their overwhelming presence in the local area, and he wondered how that was going to be possible. But his mother seemed certain they could do it, so he walked over to his suitcase and pulled it off the bed. They made their way to the closet and Michael's mom pulled down on the candlestick near the closet door. A hidden trapdoor popped up from the carpeted floor in the far corner of the massive closet. Michael's mom's brown eyes widened, and she put her index finger up and exclaimed, "I almost forgot. I need to get you some warm clothes."

Michael stood in the doorway of his closet, gazing anxiously at the door to his room. His mom tapped him from behind on the shoulder and he jumped. He thought about why the soldiers were there, turned to his mom, and said, "Why don't I just go with them and then at least you and Dad will be safe?"

His mom shook her head and said, "Absolutely not, Michael. You don't realize all that's at stake. You must trust me, Son!"

He thought of the note and the revelation about his birthday, "But I don't even know if I *can* trust you anymore. You lied about my birthday… all these years."

She placed a hand on his shoulder and said, "I'm sorry. I know that must be hard to take but we did it for your own good. I will explain more later." He nodded and she held up his winter jacket. He thought about what came next and found himself staring at the open trap door at the other end of his closet. When he didn't respond, she shook the jacket and said, "Snap out of it, Michael! We need to go. Those brutes could come check on us at any minute!"

He quickly grabbed the jacket, shocked by her tone. "Ok. I am! This is all just happening so fast."

She patted his back and said, "I know this is hard. I wish there was another way." She shook her head and pointed at where the arm of the jacket fell slightly short of his wrists. "Look at that. Even your dad's old jackets don't fit you anymore. Will you stop growing already? You're supposed to stay my little man forever."

He smiled faintly, shrugged and stepped toward the open trap door, taking in a deep breath, as if trying to suck in whatever courage he could from the foreboding air.

He made his way down a short ladder beneath the trap door to a small landing that led to a narrow set of steps below. His mom lowered their suitcases through the hole to him and climbed down the wooden ladder before pulling on the rope to close the trap door. It clicked ominously back into place. She put her finger to her lips, stepped in front of him and motioned for him to carry his suitcase.

At first, only a single light bulb dangling from the ceiling illuminated the stairway. But eventually lamps showed up on each wall and Michael noticed that the narrow stairs and walls were carpeted as if his parents had soundproofed the area. Even with this soundproofing his mom still tiptoed; she hadn't spoken since they started their descent into who knows where. When they reached the bottom of the stairs, the ground opened up into a small carved out rock tunnel and Michael whispered, "Where did this tunnel come from, anyway?"

"We discovered it purely by accident when we inherited the house from Granny, and we decided to use it as an escape tunnel," his mom replied in her quiet, lilting voice. "We think it's part of the Underground Railroad from the mid-1800s. This whole area of Indiana was at the heart of a lot of that activity, especially Fountain City." She pointed to the boarded path ahead. "Your dad and I had to dress it up a bit, but it's surprisingly still in pretty good condition. Just think of how many slaves walked to freedom through this corridor. From our research, this tunnel is very rare and may be the only one of its kind."

Michael glanced all around, trying not to think about how closed in they were. "How far does it go and what are we going to do once we have to be above ground where the Legion has all their drones and scanning kiosks?"

His mom began walking again, motioning for Michael to follow. "We have a plan for how to handle those. Your dad has connections. Didn't you ever wonder why the United Legion was never suspicious of your dad's military record?"

"Yes, I did actually. Does he have like an old military buddy who can make fake records and stuff?"

"That's right," she said. "Although he's not really that old. Your dad trained him, and he's someone we trust completely. This is something to remember, Michael. You must be careful who you trust in this world. I never thought I would say that, given that I was raised to trust first and only think the best of everyone, but I have learned that it's a balance. You must also be wise about the realities of the world and those who walk on it. Anyway, our friend Peter is one of those few that I would stake my life on being trustworthy in all things. He has created new alternative identities that we can use that should keep the Legion off our trail, at least for a while."

Michael thought about what his dad had told him about trusting Peter back at the house. "That makes sense. This is all just so unreal."

The jagged tunnel suddenly became noticeably darker and Michael realized that the chain of lamps had disappeared. His mom pulled out a small LED lantern to help light the path, but Michael was feeling a bit claustrophobic. The plywood track had run out and the path underneath was dirt, so they had to resort to carrying their suitcases. Michael had offered to switch suitcases since hers was heavier. The time passed slowly. They had been walking for roughly 20 minutes now and Michael's sore arms were screaming at him.

"Does this tunnel ever end?" he asked. "I need some fresh air. Can't we take that door we passed back there up to the surface?"

"I'm not sure where the tunnel ends. Unfortunately, your father and I never came this far before, but Peter told us to find a specific door. It has a carved sun design on it," she answered.

Michael thought of the fact that his dad was missing from this occasion, and this prompted thoughts of the Legion soldiers and the nasty sounding crows. Why had they come? The soldiers had said they were there to collect Michael for a United Legion Youth Scholarship program but that was probably just a front for some brainwashing factory they brought teenagers to. And what would happen to his dad? A sickly feeling came over him. Was he betraying him by leaving him behind?

His mind flashed back to his last moments with him before he and his mom were forced to escape. His mom had been getting the soldiers some food and his dad had used American Sign Language to communicate. They had all learned ASL to allow them to converse with his Aunt Jenna. His dad had signed, "Remember all we have taught you. I'm proud to be your father. I love you." As the memory lingered, Michael choked back his emotions and glanced at his mom, who was studying the walls of the tunnel carefully.

He thought about the soldiers back at the house and wondered how it had played out. Surely, if the Legion wanted *him* they wouldn't harm his dad. But what would he do if they threatened to hurt his dad, or worse unless Michael turned himself over to them? He knew he wouldn't hesitate to surrender himself to save his dad's life. The thought of that scenario gave him chills.

*   *   *

A few minutes later, something caught Michael's eye, and he motioned for his mom to stop. There was a small object moving on the trail ahead. At first, he thought it was a mouse, but he soon discovered that it was a bird, which was sitting there looking directly at him as if it had been waiting for them. Michael recognized it from pictures he had seen. It was a nightingale, but it had white feathers and a faint golden glow all around it.

It took flight, pausing directly in front of him. Its eyes almost seemed human. Not that they had a pupil or the shape of a human eye, but there was an intelligence behind them that he couldn't put his finger on. Was it smiling? How can a bird smile?

The bird's tiny beak opened and it chirped a beautiful melody that soared up to a final high note at the end. It was mesmerizing, and Michael felt more at ease now. A thought came to him in a soft, male voice with a rich English accent, "Please do not utter a word regarding my presence. My arrival will be announced to all in due time. Remember to trust your instincts, young Master. And know that I will always be here by your side."

From his mom's reaction, Michael could tell that she saw and heard nothing and he wondered how that was possible.

She had frozen, mid-stride, and was looking around as if trying to figure out why he had stopped. She tapped his shoulder and gave him a questioning look.

Michael pointed at a random spot further up the path. "Oh... nothing. I thought I saw something up ahead. Must've been shadows playing tricks on me. Let's keep going."

"Are you sure? You looked like you checked out for a bit there."

Michael, whose eyes were still locked in on the hovering bird, said, "No, I'm good. I just want to get out of this tunnel. That's all."

The bird flew toward him and Michael stopped in his tracks. When it landed on his wrist, he felt an overwhelming surge of happiness and contentment. Then his mind left the scene in front of him. He was in their house, hovering high in a corner of their front room. But how could he hover? Was the bird sharing a memory or a vision with him?

He shuddered at the sight of his motionless father, sprawled face down on the floor. Michael felt so helpless and terrified. His dad's pistol was lying several feet away and the man who had called himself Sergeant Rillick was standing with a strange black serrated knife poised over him. A deep chill rolled through him when he scanned the scowling face of the vicious attacker and saw his uncovered eyes. They were yellow with narrow black slits, identical to the dragon's eyes from his nightmare. What was the connection? Part of him didn't even want to know the potentially terrifying answer to that question.

As suddenly as it had come, the horrifying scene was gone and Michael was back in the tunnel. He was startled at first when he saw the bird floating in the air directly in front of him. He heard the crisp voice again, "I apologize, Michael. You were not supposed to see that. Don't fret. The Order will help you get him back." Michael fell to his knees, overcome with panic. He noticed that the bright wings of the bird were carrying it toward a shadowed area on the left side of the tunnel.

"Are you ok? What's wrong?" his mom asked.

Dread filled his chest and he jumped up and exclaimed, "I have to go after Dad! They're going to kill him. I don't know how, but I saw him, and he was hurt and the Sergeant was standing over him with a weird dagger. I can't just leave him there. Who knows what they'll do?" When he turned to run back the way they had come, his mom grabbed his wrist. She was shaking.

"Wait, Michael. Please wait!" Her voice cracked. "I don't know what you saw, and it frightens me more than anything to imagine that your father is hurt, but it wouldn't do any good to go back. There's nothing we can do for him now. We can only hope that he is still ok and that we'll be able to get him back later." Her voice softened and a tear trickled down her cheek. "Please stay... *I* need you to stay."

Michael gazed into her glistening eyes and pulled her in for a hug. "What are we going to do, Mom? I'm not Dad. I can't protect us out there. Why is this happening to us?"

Something shimmered off to the left and, as if it were responding to Michael's question, the glowing bird nodded at him and flew toward the wall. Right when it was about to hit it, it just disappeared. Michael stepped toward the edge of the path, his eyes wide, grateful that their remarkable new friend had distracted him for the moment. But he hadn't been watching where he stepped and he tripped on a rock and fell to the dirt. He wiped his jeans as his mom helped him up and she asked, "What happened? Are you ok?"

Michael pointed toward where the bird had disappeared, and said, "Yeah, I'm good. Just thought I saw something over there."

His mom stared in that direction, and said, "Ok, let's go take a look."

When they approached the area in question, he spotted an old, wooden door, which was almost invisible in the shadow of the bulging tunnel overhead. The dark door was plain except for a tiny insignia in the bottom right corner. As Michael bent over to get a better look, his heart jumped. It was an elaborately carved design in a circle that was about four inches in diameter. There was a sun design depicted with a crescent moon and a star inside it. His mom gasped and placed her hand over her mouth.

They had arrived at the door.

Chapter 2

The Door

The strange glowing nightingale had led them straight to the sun insignia door that Michael's mom had said they needed to find. But how did it even know, and how on earth did it fly through it? The door had a large keyhole above an egg-shaped knob. As Michael reached out to grasp the faded brass knob, he heard a clicking noise behind him, and when he spun around his mom was pulling something out of the secret suitcase compartment. It was a large key.

She studied the Destination 1 sheet again, unlocked the door and opened it. After checking the area, she motioned for Michael to proceed, and said, "Let's hurry. I'm ready to get out of this tunnel." Michael walked into a musty hallway and his mom stepped past him, the lantern light causing their shadows to flicker across the dome-shaped rock ceiling.

Michael noticed cobwebs in the corner near the entrance and asked, "Where does this creepy hallway lead to anyway? And where did you get that key? That thing looks ancient."

She pointed back where they had come from and answered, "That door is supposed to lead to a safe house, a place where we can lie low, at least for the night. It's an abandoned home that Peter set up for us. He gave us the key and some instructions just in case we were ever forced into a situation."

Michael pointed at the cave wall. "Well, this would definitely classify as a situation." At the end of the hallway was another door. As they approached it, the metal heavy-duty panels and electronic keypad entry lock on it looked very out of place in this primitive tunnel.

His mom lifted the Destination 1 paper. It listed instructions as to what to look for and how to use the code on the inside door. He watched closely as she typed in the 6-digit code from the paper, being sure to memorize it. Three loud clicks erupted from the door, sending his heart into his stomach. He glanced back down the dimly lit corridor but was grateful when there was no sign of activity.

Michael's mom pushed on the heavy door to open it. On the other side of the door was a steel staircase. It was at this point that Michael was reminded of the weight of his mother's suitcase, as he hefted it up the long flight of stairs. There was a regular door at the top with no lock. When they walked in, it appeared to be a panic room. He remembered seeing one in a movie once.

They collapsed onto a couch and chair and Michael sighed in relief, his mind drifting to the moment the Legion soldiers had arrived. Back at their house, his parents had been starting to tell him about why he had been trained so hard and sheltered his whole life when a flock of screeching crows, followed by the Legion soldiers had arrived at their front door.

"So, what were you guys about to tell me when the Legion showed up?" he asked.

His mother's gentle face took on a somber look and she said, "Well... I guess it's time for you to know. About sixteen years ago, your dad was stationed out of a base in Europe for a few years. We had been trying to have a baby but all the doctors we saw said that we would never be able to. While we were there, your dad and I both had a dream that we needed to go to the Chalice Well at Glastonbury in England. When we approached the area near the pool, from the dream, we saw a woman dressed like a princess, all in white. She had a strange golden glow all around her and the clearest, light green eyes and called herself Nimue. I know this is going to sound crazy but... she was floating above the water."

Michael couldn't believe what he was hearing. It all sounded so incredible. Was this the mysterious visitor they had mentioned to him before? He had always thought that they just made up that story and that there was some other underlying reason behind his intense upbringing.

"I didn't believe it at first either," she continued. Then she paused and lowered her head as if what came next was hard to say. "But it was real, Michael. She... She gave you to us and gave us a box, and she explained that only you would be able to unlock it and receive what is inside. We were not to tell anyone but you about meeting her or receiving the box. She called it a capsule."

Michael's chest hurt and his head was spinning, "Wait a minute! So, you're not my real parents? This is crazy. So, my childhood has been one big lie?"

Michael's mom stiffened. "Calm down, young man! Nothing that we have said or done has been a lie. We kept the full truth from you to protect you."

"To protect me! How would being kept in the dark about who I am and where I came from protect me?"

She grabbed his hand, her soft eyes pleading. "I'm sorry. I know you must feel betrayed right now, but we really do love you and we did what we thought was best for you." She squeezed his hand and continued, "This next part is very important. Nimue said that you were to be protected at all costs and that someday you would become a great leader and save us all. She said that the capsule would only open after your 16th birthday. She called it your Anointing Day, March 21st. And she said that the Legion must not find out when this actual day was. That's why we changed the day from the very beginning—as a precaution to protect you. She warned us to beware of the Legion and to avoid them at all costs and that they would seek to destroy all that was good in the world. As soon as the United Legion came into power, we knew it was the group she had spoken of, and we adapted our plans to protect you."

She looked around as if she was afraid the Legion might be lurking in the corner, and continued, "Nimue also told us that the Legion had ways of discovering those individuals who had just had this very important anointing event, usually through a flock of crows. She called it a pack. That is why we were preparing to leave Linkston tonight to head west. To escape the eyes of the Legion before tomorrow." She lowered her head. "But somehow the crows and the soldiers came early, and we had to use our Extreme Measures plan… Where at least one of us has to stay behind." Her lips trembled and she smiled at him. "But you escaped safely. That's all either of us really cared about."

Michael hugged her. "Thanks, Mom. I understand. I know you've both sacrificed a lot for me." He felt completely overwhelmed. He was being bombarded with so many new and unexpected things. A magnificent floating princess, different biological parents, a destiny, a mysterious and powerful box! Was this all for real? Who was he and where did he belong?

Michael spotted the mini kitchen in the corner and said, "I'm going to see what food they have in here. You hungry?"

She nodded and said, "You do that. I'm going to find a restroom."

Michael jumped up and began looking through the cupboards. She returned within a few minutes and Michael pointed to an open cupboard and said, "Ok. Looks like they have cans of stew, corn and chili. There's some jerky and different kinds of chips and snacks." He opened the small refrigerator. "And for drinks, we've got some bottled waters and various soda and juice flavors." Then a funny thought came to him and he said, "Sorry, no Kale crackers or grass juice though."

His mom laughed. "Nice. I'm sure your father would appreciate you filling in for him on the organic food teasing front. You've learned well from the master." She smiled, shook her head and said, "I'll take some jerky and a bottled water, please. Sarcasmo."

Michael chuckled, grabbed the items along with an armload for himself and plopped down next to her. "So, where do we go from here?" he asked, in between bites.

She opened the jerky and said, "I believe Destination two is a larger safe house in Dessa, Illinois. But I need to look again to see how we get out of here."

Minutes later, Michael had just finished a bag of chips and was picking up the Destination 1 paper to see if it had anything about where they needed to go when he felt cold and then a shudder rolled through him. For a split second, an image of the sun insignia door appeared in his mind. It was slightly ajar. But he could've sworn they shut it. He shot up off the couch and blurted out, "Mom, the outer door. I don't think we locked it."

He ran back through the panic room door and down the stairs, being sure to tiptoe. He entered the code into the keypad and pulled the solid door open.

The unpleasant sensation in his chest was growing, and then he heard muffled voices coming from the main tunnel. He froze and stopped breathing. As he tried to calm himself, his mind went back to a lesson his dad had taught him about not panicking. He could hear his dad's low, confident voice, "Use deep breaths and focus your thoughts to gain control of any situation." Michael went through the steps and soon had his heart down to a manageable rate and his mind re-engaged.

He could barely see that the outer door was open a crack, just as it had been in his vision. As he looked closer, he could see that the door latch was stuck in a depressed position. Stupid old door. The voices out in the tunnel were getting louder. He was under the grip of some fear-triggered paralysis and he strained to try to hear them. Surprisingly their voices suddenly came through, as if they were standing right next to him. One of them sounded like the hefty Sergeant from the house, but his voice was lower and had a gravelly edge to it. "You better hurry and catch your breath, you slug. We need to catch them or Erubamir will not be pleased."

There was a pause and he said, "What's up with you anyway, Farstus? You look like you're about to pass out. Are you a Gaddigon or some Sullite weakling?"

A higher pitched, squeaky voice responded, "Take it easy, Serrenz. It's because we had to run to make up time after that insolent human wouldn't tell us anything. Looking at those old blueprints again was a genius idea. And that was fun busting through their wall into that stairway. Who would have thought that these Sullites would be clever enough to find a tunnel and plan a getaway? At least we got the security guy. He's the main thing Erubamir wanted anyway. The puny Freedom Alliance has no idea what we have in..."

The Sergeant's gravelly voice cut in, "Silence! You talk too much, you fool... Wait, it looks like their tracks go over that way. Let's..."

Michael couldn't believe what was happening. They were about to find the open door. And here he was, frozen at the end of the hallway. He would never get to it in time to lock it. A hopeless feeling of inadequacy swelled inside and he felt a strange prompting to extend his hand. When he did, he could feel the deadbolt; in his mind, he was holding onto it. He pushed his hand outward as the door slammed shut and then he twisted as the deadbolt locked. Within a few seconds, their stalkers were pounding on the old door with great force and it shook as if it would explode. Michael rushed to type in the code for the thick metal door and was staring down the tunnel as he prepared to enter the secure hallway. He heard a thunderous crash and the outer door flew off its hinges and came careening down the tunnel. He quickly ran in, shut and locked the door and ran up the stairs.

He stopped midway up and jerked his head back. He had dropped the Destination 1 instruction sheet out in the hallway. How could he be such an idiot? Now they had the code to *that* door. He ran into the room and found his mother, who was staring in shock at the door, her hand over her mouth.

He felt like he was having a panic attack. "Mom! I accidentally dropped the Destination 1 sheet down in the hallway. They have the code! What can we do?"

She turned, her eyes wide. "I don't know. I know there's a secret exit in this room somewhere, but I didn't have time to study up on it. How could you leave it with them? That's the worst thing you could've done!"

"I don't know, Mom! I just froze and then I must've dropped it when they broke through the outer door."

The golden bird materialized above them and Michael heard his familiar, but more urgent voice in his head. "Gather your bags. Quickly! You are in danger!"

Michael grabbed his mother's shoulder and said, "Mom! We need to grab our bags. I can't explain. Hurry!"

They both loaded up right as an explosion of heavy footsteps sounded on the stairs below. A brilliant golden dome formed around them, millions of lighter gold colored swimming flecks surrounded each of them and Michael felt dizzy. Then... there was an all-encompassing brightness.

Chapter 3

The Anointing

As the world came back into focus and the dizziness subsided, Michael quickly realized that they weren't in the same place. They were standing in a small entry area, illuminated by strange cone lights. Just beyond the entry, there was a loveseat, couch and a flowered chair like you might find in an antique shop. Beyond this section was a sprawling open space with a gigantic white couch. The couch sections formed a complete circle, with periodic openings, and sitting in the center was a single large chair covered in ornately decorated gold fabric.

Michael saw several closed doors in the back of the spacious room. "That was crazy! How did we get here? Are we at the Destination two safe house?"

His mom's mouth was gaping, and she was staring around at their new surroundings. "I don't know! I just felt really strange all of a sudden and then everything got super bright… And then we were here."

So, she hadn't seen the golden bird or the dome. Interesting. But how did a little bird bring them miles away to here?

Michael thought about what he could tell her and said, "I can't really tell you all that I know but what I can tell you is that we should keep the whole teleportation thing a secret for now. I promise I'll tell you as soon as I have permission."

His mom had a shocked expression. "Permission? Permission from whom? I don't like secrets, Michael."

"Well, for someone that doesn't like secrets you sure kept a lot from me over the years."

She lowered her head and Michael said, "I'm sorry. That was a low blow. You were doing what you thought was best for me… Just trust me on this one, please. I'll tell you more as soon as I can."

She nodded. "I do trust you, Michael. It's just crazy to see how well you're responding to all this. I am beginning to understand how true Nimue's words were about you. You're a natural leader."

Michael smiled and shrugged.

Julia pointed toward the corner of the room and said, "Isn't that a Ham radio? I recall from the instructions that we're supposed to call Peter and let him know we're here?"

As she made her way over there Michael eyed the thick cushions and said, "Well, I need to try out that couch. That thing looks comfy."

"You do that. Just relax. By the way, sorry for yelling at you back there. I was just so worried we were going to get caught. I still can't believe we were teleported here somehow. How is that even possible?"

"I know. It's all so unbelievable. Don't worry about yelling. We were both freaking out. It's on me. I should've held on to that paper or just left it in the room when I went to check on the door."

She pulled the Destination two paper from the secret compartment and walked over to the radio, made some adjustments on a few of the buttons and knobs, and had Peter on the other end within minutes. Peter's voice was sharp and lively. He sounded like he was a motivational speaker type guy.

The conversation sounded tinny through the radio speaker. Peter advised them to stay put and get comfortable and that he would be there in the morning. He also told them that they must not make contact with anyone. He was sad to hear about Michael's dad and promised to do everything within his power to get him back. There was a softness in his voice when he spoke of him and Michael wondered what, from their experiences in the military, had brought them so close.

He asked to speak with Michael and when Michael addressed him, he said, "Hello, Michael. I look forward to meeting you. Your father has told me a great deal about you. Whatever happens tonight, you must know that all things will be made clear. Your life will soon change in ways that I can't explain."

This statement surprised Michael, and he asked, "What's going to happen? What do you know, Peter?"

There was a pause as if he were contemplating his answer, and his calm voice said, "What I know is that I will lay down my life, if necessary, to protect you and your family. You will learn more later. Now try to get some rest. Tomorrow will be a life-changing day for you. I'll see you both first thing in the morning. Over and out."

The abrupt disconnection left Michael thinking about what he had said. Why did Peter mention tomorrow? Did he know about the anointing? Is that what his Dad had meant when he said, "Trust Peter. He knows."

back at the house? What was so special about this anointing event anyway?

They cooked up some food that they found in a small freezer and chatted for a while, their conversation steering away from anything remotely related to their current situation. Eventually, they found bedrooms in the back and his mom insisted that he sleep in the same room with her, so they picked one of the larger rooms, which had two beds. She took the smaller of the two since she was several inches shorter and it wasn't long before she was off in dreamland.

As tired as he was and as much as he tried, Michael couldn't fall asleep. He found himself looking around at everything in the quaint room. There was a dying plant on one of the nightstands with drooping limbs and browning leaves. Right next to it was a HoloFrame with a crisp 3D projected image of him and his mom and dad, from a recent trip to Disneyland. His mom must've packed it for the trip. He couldn't believe how much he towered over them now.

Now that he knew he was adopted, all of the differences between him and his parents seemed to stand out more. His hair was light brown, whereas they both had dark hair. He had more of a pointed chin, whereas theirs were wider, his mom's more rounded. He laid back and noticed more of the unusual cone lights, but this time they were in the form of a chandelier and he wondered again what they were. Their soft light seemed to hypnotize him and he finally drifted off to sleep.

Michael was breathing heavily as he raced to escape the groping clawed hands thrashing after him. He was having the same nightmare from the night before. The terrifying dragon creature was chasing him. It stood on two legs like a man, but it had a dragon's head with a short snout. It was wearing a black uniform, with thicker dark gray sections on the chest, arms and legs. There was an insignia of a dragon blowing black flames on the monster's upper chest, near his left shoulder.

Michael turned back and saw an enormous cave entrance on the mountain ahead. There was a wall of peculiar gold light over the massive doorway of the cave, much like the light that had teleported them, and he could feel it beckoning him as if it were a safe haven. Hearing a blood-curdling screech behind him, he turned and saw the yellow, black-slitted eyes of the towering dragon figure. The imposing creature's long claws slashed at him, just inches from his back. The sight sent shivers through his body and he lunged forward. Then, right as he was about to slip into the monster's grasp, the curtain of gold-flecked light swallowed him up.

He shot up off his pillow, his pulse racing. The dream had seemed so real! Maybe it was the fact that he had seen those eyes again. It took a few minutes for him to gain his composure. Was there some message or foretelling embedded in it? He knew from his studies that every dream had certain symbolic representations, often taken from the dreamer's subconscious. He heard a faint ticking sound coming from the ornately carved grandfather clock on the wall, and he gasped when he saw that it was 11:58. Was this anointing event going to happen at the stroke of midnight? His heart raced and he began to count the seconds.

Two minutes had never passed so slowly. His heart rate grew as the seconds ticked by. Shortly after the clock struck twelve, his mom sat up, her eyes wide open, and said, "What? What am I supposed to see?"

A shaft of white light filled with tiny red particles shot through the ceiling and slowly descended toward Michael. It reminded him of the unique glow of the bird and the door from his dream. It resembled a beam of dust particle filled light shining through a window. He felt drawn to it, stood up, and raised his right hand to touch it. The tiny flecks seemed to come alive. As they flooded into his outstretched hand, waves of joy lapped over him and he wished he could stay in that state forever. The positive energy within surged and pulsed and the speckled light drifted out from his hands and chest, lighting up the room, accompanied by a high humming sound. Michael stared in awe at the incredible scene around him. Every object in the room, including his mom's bed with her on it, was floating 2-3 feet off the ground.

Her eyes were full of tears and she said, "This is so incredible, Michael. What are you feeling right now?"

Michael tried to think how to put it into words and said, "I don't know. I feel full of happiness and energy like I could leap up and fly. I can't describe it."

With a huge smile on her face, she clapped her hands together and said, "I feel some of that too. It's amazing. In my dream tonight, I saw a glowing man, and he told me to wake up, as there was something that I needed to witness. I see what it was now, and I wouldn't have missed it for the world." Her eyes drooped for a second before she said, "I just wish your father could've been here to experience it."

"I know, Mom. We'll get him back, whatever it takes," Michael said, trying to convince himself that it was possible.

Slowly the warm feeling and the speckled light faded, and he was left feeling exhausted. The floating items came to rest, and Michael found himself staring at the plant next to his mom's bed. It was now very alive, with thriving pink blossoms and fresh green leaves popping out from each healthy branch. His mom's eyes had followed his gaze, and she muttered, "That plant was all but dead when we laid down earlier. I remember thinking that I should water it, but I was way too tired. Look at it now. It came to life!"

"I know," Michael replied. His head slipping down to his propped hand. "What's weird is that I can feel its life force as if it's thanking me." What he had said sounded strange coming out of his mouth, but it was the truth. His eyelids felt very heavy. And then his head dropped to his pillow and he was out.

When Michael woke up the next morning, his mind flipped on, and the previous night's activities began playing out over and over like a video set on repeat. Why had that nightmare come again? What was the significance of the mountain and the golden door? His mind went to his anointing. What was that strange red-flecked light and why did everything in the room float? And what was it about the light that brought the plant back to life?

He felt different. Like he was bursting with energy and his mind was clearer than it ever had been. A memory of the capsule came to him and he jumped down, grabbed a fresh T-shirt from his suitcase and took off toward the main room, nearly tripping over his mom's suitcase. He had to chill out or he was going to hurt himself. But all he could think about was getting to his mom and opening the box.

He was dying to know what was in it and what the future held for him. Then a sickening thought entered his mind. What if the destiny the capsule held for him didn't include getting his father back? Part of him wanted to just bypass opening it, go and get his dad, and return to open it with him. But then he had a comforting thought. At least they had Peter to help them get him back.

When he walked around the corner, his mom was cooking breakfast in the kitchen. Everything about this place was super-sized as if it had been built for large gatherings. There was no natural daylight shining through, as there were no windows, but the room seemed brighter than most. The odd upside-down cones were providing the lighting. It didn't look like any electrical system he had ever seen and he wondered where the light was coming from.

The golden chair? An ultra-secret location? He was sure there was a great deal about this place that Peter hadn't told them. And how were Peter and the magical bird connected?

His mom saw him come in and said, "There you are." She had her usual pleasant smile but her soft eyes were puffy and red like she had been crying. "Are you hungry? Luckily I found more food in that freezer." She was pointing to the small refrigerator unit they had discovered the night before. She motioned to an enormous round wooden table in the adjoining dining area and said, "Have a seat. You must be starving."

He felt the pronounced emptiness in his stomach and said, "I am. It's weird. It feels like I haven't eaten for days."

"It may have something to do with that floating room event last night. That was the most amazing thing I've ever seen," she said.

Her comment jogged his memory and he said, "Which reminds me, Mom. We need to open my box right away." He thought of Peter.

"What are we going to do with Peter, by the way? Dad said something about Peter knowing and that we should trust him back at the house. But what does he actually know? And how is he involved with all of this magic stuff?"

"Don't worry about it, dear. Peter mentioned that things would change after today. Maybe your dad told him about your anointing. After all, like you said, your dad trusts him and he is very leery about trusting anyone, even family." She paused and said, "One thing at a time though, mister. Eat up… And just remember that Nimue said not to tell anyone about her or the capsule."

After eating more than he ever had in one sitting and finally feeling full, he put his dish in the sink. But as he turned to walk away, he heard his dad's voice in his head say, *Do your part to help out, even if your mom is willing to do it for you, and take care of your responsibilities*. He knew that what his dad had often said was right on. His mom would do anything for them without hesitation, but it wasn't fair to her if they took advantage of this. With that thought, he turned back around, washed his plate, and put it in the strainer next to the sink.

His mom winked at him and said, "Thanks, Bud."

"You're welcome," he said, turning to sprint to his room.

As he bounded across the floor, he heard his mom call out, "Ok, get the box. I know you're dying to open it."

*   *   *

Michael rushed back to their room, trying not to trip this time. He found the box in the special compartment of the suitcase. It was made of ancient-looking rich cherry wood and was about the size of a large jewelry box. There was something strangely familiar about this mysterious artifact. What secrets did it hold? He carried it carefully out to the white couch next to the kitchen area and sat down. His mother was sitting there, waiting patiently. Now she was staring at the capsule and nodded for him to go ahead.

A capsule? Why had Nimue called it a capsule? Whenever he thought of a capsule, he usually thought of a time capsule. His eyes stopped on a clear crystal inset on the top of the box, embedded in the wood. When he brushed his hand over it, he couldn't even feel it there, but he felt a surge of warmth and contentment, like the feeling the bird had brought. The ghostly magic crystal pulsed with a golden light.

Something stirred inside of him. It was as if it were a long-lost prized possession. But when would he have seen it? And why didn't he remember?

There were two clicks and the capsule lit up. Michael noticed that the beaming outline had light gold, almost yellow specks swimming around in it, instead of the white light with red specks from last night. This was the third time he had seen this magnificent light and he wondered what it was and what power it held?

His mother gasped. "Michael, where is the capsule? It's not there anymore. Is it gone?"

Michael grabbed it, just to reassure himself. What had happened? Was it invisible to her, like the golden bird?

"It's right here, Mom. But it's surrounded by this incredible speckled light like we saw last night, but gold colored this time. Maybe it's hidden from you somehow. I think it has something to do with the weird crystal. The box lit up when I touched it." There was now a thin visible lip on it and for the first time, it looked like it could be opened.

His mom was staring at his hands like if she stared long enough the box would appear. "Crystal! What are you talking about? Your dad and I never saw any crystal on it. And we have studied that thing for hours, trying to find clues."

The crystal and the light around the capsule were no longer flashing, and Michael took a deep breath and said, "I'm going to try and open it now." When he touched the front near the lip, he could feel the presence of the crystal, calling out to him. The capsule opened easily and sitting inside, in a velvet slot, was a ring with a crystal in it. But this one had six distinct facets. In the center, the crystal jutted out to a slight point, framed in by an engraved four-pointed star. He also spotted intricate engravings of what appeared to be a planet on either side of the overall setting. The crystal and the ring band were steadily flashing with the same strange red light he had seen during his anointing event.

Michael felt drawn to this unusual artifact, and he wondered if the feeling of longing and familiarity he had noticed before was actually for the ring inside. His mom had a confused look on her soft face and said, "What is it? I don't see anything at all."

So, maybe the ring was invisible to her too. "It's a ring, Mom. It has a clear crystal in it, with a point in the middle. The crystal is glowing red with that strange light from last night. And there's a star carved into it. The whole thing is flashing." His voice trailed off as he reached for it; he was in a trance. "It's beautiful."

When Michael grabbed the ring, it felt like he was holding onto something made out of low voltage charged gas. It had substance but it wasn't a solid object and there was a subtle sensation that reverberated into his hand from it. Then there were two clicks and it glided onto his right middle finger. A strong surge traveled up his arm, and warmth filled his chest. What was happening to him? All the gold light surrounding the box shot into its embedded crystal, flashed several times and the crystal disappeared.

His mother started and said, "Oh. Ok. There's the capsule. But I still don't see the ring. What happened?"

Michael's eyes lit up and he said, "Did you hear that?"

"No, what was it? I feel like I'm missing everything." Her normally subdued voice was anxious. She pointed and said, "Why would the capsule reappear?"

"I'm not quite sure. It's like once I touched the ring there were these two clicks, like the ones I heard when I touched the gold crystal on the box to open it, and then all of the gold light around the box went into its crystal. And now the crystal is gone. It just disappeared. This is all so weird." He was staring at it. "Maybe the strange light is what hides things."

It all felt like a dream. If this was real, what powers did this ring hold? What was he to do next? Almost as soon as the thought came to him, a prompting echoed through his mind. It was telling him to touch the ring. So, he reached down and touched the small, pointed face. His fingers passed right through it and touched the glowing ring band.

Then a beam of the same unusual red speckled white light floated out of it and formed a lively swarm above him. He heard a high but pleasant humming sound and the strange mist seeped through the ceiling and disappeared.

The room became eerily silent and Michael was left staring in awe at the spot where the light had vanished.

Chapter 4

The Sentry

After what seemed like minutes but was probably much less, he heard the same pleasant humming sound and a square pillar of white light, with blue dancing specks, shot down from the same spot.

A stocky figure, bursting with white light, descended in it, as if it was a teleportation beam. Miniscule, almost imperceptible sky-blue particles swam furiously all around his form in an outline. The man was wearing a uniform made out of a thin layer of dancing blue particles. It had a tunic with a white belt, matching long-sleeves and shin-high boots. There was a heavy white cape that hung down almost to the floor. It was an outfit straight out of the medieval times and Michael wondered where this guy had come from.

There was a gray amulet on the man's chest. It had an illuminated blue diamond-looking crystal embedded at its center. And all around the crystal was the same sun insignia he had seen on the tunnel door. All the wavy sun spires were lit up, and all the straight-edged outer compass points were lit up. What did it all mean?

Their mysterious visitor landed gently and touched the amulet.

The pillar shot up through the ceiling like he had turned on a light-sucking vacuum positioned above the house. The man had olive skin and was about 6' 3" with hands and forearms that were unusually large for his body.

His noble, broad face smiled, and the glowing uniform disappeared, revealing a modern-looking outfit that included a plain black T-shirt, jeans and a rugged brown leather jacket with an understated collar and several zip pockets.

Michael's mom gasped as if she hadn't seen him until that moment, and she said, her voice cracking, "Peter? But...? I'm confused."

The man who was apparently his dad's spy in training, Peter, nodded and spoke, his voice resonant and full. "Yes, Julia. It's me. I received my assignment as a sentry from King Deyan some time ago and it began with military service alongside your husband. But you must know that all that I've done has been genuine and motivated by a desire to serve my king and your son and this family in any way necessary. I don't know what the future holds for you, Michael, but the fact that the king has sent a Guardian Commander as your sentry should be an indicator that he expects great things from you. This is all very unusual. I was not expecting to be summoned. I knew that your anointing would happen today, but I am surprised to see you wearing a squire ring. Where did that come from?"

Before Michael could respond, his mom said, "Unfortunately, we're not allowed to tell anyone where we got it. Sorry."

Peter was studying Michael carefully, and said, "You have piqued my curiosity, young Squire. Especially since my son, Silvan also received a squire ring in an unusual way and we never knew why. His was given to him by Captain Gabriel on his anointing day." Peter gave a slight bow and continued, "I'm sorry to learn that Spencer did not make it here with you. Please tell me everything that happened to him."

There was something formal in the way he talked as if he were thinking carefully about everything he said. Michael related the events surrounding his dad's capture.

Peter had been standing quietly, his large eyes intent and said, "I know that what you have been through seems like a lot to take in, but I must warn you that there will continue to be danger and trials as long as the Legion has any amount of power in this world. This is why you must be protected and prepare to take your place in the Order. That is why I'm here. I am Commander Piddir Olgath of the Order of Lithegol, from the Herkili Realm within the Northern Triad, and I am your Mentor Sentry. My assignment is to protect you, tutor you, and deliver you for training and advancement. The Fortress of Camelot is where you will prepare to become an apprentice knight and enter the Order of Lithegol."

He had pronounced his name differently. Not Peter, like the standard name one would hear, but Piddir (Pi-deer). What an odd name. The commander smiled and, as if reading his mind, said, "But you can call me Peter. This is how all on this world refer to me, except for Captain Gabriel, the Overseer. But he is a different type altogether."

Michael recognized something from what Peter had said and asked, "Did you just say Camelot? Isn't that tied to the legend of King Arthur? Was Arthur real?"

"Yes, he was, and is still very real," Peter replied. "He is a Prince of Lithegol. His father, King Deyan, sent him to lead the Order in The Great War of the Meridian Times around 1500 years ago. This was a key war, in that Drakkir and the Legion were poised to overrun Prime and ultimately Camelot and seize the most important core world in the kingdom, Earth. But they were no match for Prince Arthur and the power of Sullice. Now you get to follow in his legacy and become a knight of the round."

Michael's mom was gazing proudly at her son.

Michael thought of his dad and said, "But I can't do that without my dad. We have to go and rescue him *before* we go to Camelot. I'm not going without him."

Peter took this statement in, as if he had been expecting it, and responded, "The thing that you must understand is that Camelot is not in your dimension. It's in Avalon, where time stops as it relates to your world. We can go to Camelot, where you can finish your apprentice training and prepare for what feels like months, while in your world no time will have passed by. You must trust me, Michael."

"Ok. That sounds crazy. But, given what I've already seen, I believe it. So, what is an apprentice anyway?" Michael asked.

"You have received this ring as an indication that you are ready to be made a squire," Peter answered. "Your next step will be to receive your training in preparation to enter the Order. Knights and matrons enter the Order of Lithegol as an apprentice and advance in the ranks to become a master and then a commander. Beyond that is an overseer knight, but only 13 overseers exist at any given time in the entire kingdom."

There was so much he didn't know. "So, where is this Lithegol and what is that strange light with the flecks in it? And why can't my mom see my ring?"

Peter responded, "Lithegol is the kingdom that encompasses 13 living realms, including Prime, where embodied beings dwell on each respective realm's core world. A core world is the living planet within each realm like Earth is for Prime. Each realm has its own set of knights and matrons with special gifts. Each realm also has an overseer knight, assisted by a head matron, to lead and protect its people. The particle-filled light is the power of Sullice. Sullice is the essence power of all that is good and life-giving in the Universe."

This was all so hard to fathom, and Michael asked, "How are these people from the other realms different from us and can they come to Earth?"

Peter answered, "Yes. They are much like humans from Earth, but they are from different races, including the elves, the dwarves, the faeries and my race, the giants. They can travel to Earth, using special corridors. Imagine light-based teleportation tunnels that transport someone from one realm to another.

"The ring, band and orb that I wear, which are called tokens, are made of Sullite Essence material. We are accustomed to how everything around us is solid and physical, but essence is the other stuff that makes up all living things. It is the true source of life. The essence crystals embedded in our tokens are how we harness and direct the Sullice. I assume that Julia was unable to see your squire ring because it was activated in response to your Sullite signature. Each of us has a unique essence signature. Think of it like a fingerprint but tied to our living essence body. The crystal was probably flashing, correct?"

Michael nodded. The missing pieces were coming together in his mind.

Peter pointed to Michael's ring and said, "The ring tokens contain a unique crystal with six refined facets surrounding a pointed section. The facets are tied to the SullSword, a shield, the uniform and armor, communication, the hoven and the cloaking mechanism. Each token must have this cloaking refinement to keep the Sulgons from seeing them. Although some of the more powerful Sulgons can still sense the presence of Sullice.

"The pointed crystal section within the center of the ring goes through a lesser stage of refinement called 'Skimming', which allows for it to be used to form various essence weapons and objects when needed. A raw essence crystal without any refinements can be seen by anyone and has the characteristics of a solid object. All of the tokens are created using only refined Sullite crystals and therefore will never be seen by anyone unless that person has been given the ability to see essence material.

"It is similar to how only certain frequencies of light are visible to the human eye. The ring and the other tokens are what typically provide this ability. So, normally you wouldn't have seen it either, but you did because it was assigned to you. Sometimes tokens and those objects cloaked by them can be shown to us when there is a special need. A powerful knight or matron can also display certain essence objects to those that are blind to them, when appropriate."

Peter pulled out a gray bracelet with a tiny crystal on it and said, "For now your mother can wear what we call an Illuminator Band. This doesn't provide her with the same powers as that of a squire, but it will allow her to view those things encased in an essence aura. The Illuminator band is made from Omithite and a small Forithite crystal. Unlike the other essence crystals, Omithite can be handled by anyone who has been given the ability to interact with the essence world around them. Think of when you picked up the ring. You probably felt the living essence energy buzzing in your hand. Then you were able to authenticate with it—that was the clicking sound you heard. Once that happened the Omithite drew the ring onto your finger. That's how it works."

He placed the band on his palm and extended it to Julia, motioning for her to pick it up. It was much larger than his mom's wrist and Michael wondered how it would fit. She stared at Peter's large hand and said, "But I don't see anything yet."

"Oh, but you will. You have to reach out for it and once you touch it your eyes will be opened, and it will come to you."

She tentatively extended her hand. When her fingers made contact with the thin bracelet there was a soft click. She jerked her hand back, gasped and said, "Oh my goodness! There it is. That is amazing."

Peter nodded. "Ok, now touch it again and it will authenticate and encircle your wrist."

When she did there was a double click and the band floated onto her wrist and shrank to fit. Peter pointed to the band and said, "The first click was an indication that the band recorded your essence signature and now will only work for you. The double click meant that it authenticated that signature and now the Illuminator Band is engaged. Your eyes should be open to the essence world around you now."

Her eyebrows lifted and she said, "I can see your ring, Michael. I've never experienced anything like this. It's like there's a new world out there that we didn't know about."

Peter's eyes went down to his own ring and his countenance fell. His ring was different. It had an engraving of two crossed Aladdin swords. The thick commander touched his ring, and his radiant uniform appeared again. "Ok, Michael, please get down on one knee."

But Michael hadn't been paying close attention, and as he went down, he nearly fell. He felt like a klutz but when he gazed up at the commander the majestic figure just smiled and continued, "Don't worry. It will all make sense soon. When the people of this kingdom desire to be a knight or matron, they must live by a special oath. I will now have you take that oath and will advance you to the rank of a squire. As I mentioned before, this will allow you to prepare to take the next step and eventually enter the Order as an apprentice." He raised his right arm and continued, "Please raise your right arm to the square like this and repeat after me...

I, Michael Brenlan, promise to live from this day forward by the Oath of Lithegol:

I will show love to my King and all others who may be in need
I will stand for honor, cleanliness, freedom and justice
I will serve the Order of Lithegol and will follow my knight and matron leaders
I will fulfill my mission assignments with courage, using the power of Sullice
I will choose good over evil and will heed the warnings that come to me
I will fight for Lithegol and for the Sullite people of all worlds with all my might

As Michael repeated the words to the oath, a rush of calmness and self-assurance told him that this was what he was supposed to be doing and it was right. Peter touched his amulet, reached his right hand out and placed it on Michael's chest. Michael felt an influx of warmth and comfort. Peter motioned for him to stand, and as he did, Michael noticed that the crystal in the center of his ring and the ring band itself were no longer pulsing. They now emitted a steady red glow. He thought more about why that could be. This must mean that he was a squire now. But what was he supposed to do with that?

*   *   *

Peter followed his gaze to the ring and said, "Do you see the engraving on the ring? That is the design used for all Prime tokens. We are in the times of the great gathering, which means that Earth, being the Prime core world, is a melting pot for many of the most powerful warriors from all the living realms of Lithegol."

He pointed to the etching of the crossed swords on his ring and said, "These are the engravings on the tokens from my home realm, Herkili. We are guardians. We guard the fortresses, the Dread Realms and some select Sullite beings when needed. Ours is a special role that we have accepted gladly since the beginning of time. It amuses me that those on your world have written a story of a strong hero, with a similar name – this Hercules character. My guess is that someone familiar with Lithegol was involved with the creation of that story."

Michael's mom had an inquisitive expression on her face and said, "Wait. If there is a system of knights protecting us, then how did the Legion take over our government?"

Peter's long face fell, and he said, "*That* is a very good question, Julia. We were betrayed at the highest level. Unfortunately, one of my heroes, the overseer knight from my realm, turned on the Order, and in the year 2022, he orchestrated a Legion invasion of grand proportion on Earth. Our forces were caught unprepared. Therok had done his homework and was able to infiltrate the United States government with his Legion forces before we knew what hit us."

Julia's expression was one of sympathy and shock. "So, what happened to Therok?"

"First of all—it is important to understand that Gaddin is the essence power of darkness, evil and all that is destructive in the Universe. Unfortunately, Therok allowed Erubamir, one of the most powerful Gaddigons, to take him over, and he became an extremely powerful Sulgon. A Sulgon is an embodied being that has allowed a dark Gaddite Essence being, called a Gaddigon, to take him or her over. Sulgons are a hybrid creature that take on characteristics of the host and the parasitic Gaddigon. Unfortunately, you know exactly who Therok is. He has now taken on a new identity here on Earth as David Sampson, the President of the United States."

Michael's mom gasped.

More pieces of the puzzle were falling into place in Michael's mind. So, President Sampson was the Legion leader who also formed the United Legion organization.

Peter was shaking his head now, "Therok was a mentor to me. I saw him do incredible things with the power of Sullice and help many people during his time as a leader. I just don't understand what happened.

It all went bad in 2022 when Therok captured Braster, a Herkilian senior commander who joined the Legion and became their leader back in 1865. Up until the time he was captured, Braster had been sneaking Sulgons and Gaddigons into Herkili and Prime and had become very powerful.

"The theory is that Braster offered Therok the Legion leader position in return for his freedom. Therok was already having problems with the Order so the timing was perfect for him to be drawn in. Therok thought that he should've been made Captain of Lithegol since he was the overseer for Herkili, the most dominant Guardian Realm in the kingdom. He had also become frustrated with all of the lawless and out of control Herkilians and believed that a system of government that reigned over the people and forced order would protect them and make ruling easier. The tipping point was the influence of Erubamir, who is extremely persuasive and powerful."

Peter wiped his cheek discreetly and continued, "Therok allowed the thirst for power and dominion to drag him down and ultimately ruin him. I have vowed to myself not to let this happen to me. It is a frightening example of how even someone high up in the Order can fall."

Michael, sensing how hard this topic was for Peter to talk about, asked a question to change the subject. "So, you mentioned that there are different races of people in the different realms. How do they not stand out in a crowd?"

Peter took a deep breath and said, "They... I should say we are changed when we enter that realm through a Realm Portal. The portal alters us so that we take the form of a native for the living core world in question, in this case, Earth. A visitor can only be changed to his or her natural state through the power of Sullice. It actually happens automatically whenever a knight or matron engages their armor."

Michael's mom had been watching quietly and said, "What about women? Can I become a squire too?"

Peter turned to Julia, nodded and said, "Yes, you can. So, Michael's situation is a complete exception to the norm. Normally a Mentor Sentry is sent to pick up a squire candidate when that individual has had their Anointing day and has been sufficiently prepared to receive their call. Not everyone that turns 16 is chosen right away and most don't even realize the anointing event has occurred or that anything has changed. Those that have been prepared are called when their leaders send a ribbon of Sullice that extends from a portacon and summons them to a particular fortress. The Mentor Sentry escorts them, using the ribbon as a pathway to the closest portacon and then to the fortress in question. There they receive the necessary training to earn a ring and become a squire. I've never seen it happen the way it did for Michael. It's interesting to me that my son, Silvan's advancement was the only other I've seen where he was made a squire without finishing a Training Cycle. It makes me truly curious about both of your futures in the Order of Lithegol."

Michael felt like he was in a dream—listening to a powerful figure who was pledging to help him and talking about realms and worlds and Orders and destinies that he had no idea about. And what was this boundless energy boiling inside of him since he was made a squire? His senses were all in overload mode. He was overwhelmed with stimuli, and his mind seemed to be racing with memories and information.

Michael was trying to rein it all in. He had been made a squire by a glowing visitor that had arrived in a beam of light through the ceiling, and he had learned that he was to be a knight in some Order within a kingdom where the legendary Arthur was one of its leaders. And he was filled with a new unknown power that he didn't know how to control.

He thought about what Nimue had said he was to accomplish. It had to be tied to the Order and his future as a knight. His head hurt from the weight of it all, and part of him wanted to just run and escape from it. Peter must have sensed his struggle because he grabbed his hand and a wave of blue Sullice flowed from his hand into Michael's. After that, the anxiety was gone, and he felt a ripple of calmness roll over him.

"That was the power of Sullice," Peter said. "It can provide comfort to a troubled heart, among many other things. Don't worry, Michael, you will not be alone on your quest. I will do all within my power to help you. And we *will* get your father back."

"Thank you," Michael said.

Peter jerked his head, as if an alarm had gone off in his mind, and said, "But you will learn more about all this later. We must leave right away. It is near midday, and this is the best time to travel because there are fewer Legion punks... I mean enemies, out and about."

Chapter 5

The Journey Begins

Peter grabbed a handful of items, dropped them in a backpack and led them to a secret passageway behind one of the closets. When they got to the end of the dark tunnel, they walked into an extremely well-lit warehouse area. Michael gazed in wonder at all the futuristic-looking gadgets, machines and vehicles.

As Michael's eyes scanned the enormous space, they landed on a super-sized Hummer with elevated wheels and special doors and hatches along the outside frame. It was substantially longer than any he had seen, almost like an ultra-long limo.

The entire shell of the amazingly long truck was covered with Omithite circles. As they approached, Michael noticed little clear crystals in the center of those circles, sprinkled throughout the bulging frame. Peter's wide mouth was turned up in a sly smile, like a kid about ready to play with a new toy for the first time, and Michael said, "What is that thing? A tank?"

Peter chuckled and waved the back of his ringed hand against a panel in the wall. Two rapid clicks sounded, it opened up, and some keys fell out into his other hand. On the keychain was a remote with different sized buttons and a crystal in its center. Peter nodded and said, "Yes, except this thing is more powerful than a tank. I'm going to enjoy showing you what this bad boy can do." He had a wilder expression than Michael would've expected from such a proper guy. And had he just referred to the Hummer as a "bad boy?" Peter gazed at Michael sheepishly. "My apologies, young Squire. I have been trying to talk with more of what Gabriel calls nobility and respect, but sometimes I slip back into my old ways."

"That's no big deal. You can talk any way you want," Michael said.

Peter patted his back and smiled. "Great! Thanks, bud. That makes it much easier."

"You keep mentioning Gabriel. Who is he?"

Peter's eyes lit up. "Gabriel is the most powerful knight in all of Lithegol. He has been around longer than anyone else and is the wisest, most kind and perceptive individual you'll ever meet. He is the overseer knight for the Prime Realm, and he's also the current Captain of the Round. But he's old-fashioned. Almost like the knights from the movies. Very proper most of the time."

Michael nodded. "Sounds like a cool guy."

"Yeah, he is a very cool guy to have around if you're in a fight with Sulgons, that's for sure."

They placed all their bags in the back and Michael hopped into the passenger seat of the massive vehicle. As soon as he sat back in the seat, which seemed to fit like a glove around his body, his eyes locked in on the front dash, which resembled the instrument panel for a jet. It had digital displays, buttons and gauges covering every square inch. "What are all those panels and buttons for?"

Peter touched a crystal on the dash. As soon as the second click sounded, the whole dash lit up and the doors closed. There was a high humming sound as a white Sullice force field surrounded the vehicle.

"Wow. That is cool. What kind of Sullice is that? It has gold flecks in it!"

Peter pushed several buttons on the steering wheel and said, "We call this beast of a vehicle 'Little Billy'. It is equipped with a brand new Mithite shell, which is one of the most powerful Sullite crystals available. The tokens for all knights and matrons, except for the overseers, use a Forithite crystal. Only the overseer tokens contain Mithite. This Sullite Armored Vehicle, or S.A.V., was developed by one of our leading scientists, Dr. Henry Waicroft. 'Billy' is highly protected against the weapons and powers of the Legion. We have to be careful though and only have the shell turned on when we're fighting the bad guys because when it's engaged other drivers without tokens can't see us. Billy also has some serious power under the hood."

Peter gunned the engine, which roared loudly as if it had the power to launch into space. He typed a number into the lit keypad on the dash and lights came on up ahead along the wall, illuminating a tunnel carved out of the hill. "Ok. Is everybody strapped in?"

Michael glanced back at his mom and almost laughed when he saw the scared silly expression on her face as she stared at the over-the-top four-point harness seatbelt. He couldn't resist and asked, "Your parachute secure, Mom?"

She smirked and said, "Very funny, Michael. Although that is what it feels like."

Michael pulled on his straps to make sure they were snug and he and his mom answered, "Yes," in unison.

Peter smiled and said, "OK, hang on." He flipped a gear on the side of the steering column and pushed on the gas. The force of the acceleration pushed Michael's head against the seat. The sides of the tunnel whizzed by as Peter navigated the narrow tunnel with ease as if he were driving at 10mph. Michael wondered how Peter's reflexes could react so quickly to the fast-approaching curves and twists. Within what seemed like seconds they were drastically slowing down. As they came out of the tunnel on the other side of the mountain the light of the noonday sun blinded him. A group of hedges and dense bushes slid to each side like they were embedded on a track, and they drove between the trees.

The rest of the drive was fairly uneventful, with them driving through what seemed like endless forests and open fields. They seemed to be spending their time on obscure back roads that would barely qualify as roads. Peter told them stories of growing up on his home world, Veloro, where they had castles and hovering carriages and unusual six-legged creatures. The sun was starting to dip below the horizon. They had entered Iowa several hours back and it seemed like they were passing a never-ending string of farms. When he saw a sign for Decatur, Nebraska he lifted his legs in an effort to wake them up and wondered how much farther it could possibly be. As if sensing his discomfort Peter turned onto a narrow country road and said, "Don't worry. We're almost to my place. My son, Silvan, is eager to meet you both. He's about your age, Michael. He turned

16 three months ago."

After a few minutes, Peter turned down a barely noticeable road, more like a trail, and said, "Hang on. This could get bumpy. It helps to keep out unwanted visitors." They were bouncing quite a bit as he continued, "Faren is a small town in western Iowa. We should have no trouble avoiding the Legion here. The closest major city with drones and soldiers is hundreds of miles away." They drove until the trail stopped abruptly in front of a huge hill. Peter pushed a black button on the dash and Michael covered his eyes as they drove straight at it. It split open right before they got to it and then closed behind them.

When they stepped out of the vehicle, Michael realized that this was not a normal cave. It was more like a nursery for plants with the same strange light-funneling cones that he had seen at the Safe House. They snaked up into the rock wall, light bursting to escape out the sides of their transparent skin. The area was huge, and the ceiling seemed to go up forever into the shadowed chasm above. Plants lined the floor and walls of the cave, many of them breathtakingly beautiful, with elaborate colors and shapes.

"That's Commander Sam's area," Peter pointed out. "He is an Elemental and loves all types of plants. But Elementals can be involved with lots of different things, besides the four elements, including metal, medicine, geology, astronomy and animals. Sam lives with us, but he keeps a different set of hours altogether."

The plants Michael saw were unlike any he had seen before. Some had flowered petals surrounding a clump consisting of hundreds of tiny berries. Others bore a strong likeness to a Sunflower but with what

Michael swore were barely visible tiny crystals in the center. Peter gestured at the garden, and said, "Most of these plants are new species that Sam helped to develop." He pointed at a snaking plant resembling a grapevine, except the fruit was orange, and said, "That is one of my favorites. It's a combination of some of the most potent medicinal plants on your earth crossed with some from Ellonta, Commander Sam's home realm. It can cure most minor injuries within seconds."

Michael walked over to it and stared, unable to believe what he was hearing. A plant that could cure injuries? This was a serious breakthrough. He turned back to Peter and asked, "So, why doesn't the world know about this plant? The impact would be huge."

Peter replied, "Unfortunately, in order to tell the world about it we would have to disclose all the details about the Order of Lithegol and all that goes with it. The King doesn't feel that everyone is ready for that yet. But we're close and the gathering has caused quite a bit of that knowledge to be shared with doctors and scientists of your world. Why do you think there have been so many medical breakthroughs in the last 60 years?"

He waved his ring over a section of the rock wall and a 3D hologram image of Peter's head with a thin beard appeared in front of it. The commander's stern floating face said, "Please step forward and look into the two provided targets to authenticate your identity."

Peter stepped forward and two miniature eye hole targets shot out into the air. Moments later, a pleasant dinging sound came out of the small console speaker and the image nodded and said, "Identity confirmed. You may enter. Welcome home, Peter. Father to Silvan the Great."

Peter smirked and said, "That's what happens when you let your teenager configure the door greeting system." This announcement was followed by a series of loud noises, as a section of the rock wall sucked in and slid open. Michael wondered how much horsepower was needed to move such a heavy object. This door was at least 20 feet tall, and Michael couldn't help but think back to the gigantic door from his nightmare. What was the deal with these doors, and who needed them to be that tall? Were Peter's people that big?

Peter pointed to the projected image and chuckled. "That silly beard. I used to wear that thing for Silvan. He loves Chuck Norris, and Chuck has a beard. That guy is ageless. He's like in his 80's and looks like he's only in his 60s. Silvan loves to quote the Chuck jokes. Some of them are actually pretty funny."

After they stepped through the opening in the rock, Michael noticed right away that this was definitely different from the Safe House they had just come from. Aside from the intricate carvings on the rocky walls, this was more like a bachelor pad. Peter shook his head and said, "Since the Legion took over, we've all had to go into hiding in places like this. I really do miss my house. I built most of it myself."

Without anyone touching a remote, a large ultra-clear 3D projected image popped up in front of a set of couches and the news, with no volume, scrolled through the air. There was a kitchen with an island in the far corner and a game area with a pool table, foosball and air hockey to the right. He spotted the wireless headsets and recognized one of the new virtual reality stations, called VRT-Pods, in the corner.

Michael's friend Jeff had one too and Michael remembered playing "Epic Combat: Zombie Invasion" on it right before his crow encounter and the Legion's arrival. Was that really only yesterday? He continued to check out the house. The cabinets and furniture were custom-made with some of the best detail work Michael had ever seen.

On the coffee table was a photograph of the bearded Peter and a teenage boy. He was slightly taller than his dad and had a mini-faux hawk. Peter picked up the picture and said, "That's Silvan. Man is he getting big. He's a great kid. We kept his anointing day a secret from the Legion. They think it's coming up next month. That is what we do through our inside sources in the government. If we ever lost them, we would be in trouble. Your parents were wise to hide your true day from the Legion."

Peter walked to the back and went into one of the rooms. In the meantime, Michael wondered what it would be like to live in a hill. This knowledge brought a comforting realization. He wasn't the only teenage boy living in isolation who had been hidden away from the Legion and was being prepared for some unknown destiny.

*　　*　　*

Peter came back out a few minutes later, chuckling for some reason. Michael's mom had found the restroom and came out looking refreshed. They were all working their way toward the enormous wrap-around couch. But before Michael could ask what was up with Peter, the rock door they had come through clicked loudly, lunged inward, and slid open.

Peter leaped through the air, sailing over their heads, and touching down softly between them and the door. His eyes narrowed and he motioned for Michael and his mom to get down behind the loveseat.

His body shot up into a gigantic, muscular form, with bulging arms and legs. From how he dwarfed the furniture, Michael guessed that he was over eight feet tall. Glowing armor, consisting of concentrated areas filled with blue speckles, covered his arms, legs and chest. It looked like an extremely streamlined version of the traditional armor from the medieval days, with white contours and accents. A sleek blue speckled helmet appeared. It covered everything but his eyes and then it shot back and all the tiny specks gathered up in a circular disc behind his head. Their protector had the familiar sun insignia on his white glowing cape.

His features were all pretty much the same except on a much larger scale. Michael wondered if the reason that his hands and forearms had been so big in his human form was a carryover from how big they naturally were. A blue Sullice sword materialized in his monstrous right hand. The radiant sword had a broad blade toward the tip and a sharp edge protruding off the back. He was also holding a blue shield and was posed in a braced position, facing the entrance.

Michael's mom had a shocked expression, her mouth agape. She turned to Michael and said, "What's going on? How did he get so huge?"

Michael pointed and whispered, "I think that's what he actually looks like." He put his finger to his lips and pointed toward the door.

A small man had entered the main area, but he didn't seem threatening. His skin was pale, and he was stumbling as if he were about to pass out. His long hair was wavy and feathered back, revealing slightly pointed ears with tiny earlobes. Peter's armor and weapons vanished as he shrank to his human form and ran toward the small man. "What's wrong, Sam? Are you ok? What happened?"

When the man lifted his head, the first thing Michael noticed was his eyes. They were pale blue, almost white. He had never seen eyes that light. The man was panting and sweat dripped down from his forehead. "They know about us. I don't know how. But they know. They said they were going to come for you. I was so worried about you and Silvan." He turned his gaze toward the back of the room and said, "Oh, good! He's here. I see him in the training room. Thank the stars!"

Michael followed his eyes and saw nothing. What was the man talking about? He had said something about the training room. But how could he see into another room?

The man paused and shook his head. "I just knew that if I didn't escape you would have no idea they were coming. There were scary moments when I almost fell, but I managed to get away and was able to use The Portacon of Geraint to get a head start on them."

He paused to breathe, a tear trickling down his cheek. "I snapped when I thought of losing you both. You are so precious to me, especially since Lisa died." His countenance changed and his breathing slowed. He closed his eyes and when he opened them again he was completely calm. "I must quiet my inner essence and ponder on what I can do. We must travel west to California. There's some Legion event about to transpire there and we need to stop them. Our intelligence has been seriously compromised."

Peter glared at the entryway, his jaw clenched, as if in his mind he was daring the attackers to come through and face him. He put his hand on the man's slight shoulder. "I'm sorry you got attacked, Sam," he said. "You truly are like a brother to me. If anything had happened to you..." His face was somber, and he asked, "What happened out there?"

Sam's features were calm and collected, and Michael thought about how different this face was from the panic-stricken one he had seen several minutes earlier. There was something different about his eyes and the way he looked around. Was he blind? If so, how did he fight with the Legion soldiers and see into the other room?

Michael had been watching the interaction between the mysterious man and Peter play out by barely peeking around the corner of the loveseat.

Peter motioned for his mother and him to come out. "One thing at a time," he said. "Michael, this is Commander Samas Perren. Or you can call him Sam or Commander. Sam, Michael. Sam is a fellow commander in the Order and one of our most valuable knights, especially among the Shadow Sentries."

Sam's eerily transparent eyes studied Michael and he stepped toward him. "So, you are Commander Peter's mystery assignment. I see why now. I have never seen an essence aura that powerful in one so young. Amazing."

Michael's mom had been standing silently, observing as she usually did. In this case, she was staring at Sam and finally broke in. "Hi, Sam. I'm Michael's mother, Julia. I hate to cut introductions short but... are you injured?"

Leave it to his mom to step into nurse mode. Peter turned to Michael's mom and said, "Good eye, Julia. That's right, you were a nurse at one point, right? Isn't that how you and Spencer met when he got injured in combat overseas?"

She nodded. "Yes. He had some shrapnel in his arm." She approached Sam, reached out her hand, and said, "Nice to meet you, Sam."

Sam gazed in her general direction, extended his hand, and said, "Very nice to meet you, Julia. I regret we're not meeting under better circumstances. In answer to your question, I took some Renber juice, which fixed my slightly sprained ankle, but I desperately need a vial of Sullflora extract to replenish my Sullice. That confrontation really sucked it out of me."

Peter glided quickly out of the room and Michael's mom offered to help Sam. Within seconds, she had his arm over her shoulder and was walking him toward one of the couches.

Peter returned right away and extended a small tube of milky liquid to Sam and said, "Here you go, Commander. I grabbed the maximum strength vial."

Commander Sam grabbed the vial and took a small sip. Michael noticed that Sam's arms and fingers were unusually long. Within less than 30 seconds, the color returned to his face and Sam's countenance seemed to light up more.

Michael and his mom gasped, and Michael said, "It's incredible how quickly that worked. What is that stuff?"

"It is an extract from the plant I showed you from Sam's garden, and it replenishes a person's Sullite reservoir quickly. It is like your Sunflower, but it has actual Sullite crystals in it and is called a Sullflora. It usually only takes a small sip from a vial to replenish in most cases. The

Renber juice that the commander mentioned is orange. It's the one that cures minor injuries, although if you get a high enough dose it can even heal broken bones. With that, you definitely have to understand the potency and add the right number of berries to the mix. Our knights and matrons carry both of these, along with a special Sullite bar as part of what we call a Replenishment Pack or RP for short."

Commander Sam sat up, stretched and said, "Thanks to both of you. That's much better. Now let me finish telling you about what happened." He went on to explain that he had been attacked. But then the tone of the retelling changed when Sam mentioned a detail about their attackers. He said, "Then Braster and his soldiers ambushed me. I'm still not sure how they approached me undetected. They surrounded me and Braster said that he was going to make you pay for betraying your Herkilian brothers and that he was going to raise your son up to become a powerful Sulgon soldier."

Peter held out his hand to interrupt Sam and said, "Did you say Braster? How did they sneak up on you? For sure you should've sensed his nasty presence." With Sam's reaction to the arm signal and the other things that Michael had seen he was starting to doubt his blindness theory. But then why didn't Sam look people directly in the eye when he spoke to them?

Sam nodded and said, "Yes, Braster. I don't know how that happened, but I sensed no Gaddite presences and then there they were on top of me. I was lucky to escape with my life. He attacked me with a volley of Gaddite macers while one of his soldiers pinned me against a rock. We fought for a while. I don't know how they did it. It has to be a cloaking device of some kind. It's almost like they have figured out a way to manipulate the cloaking facet on their Gaddite tokens." Sam was staring off into space now as if his mind were elsewhere. "During the attack, all I could think about was getting to you to warn you."

Peter had been listening carefully and said, "You're fortunate to have escaped. How did you get away from Braster? He can hold his own against almost any knight, except maybe an overseer."

"It's funny that you should mention overseers. It was actually the elite move that Gabriel has been working with me on that saved me. Then I used the trees to lose them."

Peter said, "The trees? Yeah. They would definitely not be able to catch you in the trees." His jaw dropped and he said, "You attempted 'The Sweep?' You're lucky you didn't put yourself in a Sullite coma or worse. That's crazy, Sam. What were you thinking?"

"I was thinking that I didn't want my brother-in-law killed and my nephew taken and corrupted by the Legion."

Peter nodded, his eyes studying Sam. "Maybe that's why it worked, my friend. You were willing to sacrifice yourself for another. That's incredible. Gabriel will be very proud."

Michael had been thinking about the bad guys that Sam had mentioned and asked, "So, you mentioned this Braster guy before. What's his story anyway?"

Peter's dimpled cheeks fell, and he said, "He was a Herkilian senior commander for the Order. But he has surrendered himself over to one of the nastiest Gaddigons, Veeral. Braster turned on the Order when something tragic happened back in 1865. He will not stop until he has enslaved or killed all those within the Order of Lithegol who oppose him. Veeral and his band of traitors have been at it for centuries."

Michael's mind had filled with questions. "So, was that huge thing your natural form before? And what is a Shadow Sentry?"

Peter smiled. "Yes, that big ugly guy was me. We Herkilians are much larger than you and the other beings of Lithegol. You probably noticed that my hands and forearms are bigger than normal when I'm in my earthly form. Some characteristics of our true embodied selves carry over, regardless of which form we're in.

"As far as the Shadow Sentry question: The Shadow Sentries are an elite organization within the Order that is assigned to perform special operations, many of them in the dark hours of the night when the Legion is at their worst. They are a special breed and some of the toughest knights and matrons out there."

Michael's mind was racing. What he thought he understood about life on Earth had completely been flipped on its head. He thought about the overwhelming powers and sensations he had started feeling since being made a squire. A feeling of loneliness sank into his chest like he had left his mom's side somehow and he was in a place she couldn't go or understand. Who could he confide in now who would understand? He tried not to think about it and focused his thoughts on what Peter and Sam had said. What came next?

"So, tell me more about these Gaddites. And what is this gathering you keep talking about?" Michael asked abruptly, his question pot boiling over.

"Gaddite Essence beings are called Gaddigons," Sam replied.

"Imagine dark ghosts with no physical body that are in the form of a nasty black dragon. They were once Sullite Essence beings like us, but they committed many terrible acts against the Order and were tried and found guilty of the highest atrocities and crimes. They were transformed into Gaddite Essence beings and banished to a Dread Realm, a place of darkness within Lithegol, where Gaddigons dwell after being exiled from their home realms. There is a Dread Realm for each of the Triads. It is not a living realm and they dwell in misery, knowing that they will never be allowed to become embodied beings.

"During the beginning of days, a large group of them found a way to enter Prime through the Dread Corridors, which are used, within the four kingdoms, to transport prisoners from the Guardian Realms to the Dread Realms. Drakkir, their powerful leader, was a part of that first group and wreaked havoc while he was free to roam the Earth."

Peter chimed in like he was dying to tell part of the story. "But Drakkir and most of his traitorous thugs were put down and imprisoned by Prince Arthur during The War of the Meridian Times. The secret migrations, including the ones in 1962 and 2022, have led us to believe that the events mentioned in the prophecy about The Gathering and the End of Days War are happening. In this last unsanctioned migration, Therok snuck through hundreds of thousands of Gaddigons. This is why he has been able to build such a large Sulgon army."

The mention of Gaddigons triggered a memory and Michael asked, "So are Serrenz and Farstus the names for some Gaddigons?"

Peter's eyes widened. "Yes, they are. Where did you hear those names?"

Michael explained how he had heard the two Legion soldiers talking down in the tunnel and that they had referred to each other as Serrenz and Farstus.

Peter stared off into space as he said, "Serrenz and Farstus are Gaddigons that are supposed to still be trapped in the Northern Dread Realm. How did they get onto Prime? This is not good. We will definitely need to communicate all of this to Captain Gabriel so that he and his team can begin a full investigation. If they were able to keep the presence of Serrenz and Farstus from us, who knows what other lizard-heads they have waiting to be unleashed." His orb flashed and he stepped away.

At the mention of lizard-heads, Michael smiled. He definitely liked the laid-back version of Peter better than the stuffy one.

Peter stepped back toward them, his orb no longer flashing, and Sam said, "I guess it could be much worse. At least they haven't snuck Bamith through."

Peter nodded and said, "That we *know* of. Man, can you imagine? That guy is pure evil. And he would be nearly impossible to track down. I just don't get it. How are they sneaking these Sulgons through? Didn't we lock everything down?"

Commander Sam responded, "We don't know yet. But we will find out. The Legion is up to something and I'm afraid, given all of the evidence, they have powerful knights within the Order helping them. And with this latest discovery of their new cloaking weapon, they might be right under our noses."

Chapter 6

A New Development

Peter turned back to Michael and said, "Let me explain. All individuals that participate in the migrations between realms must be sanctioned by someone at the rank of a senior commander or higher for regular migrations, which happen at various times.

"The Inter-kingdom migrations allow knights and matrons to travel between Lithegol and the other three kingdoms. It is much harder to sneak someone through on one of those. The next one is coming up on the day of what you call the Summer Solstice, June 21st. The Supreme Council is the one that approves those migrations. They are a council chosen by the kings from each of the four kingdoms. For someone to come across from another kingdom without being sanctioned they would need help from multiple high-ranking individuals with access to those special corridors and the relative portals."

Peter shook his head. "A migration of new Sulgons from other kingdoms could really strengthen their army. But they're not the only ones gathering. Our forces are working nonstop to find more knights and matrons. We will not let Camelot or Earth fall. But we need to be watchful."

When Michael thought about what Peter was implying about more evil dragon beings coming to Earth, he shuddered, and his mind slipped off to thoughts of his dad. How were they going to get him back from such a powerful group and what would be left of him? A dull numbness rolled over him and he pushed the depressing thoughts away. He had to pour his energy and thoughts into their mission. That's what his dad would want him to do.

Peter and Commander Sam had barely finished talking about the migration when Peter jumped up from the couch and said, "Look! Unbelievable!"

There on the TV was a reporter next to pictures of Michael, his mom, Peter and Silvan. All of their faces had been altered to give them hateful expressions. Peter spoke abruptly, "TV volume 25."

The reporter's nasal voice broke through. "A tragedy strikes. Our sources say that Julia Brenlan and Peter Olgath, believed to be part of a Freedom Alliance terrorist cell, are suspects in the bombing of a United Legion base in Des Moines, Iowa. They are on the run with their children, Michael and Silvan." Crisp hologram images of what remained of a group of barracks appeared and everyone gasped as the camera zoomed in on a woman and two children, lying motionless amidst the rubble. The reporter continued, "A bomb was detonated last night, and two barracks were all but destroyed in the violent blast. Fortunately, the residents of one of the barracks were not home at the time of the attack. However, Davina Jasser and her two small children were not as fortunate. The father of the family, Colonel Bradley Jasser, was out on assignment at the time of this heinous act. The President issued a statement about this tragic attack earlier today."

A new screen came up and the tall, stout leader in a suit was standing in front of a podium, surrounded by reporters. His thick lips were turned down and his square jaw moved as he spoke, "We are all in shock after witnessing this malicious and senseless attack on our *innocent* families. We will not allow this terrorist group to continue their horrific crimes unchecked. They preach a message of freedom but yet strike out to destroy the lives of those who seek *true* peace and freedom. We are offering a $100,000 reward for information leading to the arrest of any of these dangerous fugitives. They are on the run and our sources believe they are heading west to California. If you have any updates as to their whereabouts, please notify the nearest United Legion authorities. Our deepest thoughts of sympathy extend out to the family and friends of the victims. I can promise the people of America one thing. We will see that justice is done." Michael noticed his massive hands as he raised his thick fist in a final stirring gesture.

The screen faded and the reporter came back on, shaking his head in disbelief, "Please keep a watchful eye out and do your part to help the President and his forces capture these violent terrorists. We will update you as more information is provided."

The newsfeed moved on to an unrelated story and Peter commanded, "TV volume mute." His eyes narrowed and he growled, "I can't believe they bombed their own people to make *us* look like the bad guys. What kind of animals murder their own women and children?" His expression softened. "That poor family." He gazed inquisitively at Sam, his thick brows furrowing, and said, "How do they know where we're headed? We need to go over every detail from your undercover findings and assess our next steps."

Michael was still staring blankly at the screen. He could see the faces of those small children, ashen and lifeless. The Legion had killed them just to pin it on the Freedom Alliance. How could the American people not see what was really going on?

Commander Sam's high voice brought Michael back and he tried to push the horrifying images out of his mind. "I will tell you all that I have learned."

Before Sam began, Peter turned to Michael and said, "Because Commander Sam is an elf, he has a greatly enhanced sense of hearing. In the right circumstances, he can hear a conversation from as far away as a half mile."

Commander Sam went over what he had learned. He said that he had overheard some Legion officers talking about new weapons they were going to use against the Order and that there was some big discovery of a dark crystal sphere in northern California that made it possible. The only valuable detail regarding the discovery was something about it being hidden in a secret government facility near Sildonia, California. But somehow the Department of Defense was keeping them from obtaining it.

Michael's mind was still fixated on the images of him and the others on the TV. How did the Legion know so much? When Sam mentioned the government facility Peter shot up and snapped his fingers. "That's it!" He glanced at Michael and his mom and said, "No way. But that means that..."

Sam stopped and listened intently. "What is it, Peter? Did you think of something?"

A door opened in the back and a tall young man, who matched the picture on the table, strutted out. He was wearing jeans and a T-shirt with a guy dunking a basketball on it. His dark hair was spiked in the front and his hazel eyes were fixed on his dad. He stopped near the couch and said, "What? What's going on, Dad? You look freaked out."

"Hi, Silvan," Peter said. "This is Michael and his mother, Julia."

When he shook Silvan's hand, Michael noticed right away that the large hand gene ran in the family. Peter said, "Julia, do you remember living in northern California when Michael was young?"

She nodded. "Yes, I do. Why?"

"That facility that the commander mentioned overhearing about sounds like it is the same one that Spencer was Head of Security for when he worked for the government nearly 12 years ago. It is one of those top-secret government facilities that is not on the books."

His mom's thin eyebrows lifted. "So, they *were* after Spencer? That must be what they were talking about when they said they got the security guy they needed. But how did they know? I thought you guys were able to keep all of that a secret from the Legion?"

Peter's head was down and he said, "That is the disappointing part of it. I now have a pretty good idea of who the mole is. Only one other person of authority knew about Spencer's role before."

Before he could say who it was, Commander Sam exclaimed, "Durrill... your senior commander friend from the Ralesta Realm? That can't be right."

Peter's expressive face fell, and he said, "It's the only answer that makes sense. He works for another group within the D.O.D. that oversees space research projects. Durrill's assignment is one of the most critical within the entire Shadow Sentry organization. He has been working for the Freedom Alliance trying to infiltrate the Legion communication channel to figure out their next move for almost a year. But why would he sell out to the Legion? And if he sold us out, why would he and his group keep the Legion from getting the weapon? We're missing something here. Maybe he's actually gone rogue and isn't on either side."

Peter turned to Michael and said, "I think in this case we're going to have to do some of our training on our way to Sildonia, as this is more pressing. We'll have to get you to Camelot after we deal with this Gaddite weapon situation. But you need to stay back and not get directly involved. This can be a watch, listen and learn experience."

Peter shook his head and said, "We should've learned this sooner and we could've protected Spencer. I'm so sorry."

"It's ok, Commander. There's no way you could have known," Michael's mom said.

Michael couldn't believe it. So, the Legion was after his father. Was it only *him* though? Part of him felt some sense of relief, knowing that his father's abduction was not entirely his fault, but then he thought about what would happen to his dad after he got them this cluster thing. They wouldn't need him anymore and he could be in real danger at that point. And what was the Legion doing to him now? What if they brainwashed him and he became one of their dragon-eyed slaves? The thought brought a heaviness to his chest and he fought back the tears. They had to get his dad back right away. But how?

Silvan was staring at Michael and it was making him uncomfortable, so he said, "What is it, Silvan? Do I have something hanging out of my nose?"

Silvan jerked like he hadn't realized he was doing it, and said, "Oh. Sorry. There's just something so familiar about you. Have we met before?"

Michael studied his long face and said, "No, not that I remember. But I do have one of those faces that always reminds people of someone."

Silvan shook it off and said, "Oh, ok. My bad. Must be a mistaken identity thing." He shot a glance down at Michael's hand and said, "Hey, you're a squire. You want to check out our training obstacle course? It's super cool!"

Michael, keen for a break from all the depressing Legion talk, jumped up and said, "I've only been a squire a few days, but yeah, sure. Sounds fun. Hey, do you play basketball, by the way?"

Before Silvan could answer, his dad said, "But, you only have ten minutes. Then we need to leave. I'll pack up some stuff for you. Make it quick, boys."

Silvan turned, mid-stride, and said, "Ok, Dad. Thanks. It won't take long. I'm the master of this course." He turned back to Michael and said, "As far as basketball goes, it's my favorite sport, by far. I'm a starting forward for the Faren High varsity team here in town. What about you?"

Michael noted that Silvan was taller than he was, probably at least 6'4", and said, "I can see you as a forward. You're tall. I play point guard for our local club team back home." Saying this brought back a flood of memories, and he thought back to playing pickup games with his friends from the team. Jeff and he had shocked everyone by how easily they were able to play off of each other. He wondered how his goofy friend was doing. He could really use his funny personality right now. Would he ever get back to that life?

He was jarred back into reality by Silvan's voice. "That's cool. Good point guards are hard to find. Let's check out the course. You're going to love it."

Silvan led Michael through a door at the end of a long hallway. As soon as they walked through the door, the area lit up and Michael's jaw dropped at the sight of a huge gymnasium-sized room.

The entire space was filled with a wide variety of obstacles. Some of them seemed unsurpassable, like one where you had to step across golf ball sized metal circles, extended up from 20-foot poles, leading to a platform. Michael was about to ask about them when Silvan called to him from a porch area about 10 feet up.

Michael called out, "How did you even get up there? There's no ladder."

Silvan chuckled and said, "You don't need a ladder when you have a hoven." A red Sullice platform formed around the excited teenager's feet, and he said, "Ok. Check this out. What I've learned from the commander and my dad is that you have to channel the energy from the ring and listen for your instincts to guide you through the obstacles. It's so much easier when you just give in and let yourself feel what to do."

With that, he touched his ring and the young Herkilian's body changed. He shot up and everything was bigger - his shoulders, arms and legs. He had to be over seven feet tall. He was now wearing a red glowing uniform with a white cape, like Peter's. Thicker areas of red-flecked armor formed on his chest, arms and legs. He was studying the first obstacle, which was a series of giant rings with a rubberized swinging pendulum that was in line to knock a person off the round elevated platform on the other side.

The hulk of a boy leaped toward the hoops. Then, he paused mid-air as the pendulum began to swing more quickly, almost like it was responding to him being close to it. The giant arm, that resembled an upside-down hammer, was rocketing across the hoops at a super-fast clip now. Silvan watched and waited and got close to the hoop. Then, right as the pendulum passed the hoop on its way back, he jettisoned through, barely escaping the returning arm. Next was a corridor with small, saucer platforms. You had to jump from one to the next while rubber arms sliced at you from different angles and heights. Silvan blew through every progressively difficult obstacle with the same fluidity and ease until he reached the tall final obstacle. It resembled a trail of over-sized lollipops.

Michael wondered how Silvan was going to get across. He saw him pause and close his eyes and Michael's jaw dropped as Silvan's towering figure jumped onto the first golf ball sized circle. The round glowing platform emanating from his feet seemed to surge and tilt as if it were keeping him afloat. The platform steadied him as he sprang from one miniature ball to the next and onto the elevated platform at least 10 feet above where he had started. Upon landing, Michael saw him open his eyes and he gasped. He had done the entire last, ultra-difficult obstacle with his eyes closed. This was nuts.

Silvan raised his muscle-bound arms in a triumphant celebration and yelled, "Yes! That was incredible! You have to try it, Michael."

Michael shuddered at the prospect and said, "No way, man. I'm not there yet. That was incredible. And you're so huge. How did you get that Sullice platform thing under your feet by the way?"

Silvan smiled. "That's the thing I mentioned before. It's called a hoven."

Before he could continue, the door to the enormous room opened and Commander Sam stepped in. "It is a gathering of Sullite particles that even a squire can produce. It can lift you off the ground, extend your jumping abilities, or steady your balance as you saw in Silvan's case. The overseers have mastered this power to the point where they can actually fly for short periods of time with it."

The commander was studying Michael and motioned toward the platform. How Sam knew which one was him Michael still didn't understand. "You must remove all doubt from your mind, Michael. I believe that you can handle this course without much problem. Silvan, you are about to witness something amazing. Michael, touch your ring and call up the love that you have for your father. Focus all your desires to rescue him toward your feet."

Michael did as he asked. He closed his eyes and an incredible wave of energy rushed through him toward his legs. When he opened his eyes, there was a red buzzing platform, even larger than Silvan's, below his feet and he was floating several feet off the ground. At first, his heart raced at the prospect of trying to control this foreign thing, but when he saw Sam smiling confidently at him, he felt better.

"Don't be frightened. That is a powerful hoven for a young squire like you to have, but it doesn't surprise me, given the strength of your essence. Now concentrate on encouraging it to lift you to the platform but don't push too hard on it. It knows what you want," the Commander said.

Michael did as he was asked, and it felt almost like a conversation. Like the Sullice was a partner working with him to accomplish something. Within a few seconds, he was standing on the starting platform, gazing out at the daunting obstacles in his path. Silvan's mouth was open, and he was staring at him. It was so weird.

Commander Sam continued, "Now, focus on the path to each of your destinations. For instance, think of each of the platforms along the way, then reach out to the power and guide it to take you to them. One at a time. But don't feel like you have to rush it. This is all new to you."

Michael took a deep breath and tried not to think about the long 10-to-15-foot drop to the floor. The good news was that there were mats laid out, but it was still a fair distance to fall. He mapped out what he would need to do to overcome each of the daunting obstacles, factoring in what he had seen with Silvan's run, and reached out to what he had come to recognize as the power of Sullice. He then leaped through the hoop, easily dodging the large rapidly swinging pendulum. His body moved quickly, and it was all a blur. It was as if he had put the coordinates into his mind and his body and the Sullice had executed the actions needed to overcome each obstacle 10x faster than normal. Within seconds, he was standing on the precarious metal balls, suspended high in the air, his hoven steadying him like it was an animate object. Hop, hop, hop and he was standing beside the gigantic Silvan, who was displaying even more shock- if that were possible.

Looking down at the course he had completed, Michael was overcome with exuberance. He raised both arms and exclaimed, "Wow! Did you see that? That was awesome!"

Silvan did a fist pump and high-fived him so hard he almost fell backward off the platform.

"That was impressive, Michael," the Elf Commander said. "You really are gifted at partnering with the power of Sullice. But it is important to always remember that the power of Sullice is fueled by your feelings of hope and love."

Silvan had calmed down slightly and was shaking his head. "Dude, that was lit. How did you do that? It took me weeks of hard work and training to finish this course, and most squires take even longer! Where did you come from?"

Michael smiled sheepishly and said, "A farm in Linkston, Indiana, actually. In the middle of nowhere."

Silvan chuckled and said, "Well, I would like to get my hands on whatever they fed you on that farm."

Michael laughed and said, jokingly, "It must have been the fresh cow's milk."

The door swung open and Peter walked in. Upon seeing the boys on the uppermost platform, his brow furrowed. "Hey, what's going on? How did Michael get up there?"

Silvan put his hand on Michael's shoulder and exclaimed, "Dad, you should've seen it. Michael shredded this course like it was nothing. He finished it in like ten seconds, and his hoven was huge."

Peter stared up at Michael, as if not believing it, and said,

"Really?" When Sam nodded, he exclaimed, "That's incredible! I really wish we had time for you to show me, Michael, but I'm afraid we have to go now."

Silvan leaped and glided down, his hoven slowing his descent. Michael hesitated and then followed. Using what Commander Sam had taught him, he tried to control the platform and its power as he glided down. An unpleasant dark feeling seeped in and he wondered what or who was triggering it. Was the Legion closing in on them? Before he knew it, he was falling rapidly, and he was shocked to see that his hoven had all but disappeared. He immediately pushed hard, and a massive glowing platform shot out and sent him careening off toward the wall. He yelled out and right before he hit the wall, his momentum slowed and he drifted slowly down to a position next to Commander Sam. The noble elf lowered his arm and asked, "Are you ok? What distracted you, Michael?"

Michael looked around. The ill feeling was gone, and he thought about the fact that no one else had felt anything, and said, "Oh, nothing. I just lost control for a second. You really have to stay on top of this stuff."

Sam peered at him curiously, patted him on the back and said, "Don't worry yourself. You're doing very well. Just keep practicing. All in due time."

Before long, they were packed and traveling in "Little Billy" to their next destination. "Little Billy" was definitely not little and did not resemble the childlike simplicity the name inferred. Michael realized on this trip how much he really hadn't explored the vehicle before on their jaunt with Peter. From the outside, the Hummer appeared to be the longest SUV limo one could ever imagine. But the inside was closer to something out of a Sci-Fi movie.

As they traveled, Michael thought about how refreshing it was to have someone his age to talk to. He and Silvan discovered they had a lot in common. Silvan reminded him of Jeff, and he thought about how much he missed his friend. He wondered when or if he would ever see him again. Late that night they made it to another safe house and Michael stumbled into a simple room with just a bed and nightstand and slipped into a deep sleep, grateful to be safe and on a bed.

When Michael woke up the next morning and walked out of his room, he noticed right away that this was definitely a smaller safe house than the hillside one they had stayed in. It had the same strange lighting in the main area and when he approached Peter he asked, "So, what are those cone lights? I saw them in the other safe house too."

Peter gazed up at them, and said, "Those are made with Radiathite sand-sized raw crystals. The scientist we mentioned, Dr. Waicroft, figured out a way to funnel the Sullite energy from the Sun into those cones and illuminate the floating crystals. The pure Radiathite crystals are an excellent source of light and use very little Sullice, so we can power several of those chandeliers for a month on only one day's worth of sunlight. It really is amazing."

Michael thought about this scientist they kept mentioning. He sounded like the Thomas Edison of Lithegol, and he wondered if he would ever have the privilege of meeting him.

Commander Sam and Michael's mom had prepared a delicious breakfast and Michael wolfed it down. Then they were back on the road. As had been the norm, Peter drove while Commander Sam spent the next several hours talking about the different races and cultures of Lithegol. He talked about his home world, Fluren. It sounded like such a peaceful place with various communities of Elemental Elves all working together using their respective gifts. It all seemed so surreal.

Chapter 7

Discoveries

They stopped later that afternoon at another safe house, this time somewhere in Wyoming. This one had a Fitness Center and they decided to put in a quick workout before they left. Michael was watching Silvan bench press an unbelievable amount of weight, the bar sagging from the exorbitant load, and he asked, "How much is that anyway?"

After rattling off ten reps, the last two requiring a little extra effort, Silvan set the bar on the hooks and said, "These are special weights that one of the Cogs from Ralesta helped to invent. The big ones are a hundred pounds and the medium-sized ones are fifty. So, this is 700 pounds."

Peter walked over and patted Silvan on the back and said, "Great job, Son! You're a beast."

Michael's mom was off in the corner of the room doing crunches. Commander Sam had been jumping rope at like 100 miles per hour and set his rope down, walked over and said, "I think it's time for Michael to continue to discover what he can do with the power of Sullice."

Peter stared at him as if he were joking. The small commander nodded at Michael and said, "Go ahead. Be sure to guide the Sullice into your arms and chest. Your power will enable you to lift it more easily than you could imagine."

Michael thought of what Silvan had said. *700lbs.* How on earth could he even dream of lifting that much weight?

Peter shrugged his shoulders and walked behind the bar to spot him while Michael stepped toward the bench, looking one more time at Commander Sam, who just smiled and nodded. As Michael lay down, he tried to control his breathing and put aside the doubt that kept creeping in. He thought of the commander's instructions and visualized himself pushing down a door to get to his imprisoned father and felt the Sullice surge into his arms and chest as he gripped the bar and lifted it off the supports. It gave way immediately and Michael felt like he was lifting just a weight bar. He stared up at the sagging bar and said, "How is this possible?"

Commander Sam motioned for him to continue and said, "I have tried to tell you that the power of Sullice within you is beyond anything I have ever seen. You have only begun to tap into your true potential. Go ahead and try twenty reps."

Michael continued to focus and was able to easily lift the weight up and down. He was on rep 16 and it was getting harder to hold the Sullice in place when the activity prompted a flashback of working out with his dad and his mind went elsewhere. Luckily, Peter was paying attention and caught the bar before it crushed his chest, and asked, "What happened, Michael? Are you ok?"

Michael concentrated on calming himself down, and said, "I'm ok. I was distracted by a flashback to a time I worked out with my dad. I really miss him."

Peter nodded. "Yeah. I worked out with him like this too. He's an animal in the weight room." He shook his head and his eyes softened. "I'm sorry, bud. I miss him too. I will do all within my power to get him back." He helped him up.

Sam put his hand on Michael's shoulder, and said, "You will learn to maintain your focus, regardless of what is happening around you or in your mind. This is paramount, as the Legion will try to use distraction and attacks on your mind and essence to defeat and subdue you."

Peter was shaking his head. "It's just so crazy what you did with that weight. I never would've imagined that you could be that strong. Silvan and I are able to lift this amount of weight only because of our Herkilian genetics. You continue to astound me, Michael."

"All I did was focus the Sullice by thinking of saving my dad like Commander Sam said. But can't anyone do that?"

Peter was studying Michael now and said, "No, definitely not. Normally each realm has specific Sullite gifts that they bring to the Order. Those from Guardian Realms are normally stronger, more agile and better fighters and have excellent eyesight, especially in the Herkilian Realm.

"But in your realm, Prime, these abilities are usually diluted for those humans that are native to it so that each knight or matron has a modest aptitude with each of the abilities from all of Lithegol. In other words, for you to be stronger than someone at your level, like Silvan, who is from Herkili, is unheard of. And most don't have that amount of Sullite power until they become a senior master or a commander. Part of what is skewing your perception right now is that you're comparing yourself to

Silvan. But what you don't realize is that Silvan is probably among the top three most powerful squires out there. Compared to your average squire you're off the charts." After they finished and did a few runs in the small training room, Peter said, "Ok. Now it's time for a cool surprise."

The muscle-bound commander stood up, pushed inward on a wall tile near where he had been sitting as a series of clicks sounded. The wall slid to the side and there, resting on pegs was an arsenal of various weapons. Some of them didn't look like anything Michael had ever seen before and when Peter pointed to a huge, futuristic-looking bazooka rifle, he had to ask, "What kind of a gun is that?"

"*That* is a Sullera Rifle." Peter said. "They are designed by the scientist I was telling you about before, Dr. Henry Waicroft. Each one is made from Omithite and uses a special custom mechanism to harness the power of Sullice and can take down those butt-ugly Sulgons like nothing." Commander Sam shot him a look and Peter shrugged and gave an apologetic smile, saying sarcastically, "I mean, those evil Sulgons."

When Michael looked closer at the sleek gun, he noticed the oversized crystal nestled right where the bolt action would be on most rifles. He wondered how the energy was harnessed and directed down the massive gray barrel. There was an Omithite cone-shaped object above the crystal chamber and before he could ask about it Peter pointed to it and said, "That is Henry's special creation. It works like a solar funnel and harnesses the Sullite rays from the Sun, and channels them into the crystal for the gun. But the genius part of it is how he uses the Sullite signature for each weapon. Each gun is personally activated to a specific individual. When that person touches the weapon their Sullite signature is recognized and the gun is authenticated and can be fired. The other nice thing about these weapons is that they can also be used by those who have not yet entered the Order."

Peter grabbed the hefty rifle and when his hand made contact, there was a familiar double-click. The gun lit up white with a blue speckled glow, especially immediately around the crystal itself. It was the same white colored aura with blue flecks that he had seen surrounding Peter previously. Peter flipped it from one hand to the other as if it were a toothpick.

Silvan was staring at the impressive rifle and asked, "Can I check it out, Dad? That thing is cool!"

His dad carefully handed it to him. As soon as Peter let go of it the overall Sullite glow disappeared, which startled Silvan at first. Then he chuckled and said, "That's wicked! When do I get one?"

His dad nodded, smiled and said, "Soon, big guy. Soon."

Peter's attention went back to the rifle, and he pointed to a knob on the side of the rifle, with carved notches and writing around it. "This particular Sullera rifle can fire a volley of single stunning pellet-like shots, baseball-sized stun shots, spiked ball extraction shots, or a grenade shot to take out a group of Sulgons."

"That's cool," Michael said. "So, with a refined crystal, each facet is tied to the type of shot you fire? Is that how the orbs work too?"

"Yes, exactly," Peter replied. "Each of the twelve facets in the orb is refined or locked in, like we talked about before, to perform a specific activity."

"So, what is an extraction shot?" Michael asked.

Sam stood up and opened a different side cabinet door in the corner, and Peter said, "An extraction is when you use the power of Sullice to remove or extract a Gaddigon from an embodied host. It can be very difficult, depending on the grasp that Gaddigon has on its victim's essence core. For instance, this rifle would not have sufficient Sullite power to extract Veeral from Commander Braster. Sometimes the poisoning of Gaddin is so prevalent in a host that an extraction is not possible without killing the embodied being in question." He set the rifle aside and said, "But I'm still taking this beauty with me... just in case."

Commander Sam reached into the new cabinet and pulled out a heavy-duty spandex jumpsuit. "We've been discussing a lot of offensive weapons and now it's time to talk defense." He handed the black, long-sleeved full body wetsuit to Michael, and said, "This is what we call our 'Undershield.' It is made from a material engineered by one of our Cognitive scientists, Dr. Zamerin Blissel, from the faery Realm of Tisdek."

"Good old Dr. Z," Peter chimed in.

"It is ultra-light, breathable and flexible. But it will stop virtually any physical weapon from penetrating the skin, including knives and bullets."

Silvan reached over to touch the fabric, his eyes wide. "That's awesome. When do we get to wear it?"

"Right now, actually," Sam said. "That pair is for you, Michael, and we'll find some for Silvan and Julia also. Keep it on at all times, as it will likely save your life. You won't even feel like you have it on most of the time. It stretches and shrinks, as needed, in case you're wondering."

Peter smirked and said, "Sam is used to wearing Leotards from his gymnastics days!"

Sam shook his head and said, "I am, actually. It's funny you should mention that Mr. Ballet dancer." His smile broadened and he said, "What's your nickname again… Twinkle-toes?"

Peter did a double take and laughed, his whole body shaking. "Nice. You haven't called me that in years. Brings back memories. That was some night of dancing with the ladies down in Mazatlán. Sometimes you surprise me when I least expect it, old friend." He turned back to Michael and Silvan, who were looking at each other questioningly, and put his finger over his lips, winked and whispered, "The Ballet helps me with my agility."

Peter leaned down and swept his ring in front of the gray bench he had been sitting on. There was a double click and the top popped up, revealing a hidden area beneath. He pulled out a granite-like, Omithite ball that had several crystals embedded in it. It was about the size of a softball. "This little guy is one of my favorites. We call this the mini-S.S.B, which is short for a Sullera Smart Bomb, or many just call it a SullBomb. It can take out most Gaddigons within a 15-foot radius. We have different versions of this, but they all have buttons on them with various timer settings. The small black button disengages the bomb. The green is for a one-minute timer. The yellow is for a 30-second and the red for a 15-second detonation wait time.

"We teach all knights and matrons from early on in their training to avoid the blast from one of the Sullera weapons, especially the bombs. Our physical bodies can be damaged from the blast, as too much of an influx of Sullite can be more than our bodies can handle. Take water, for example. Water is good and essential for us but too much of it can be harmful to our physical bodies, whether we ingest too much and drown, or we get crushed by it."

Commander Sam had been quiet during Peter's S.S.B tutorial and put up his hand as if to signal that he had something to say. "Ok. That's probably enough about weapons, Commander. This is not your training cycle weapons class." Peter smiled and shrugged, and Sam continued, "I am living proof of what can happen with overexposure to Sullice. I was caught in the line of a blast during one of our excursions with the Legion and this is why I am physically blind. The only reason I lived through the experience is that Captain Gabriel was present and was able to stabilize me and lessen the damage. The unique thing about the effects of the blast is that it left me with enhanced Sullite perceptive abilities, and my other senses are also heightened dramatically. The one bad side effect, besides the blindness, that has posed some challenges is the imbalance in my Sullite Essence. I have had to spend a lot of time molding and shaping and learning to control my new essence. It makes me extremely easy to track and identify since my Sullite Essence is so unique compared to anyone else. But I am fortunate to have come away from the experience without further challenging side effects. I owe the Captain my life and I have tried to put my new unusual abilities to good use for the Order."

Peter, who was sitting next to the commander, patted him on the back and said, "You're an inspiration to us all, Commander. The way you have turned all of what happened to you into a weapon for the order is inspiring."

"Thank you, sir," Sam said. "I couldn't have done a lot of it without your support, my friend."

*   *   *

He proceeded to relate some of their experiences fighting the Legion. He went into more detail on the Freedom Alliance. It was a group, closely affiliated with the Order of Lithegol, that had formed shortly after David Sampson—or rather Erubamir— was elected President of the United States. The Freedom Alliance was dedicated to keeping the United Legion from taking over the world. Michael couldn't believe the outrageous stories they were telling about taking on a dozen Sulgons at a time and using their rings to form various weapons in each battle. All this talk of battles triggered a memory, and Michael asked, "You mentioned that Sweep move before. What was that?"

"That is an elite move," Sam replied. "Elite moves are those special defense and attack moves perfected by the overseer knights. There are only thirteen overseer knights in all of Lithegol, well – twelve right now."

He paused and Michael wondered why 12 at first and then he remembered what had happened with Herkili and Therok the Overseer.

Sam continued, "There is one from each realm plus a captain, who is currently Gabriel. We must learn at least one of these elite moves as part of our rites before we can become commanders. As I mentioned before, for my Commander Rites I chose one of the most difficult elite moves ever, The Sweep, which was perfected by Captain Gabriel over a thousand years ago. The move took me years of practice and preparation to learn. It was the most difficult thing I have ever done, and I still don't consider myself anywhere near a master of it."

Peter cut in and said, "Don't sell yourself short, Commander. There are only a handful of knights who have even attempted The Sweep at all, and Gabriel has been very pleased with your progress on it."

Something from that statement triggered a realization in Michael. "Wait a minute. Did you say 1000 years ago? How old *is* Gabriel?"

"*That* is a very good question," Peter replied. "No one actually knows. Let's just say he's been around way longer than anyone else from the Order. And there is no single Sulgon that can even come close to matching up with him in battle, not even Erubamir."

"Awesome! So, when am *I* going to learn some moves?" Michael exclaimed.

"All in good time, Michael. Patience. First, you must continue to learn to feel the power of Sullice and channel it. Just like back at the obstacle course," Sam said. "What you must come to know is that the core worlds and all the living things on them are filled with Sullite Essence. It is a symbiotic partnership, and we can tap into it in our quest to help those we are called to assist."

Michael's mom leaned forward and said, "So, that must explain why the plant came back to life the night of your anointing."

Peter's dark eyebrows lifted. "A plant came back to life? Really? What else happened that night?"

As Michael explained how the bed and everything in the room had lifted off the ground, Peter's slightly bulging eyes widened.

Commander Sam had been listening to Michael with his eyes closed as he relayed what had happened. He opened them slowly and said, "I am interested to discover what your future is within the Order, Michael. I am sure that you will become one of the more powerful knights in the coming years. It's no wonder King Deyan sent a Guardian Commander to deliver you. Peter, are you sure we want to take Michael with us on this adventure? It will be very dangerous. Maybe we should take the boys to Camelot first."

"I know that would seem like the right choice, but I feel like he needs to come with us. I can't explain it. There is some reason he is needed on this mission, but I can't pinpoint it yet. You must trust me, Sam. You, of all people, know me. I would never allow anything to happen to our new friend here. Even if I had to lay down my life to protect him."

"Let us come, Uncle Sam. We're ready. Give us a chance," Silvan pleaded.

Sam's eyes were closed again, and he was concentrating deeply as if he hadn't even heard Silvan's comment. "Ok. I can sense what you are talking about now, almost as if the King has chosen to communicate it to me. It still makes me very nervous though. If the Legion finds out about Michael's potential, they will do anything to capture him. We must be extra vigilant and keep Gabriel apprised of everything that happens. Everything."

Chapter 8

Training

They left early the next day. By late afternoon, they started seeing signs for California. They eventually pulled over for a break and Michael had an interesting discussion with Peter and Sam. During this chat, he learned that they had first come to Earth back in 1970. When Michael asked how it was that they weren't older they explained that as they advanced as knights the power of Sullice preserved and heightened their body's ability to fight off age and overcome illness.

Sam pointed to the amulet on his chest. "This is one of the Tokens of Lithegol. It is called the Orb of Merlin. On all knights and matrons, the straight-edged compass points within the sign indicate which Realm Triad they are assigned to. Those like me, who are assigned to Prime, have all four points illuminated.

"The bracelet is the Band of Gawain and the other is the Ring of Lancelot. Each of these three namesakes were part of the Royal Guard for Prince Arthur in the days leading up to the Meridian Times War and became known for their mastery of each respective token.

"Each realm's tokens are slightly different, depending on the nature of their domain, but they all have the Sign of Lithegol. In it, three powers of light are symbolically represented. The Sun stands for the light and majesty of the skies and the heavens, the Moon is tied to the order of the planets, and the Star symbolizes the power of each living being's Sullite Essence Core."

Sam had touched the orb while talking about it and Michael could see again that it didn't move. Feeling highly curious, he asked, "So, how does the orb stay in place? There's no chain on it or anything."

Peter gestured toward his chest and said, "The orb and the other tokens synergize with our essence cores. Which means threads of essence energy from our core hold them in place. Our Sullite Essence Cores are located near our hearts. During the crystal refining process, each of the facets on the token crystal is tied to specific powers or capabilities."

"So, what are the powers in the orb?" Michael asked.

Sam reached down, removed his orb, and held it out for Michael to see. Michael could see veins of blue speckled light extending from the back of it into his hand and he thought that those must be the threads he had mentioned. The etchings of all the elements were intricate and Michael wondered whose job it was to carve them.

All of the material in the orb, except for the diamond-like crystal in the center, was the same gray granite substance Peter had called Omithite from Michael's ring. In the upper right shadowed area, between the north and east star points, an engraving of what looked like a pointed ear surrounded by the four elements, earth, fire, wind and water shone brightly. Michael assumed those were his realm's sign, since he was an Elemental.

Sam said, "There are several different powers and abilities locked into the orb during the refining process, including teleportation, the power to advance knights and matrons, healing, the capturing of Gaddigons, elite moves, and the activation of Sullite crystals."

Peter jumped in and pushed some buttons on a wall panel and an ultra-clear 3D projection appeared floating in the air toward the center of the room. The detail of the images was beyond anything Michael had ever seen. He recognized Earth, and it was inside what he guessed was an outline representing Prime. It was right in the center, plus he counted twelve other, what Peter had called realms, surrounding ours in a circle—just like on the Sign of Lithegol. The wavy sun spires represented the other 12 realms and the crystal in the center of the sign was Prime. It was all making more sense now.

Peter pointed to the northern three realms and said, "This is the Northern Triad, where giants like me live. This center realm in our triad is Herkili, the Guardian Realm. He pointed to the left realm and said, "And this is Pratea, the Elemental Realm. On the right is Ralesta, the Cognitive Realm, where all the geniuses live.

"Each triad has each of these types of realms. The giants in the north, faeries in the south, elves in the east and dwarves in the west. The living realms are what scientists on Earth call Solar Systems and, like your Earth, each core world rotates around at least one sun. Many from each living realm are tested on missions or quests on their home core world. But all are hoping to be considered for a mission or a long stay on your core world, Earth. With your more Sullice-filled Sun, everyone's Sullite powers are enhanced and because of its strategic nature the more challenging missions are here." He pointed. "Any questions? Nothing unusual about any of this, right?" he asked with a wink.

Michael smiled, nodded, and said, "Nothing unusual at all. I hear this stuff every day... Actually, that does help. Visuals help... So, how bad off is Herkili from what Therok did, by the way?"

At the mention of Herkili, Peter frowned and shook his head. "Unfortunately, Herkili is overrun by Therok and his family and their followers. Many have evacuated, and some have sought refuge on Earth, but there are still many trapped there, unable to escape the evil clutches of the Legion."

"I'm sorry to hear about your home. That has to be hard for you to take," Michael said.

"Thanks, Michael. One of the saddest days for me was when Captain Gabriel had to call off missions to my home world, Veloro. And soon the other realms within the Northern Triad will follow. I can't believe it's really happening." His expressive face had a profound look of sadness on it and he said, "Fortunately, I was able to get my family out safely, but many of my friends are still trapped there." He clenched his thick fist and growled, "I can't wait to storm in there and crush those Legion traitors." Then he took a deep breath. "Sorry about that. Sometimes I get angry. The Captain has been working with me on that."

Commander Peter pushed several buttons on the console and the image on the map changed. The viewpoint zoomed out from the center, where Prime and Earth were located. A huge glowing white overlay with what appeared to be a transparent continent hovered in the sky over Earth. It had a label that said 'Camelot' above it. "This is Camelot," said Peter.

"It is in another dimension, called Avalon. And as I mentioned before, Avalon operates within its own time system. Knights and matrons can be trained and receive their advancements at Camelot or one of the other fortresses in Avalon while no time passes on the core worlds. One key point about the fortresses is that one can only enter an associated Avalon fortress for a given realm *from* that particular realm. So, I couldn't enter the fortress for Herkili, which is Dornin, from any other realm or core world, including Earth for instance. Camelot is the most important fortress and the most highly protected in the kingdom. Many of the most powerful Gaddigons are imprisoned there in a secret dungeon, including many of Drakkir's most prominent leaders."

Michael remembered hearing about Drakkir and how Arthur had imprisoned him and said, "So, where is *he* imprisoned? Could he ever break out? It sounds like he's bad news."

Peter bowed his head and said, "That slimeball is imprisoned in the Kingdom of Siock, his home kingdom. And yes, he is the epitome of bad news. If he were ever to be set free, the Legion would gain immense power and their overall level of cunning and cruelty would grow in frightening ways. He is the vilest, most powerful Gaddite in the four kingdoms."

Peter forced a smile and said, "But enough doom and gloom. When the time comes, as far as your trip to Camelot, here is what we're looking at." He typed something on the console and the floating image changed to a 3D rendering of a map of the United States. Certain cities were marked with a glowing Lithegol insignia. He pointed to one of them in northern California, and said, "The closest gateway to Camelot, from where we will be at, the Portacon of Galahad, is located near King Peak, which is about 50 miles from Sildonia."

He touched the glowing insignia and an incredibly clear 3D visualization of a mountain appeared. The image sharpened, zoomed in and spun around and Michael's jaw dropped. There in the door of a cave at the base of the mountain was a golden door. It was exactly like the one from his nightmare.

He stared in awe at it, unable to grasp what was happening. He finally pointed and said, "What is that? I had a dream about a door just like that."

"Really? *That* is a LumiDoor. It is the entrance to a portacon and to Avalon. What happened in your dream?"

Michael stared at the image as if the attacker from his dream lurked in the outlining trees and said, "In my nightmare, a dragon-man was chasing me, and I felt drawn to a mountain like that. I woke up after falling through that golden door."

Peter was looking at the map, then back at Michael, and said, "Wow! You're a mysterious kid. You know that?"

Michael shrugged and said, "I guess." He pointed at the hovering 3D mountain image and said, "But not as mysterious as all this."

Michael saw something move near the mountain on the holographic display, and as he leaned in, he spotted a rabbit hopping toward the neighboring forest. He pointed and said, "Did you see that? There was a rabbit. Is this an actual video feed of the location?"

Peter nodded. "Yes, it is. The image is being generated by strategically placed Visithite crystals in the surrounding area. Just think of it this way. You can send high-resolution video across glass fibers in your world today using optical cables. Imagine that same technology but without any type of wire or cable and with much more power and clarity and from great distances. The technology and the capabilities of the Order are way beyond anything you have here on Earth. That's how I was able to transport to you from a portacon. But not just any knight or matron can teleport this way. As I mentioned before, we harness the power and direct it using our orb tokens. Teleportation requires a great amount of Sullite power and control. Because of this, it is only given to those at a commander level or above. And only the overseers can teleport without using a portacon." Michael thought about how he and his mom had been teleported to the safe house. Did that mean that the golden bird was somehow an overseer knight?

Michael's thoughts went back to his dream and he asked, "So, what's up with the Legion's slitted eyes, anyway?"

Peter's face tightened. "Their eyes are slitted because in their Sulgon form they are half Sullite and half Gaddigon, or half human and half dragon if you want to look at it from your point of view. Basically, the Gaddite essence beings, once they're invited in, take over an embodied being. The host's Sullite tokens become Gaddite and they latch on to the essence core of that individual. At that point, they become a hybrid being called a Sulgon, which is a being with great power but limited by its surroundings. For instance, because of the amount of Sullite energy given off by the Sun in the Prime realm, the Legion hybrids cannot change into their Sulgon form during daylight hours here on Earth."

It was beginning to make more sense now. That was why the

Legion soldiers wore sunglasses. But he still didn't know how he fit into this world.

*　　*　　*

Later on that day, they pulled into a rest stop in California. Peter had given Michael and Silvan special ultra-light plastic swords to spar with. He called them Prindos. So, that's what they were called. He was teaching them about lunging, blocking and counter-parrying. He was a good teacher and had taken a Prindo to demonstrate each movement, whether from the body, the torso, the feet or arms.

As he sparred, Michael felt the same instincts that surfaced from his experience with his dad, multiplied by ten. He could sense what moves Silvan was going to make before he made them. Silvan was getting frustrated and was trying to mix up his moves and unleash stronger attacks. But even though Peter had to correct Michael's form on some of his defensive moves, he still had not been struck by Silvan's blade. At one-point Silvan seemed to be moving faster than any human should be able to but Michael's ability seemed to adjust and respond accordingly.

When Peter finally called for them to stop, Silvan threw his Prindo on the ground and stormed off. Michael felt bad and said, "Sorry, Silvan." He didn't know what else to say. How could he really apologize for something that just was?

Peter called Michael over, motioning for him to sit next to him and Commander Sam on a park bench. "You have nothing to apologize about.

You have incredible natural abilities that allow you to be a step ahead of your attacker."

Michael nodded and said, "That's what it feels like. I can't explain it, but I could sense what he was going to do right before he did it. I have always had this ability, but now it seems to be even more powerful. Where do you think it came from?"

Commander Sam pointed toward his chest. "It flows from the power of Sullice that is within you. Everyone has a Sullite Essence Core, but yours is different from most. It is highly 'tuned in,' as Commander Peter would say, to all things around it. Your fighting sensor reminds me of what I've seen with some powerful dwarfs, who have an ability similar to Echolocation. This is an extremely unusual gift for someone from Prime and implies that, as I've said before, you will become a great and powerful knight within the order. It also means that when the Legion discovers your power, they will want to turn you to their evil ways and inhabit you so that they can use you as a supremely powerful and dangerous Sulgon in the End of Days War."

Peter patted Michael on the leg and said, half-chuckling, "All I have to say is I'm glad you're on our side, buddy." He turned his gaze toward Silvan, who was moping on a tree stump. "I'd better go talk to my little squire. He looks pretty lit." He leaped up off the bench and Michael laughed to himself at how Peter had misused their slang. He thought about his first experience with Peter. He had been so formal. The huge commander had definitely loosened up and Michael liked it. He had a playful, childlike quality about him.

When Silvan came back, he seemed to have cooled off. He shook

Michael's hand, and said, "I'm sorry I got upset, Michael. I know you're just doing your best, which is what you should be doing." He turned to his dad and said, "Can we try it again? I'll try to use the power of Sullice more to help me."

Peter nodded and said, "Go ahead. I want to teach you a few more advanced moves, too. I think you're both ready." He proceeded to teach them the Riposte and the Reprise. It took some practice, but after a handful of tries, they were both responding to the opponent's parry differently depending on what Peter shouted. He was encouraging them to listen to the power of Sullice and allow it to guide their movements. Michael was learning how to recognize this as he thought back to the exercises Peter and Sam had been working with them on.

Silvan was doing better this time, but he still was unable to get in any strikes, despite approaching it with more patience. He would try a certain attack and if Michael countered, blocked or parried he would adjust and try something different. In the middle of an intense volley, the golden bird appeared and Michael heard his familiar voice. "Be wise, young Master. It is not always about winning. When those who fight for your cause win, you all win."

Michael stared at his hovering friend, pondering what he had said. Silvan capitalized on the distraction and landed a hit on his shoulder. You would've thought he'd won the lottery by his celebration at that point. He jumped up and down, pumped his fists and yelled, "I did it. I finally did it. Yes!"

He ran over, gave his dad a high five, and then with his dad's head motion he nodded and went over and shook Michael's hand. "That was a great match. You're awesome."

"No, good job to you. That was a great volley. Way to stick with it."

Peter patted them both on the back. "It looks like we need to work on Michael's concentration as part of his training regime." He winked at Michael. "Now, it's time to introduce you to the real weapon you'll be using in battle- your SullSword."

"Really, Dad?" Silvan exclaimed. "I have been begging to be shown how to use the SullSword. Why now?"

"I feel that you're both ready," Peter said. "It was important for you to learn the fundamentals before moving to the next step of training."

When Michael searched for the bird again, he was gone. Peter proceeded to show them how to call up the SullSword from the ring by thinking about what they wanted and summoning it at the same time. It felt like the hoven except that when Michael was finally able to bring his out, he had thought of fighting to free his dad from the Legion. It was almost like the Sullice needed to sense that he was motivated and ready for that action. Michael's SullSword was nothing spectacular. The points on the cross-guard curved downward, with ridges of red Sullice in the handle. The blade of speckled light came to a gradual point and was about three feet long. Michael noticed a pulsing sensation flowing from him into the sword and asked, "What is that surge I feel?"

"That is the power of Sullice coursing through you. It is what you harness, and it gives you your power in battle," Peter answered. He had them swing their glowing blades and repeat the moves he had taught them until their arms felt too heavy to lift. Afterward, Peter handed them a Braiz bar, which was the size and shape of a protein bar but had a unique purplish-brown color to it. Peter held one up and said, "Commander Sam was one of the Elemental scientists who helped develop this useful snack. It has a super high dose of protein and some special potent ingredients from his concoctions that replenish our Sullice power. The lead scientist was a dwarf Cog named Hilligan Braiz. Thus, why we call this the Braiz bar." Peter further explained that they couldn't spar with each other using SullSwords because only the dark power of Gaddin would clash with the Sullite blades.

Michael and Silvan's lessons continued, with the first being a mini-lesson from Peter on swordplay where he showed them more defensive moves. He told them when they engaged their 'SullSword', they could use it to battle the Sulgons, who used the dark equivalent, called a GaddBlade. He reminded them that the squire ring could be used to also provide a shield, the hoven, the uniform and armor, and it could enable communication with others. The giant commander went on to say that any weapon that they could imagine could be formed utilizing the pointed crystal part of the ring.

He also explained that as they advanced in power and became apprentice knights, they would receive their tokens and would learn to use the four facets on the band token to create other types of shields, such as a dome, a net or a cocoon. The armor that each soldier engaged when in battle would protect him or her to some degree, but the shield was more powerful and could fend off much more Gaddite firepower. He went on to clarify that the squire shield normally wasn't as powerful as those summoned from a band.

Peter seemed intent on going through certain training exercises before they embarked on the last leg of their trip and Michael asked, "Why are we training so hard? Are we going to actually see action?"

Peter placed his huge hand on his shoulder and said, "There is always a possibility, young squire." He looked at Silvan, concern in his eyes, and said, "And you must be as prepared as possible. I must *protect* you both at all costs." His voice cracked on the word protect and then he took a deep breath, smiled and jumped back into training mode.

He had them incorporate swordplay with their SullSwords while navigating on their hovens. Peter and Sam pretended to be Sulgons, slashing at them with Prindos as they moved through a set of obstacles. The exercise was exhilarating, and it felt like all of the things they had been learning were coming together. At one point, Michael dodged one of Peter's blows and Silvan came crashing down from behind and knocked his dad to the ground. Peter laughed as Silvan said, "Take that, you lizard-head!" Pretending to stab him.

Peter also had them continue to work on moving things and even controlling the intricate parts of objects, which was definitely harder. The last thing he had them try was to unlock a door in the back of the S.A.V. He talked about how they had to feel the internal spring-loaded pins within the lock with their minds. He described pushing on them one at a time with the power of Sullice until they each clicked and then twisting the whole mechanism. It took Michael three tries, but he was finally able to do it, which was apparently a surprise to Peter. "No way! How is that possible? You're a squire." Silvan was unable to do it, but they had heard clicking sounds from the lock as he pushed on it, and his dad said that that was an indicator that he was close.

After their lockpicking session, the elf commander patted Michael on the back and said, "Now, come. Let's take a walk."

When they stepped outside Michael noticed immediately that the air was substantially colder. It was late afternoon and darkness would be settling in soon. Somehow, that meant more to him now than it had days earlier. There were things in the night that frightened him—otherworldly things. And they were after him. His mind cycled back to the story of how his parents had come to have him; how he had been delivered to them by a mysterious princess. Who was she? Who was *he* for that matter? And who were his real parents?

Sam's calming voice broke his trance. "I sense frustration. You must quiet your fears of the unknown, Michael. These can cloud your vision and ultimately hamper your abilities as a knight." He paused and swept his gaze across the dense forest ahead. Michael wondered what Sam actually saw out there. The elf commander pointed toward a particularly overgrown area of trees and bushes and said, "What do you see out beyond those trees?" He turned his slightly pointed ear in that direction and said, "I hear movement, but I need you to take a closer look."

Michael stared at the overrun patch, searching for anything special there. The area was covered with spruce trees, aspens and small bushes, wild grass rampant throughout. "What do you mean by beyond? I can't see through it because it's too thick. What am I supposed to see?"

"You don't see anything because you're only looking with your physical eyes. Sometimes our physical eyes and our skewed knowledge of what is real and tangible can get in the way of what is right in front of us, waiting to be seen." Sam put his hand gently on Michael's shoulder and said, "Now, close your eyes and look again. Reach down into your essence. Think back to what you felt the night of your anointing. That is how you will learn to gain your SullSight. You must gather your power from within and reach out to nature and the creatures all around to help you see. They are your partners in this activity."

Michael had no idea what he was talking about, but he did as Sam suggested and closed his eyes. He thought back to the warmth and the surging power he had learned to call up. He was able to find it and access it without any issue. But he didn't know how to push it outward toward animals or anything outside himself. He felt like he was missing something. "I don't know what I'm doing. I think you're expecting too much from me."

"Push aside your frustrations," Sam whispered. "We have been asking you to reach *in* to find and channel the Sullice. Now you must grab it and extend it outward and call out to other Sullite beings for help. Once you experience SullSight, it will be easier to reproduce. Place your desires and your love away from you – in the sky – in that forest. Reach out with it."

With that, Michael pushed the fear away and extended his reach outward. He thought of his dad, captured and lost. He must stretch himself, extend his influence, and find some way to rescue him. A sudden feeling of awareness settled over him. He felt like he had transported part of himself high into the sky, and he was looking down on the forest below, but with a level of detail that shocked his senses. He could see the insects on the leaves, scurrying about.

There was a stump beyond the patch of trees. A mouse scampered into it through a miniature opening. The stump was the mouse's home. How was he seeing this? His eyes scanned over the other direction and he saw two people standing in the clearing. He could clearly identify them. It was Sam and him! The link broke and his eyes shot open. "How did I do that? What just happened?"

"Why? What did you see?"

Michael was trying to slow down his pounding heart, and said, "I was high above the forest, but I could see every little detail, including the big stump beyond those trees you pointed to and the mouse running into it." He was staring at Sam now. "But how?"

"You have done well, Michael. *That* is SullSight." He pointed to the sky and said, "There are SullSight partners all around us." As if on cue, a screeching sound echoed overhead, Michael's eyes shot up and he saw a hawk circling them.

A shudder rolled through him and he said, "So, are you telling me that I was inside that hawk just now?"

Sam chuckled slightly. "No, not really. More like you saw through his eyes for a moment. What you must come to understand is that we're all living as unified beings together in this kingdom. And we are all made of the same essence material - Sullice. It's a symbiotic relationship, meaning we can help each other. Usually, when we approach animals and living nature for the right reasons, they are more than willing to help us in our quest to serve Lithegol and protect its inhabitants. What you accomplished is amazing considering how young you are in the Order, and I'm sure you'll have many more remarkable experiences on your journey to becoming a knight." He gazed out in the direction of the fading sun and said, "But we must go in for now. Night approaches."

When they went back inside, Michael's mom was straightening and dusting. Peter was sitting on the couch, his eyes and attention focused on the rear of the S.A.V. What was he up to? He did an upward head nod and said, "So, how did your tuning into nature session go?"

Sam smirked and shook his head. "It went well. Michael was able to use his SullSight for the first time... with a hawk."

Peter's playful look changed to an expression of shock. "He did what? Already? Hawks are very hard to partner with."

Sam beamed proudly and said, "Yes, it was very impressive. Although, I think it gave him a bit of a shock."

Michael nodded. "Yeah, when I saw myself down on the ground it freaked me out a little. But it was cool. I saw a mouse running into a stump like I was right above it."

Peter motioned for Michael to sit down next to him and said, "Yes, hawks have incredible eyesight. I've heard that eagles are even better, but it's very rare for knights or matrons to be able to partner with an eagle."

Michael looked around and said, "Hey, where's Silvan?"

Peter smiled and said, "He's been working on using Sullice to hear from far away. He's in the very back of the vehicle and I have been whispering to see if he can hear me. He's doing really good so far. But he can't quite hear when I whisper." He pointed to the back and said, "Why don't you try it? Silvan can whisper something to test you."

Michael shrugged and said, "Ok. I'll try."

Sam had sat down in the chair across from them; his strange

extremely light blue eyes locked in on him. "You can do it, Michael. There is Sullice in you yet that you need to find."

Michael didn't know what he was talking about, but he was going to try. He closed his eyes and concentrated on what he had done outside when he had partnered with the hawk. Immediately he felt like he was in a bright chamber and was reaching his hands out to feel for something. Something elusive. Something that he didn't fully understand. Nevertheless, it was something that he was starting to recognize. At first, it seemed like there was no more Sullice to be found and he was flustered like maybe he wasn't as powerful as they thought he was.

Then Peter's edgy voice broke through. "Don't try so hard. The Sullice is part of you, give in to it."

With that, Michael tried a different approach. He surrendered his search as if turning it over to an unseen force within. The room became completely silent and Michael reached out with everything left in him and chuckled when he heard a faint voice echo in his ear.

Silvan came running into the room with a huge smile on his face and Michael said, "Really? That's what you thought of to say?"

Peter smiled and said, "What? So, you heard him? What did he whisper?"

Michael shook his head and said, "He said that I'm a big moron."

Silvan busted out laughing and Peter nearly jumped out of his seat. "Very good. You figured it out. How did that feel?"

Michael saw a glass of water and a Braiz bar on the table and suddenly realized that he was extremely thirsty. He turned to Peter and said, "Are those for me? I'm so thirsty."

Peter smiled knowingly. "You're thirsty because you have used your essence power. This will drain your overall energy until you're able to gain more Sullite strength and stamina. It takes time to build this up and deepen your reserves."

Michael downed both of them as he felt the familiar surge of Sullite energy rising up inside. Inside where though, he wondered.

He set the glass down and said, "It was like I just gave in and some other force within found the Sullice somehow. I can't explain it."

Peter jumped up and blurted out, "And what you did to listen using Sullice from that distance was amazing, Son!"

They high-fived and Silvan exclaimed, "That was awesome! I'm ready to take on some Sulgons!"

Peter smirked and shook his head, "You're not quite ready, big guy. But great job."

Sam had been sitting there, beaming, and said, "That is how Sullice works. It knew what you both wanted was to build your Sullite strength to accomplish righteous purposes, so it funneled the power needed toward that act for each of you."

A sense of comfort settled over him as if this was all familiar. Michael felt like he could take a nap or even fall asleep for the night.

"Are you ok, Bud?" his mom asked. "You've been through a lot today. Maybe you should go to bed."

Michael glanced at his watch. It was only 7:00 pm.

Sam stood up and said, "Not until he has my special Ellontish fondue though, Mrs. Brenlan. It won't take me long. You all can sit back and relax. You are our guests, after all."

Michael caught Silvan staring at him again and said, "What? What is it? You keep staring at me."

Silvan shook his head and said, "I don't know. It's really weird. It's just a familiar déjà vu type feeling. Maybe someday we'll figure it out."

Michael nodded and said, "I'll add it to the list. I feel like there is so much I still need to figure out. Maybe you can help me." He rubbed his eyes, trying to force the tiredness out, and said, "This stuff definitely sucks out the energy."

As expected, the dinner was delicious and Michael was stuffed. He had never had Fondue quite like that. They had dipped strange-looking vegetables in some thick blue sauce that tasted like a cross between pesto and chorizo. He thought about all that had happened in the last several days. It was mind-numbing when he recalled waking up that fateful morning with nothing on his to-do list except milking the cows and gathering eggs from the chickens.

Part of him wished that he was still in that situation. Milking the cows was relaxing and not complicated or scary. As he thought of the scary factor, an image of the dragon-man from his dream and those black-slitted eyes popped into his mind, and a dizzying sting of fear bit him. How was he supposed to become a knight and fight against superhuman beasts like the commanders had described?

Everyone went to bed shortly after dinner. The plan was to leave early in the morning with a goal to reach Sildonia by the end of the day. Michael dreaded bedtime since his dad's abduction. He never wanted to see the vision of his unconscious father ever again. And that wicked-looking dagger...

He lay on the bed, with Silvan on the pop-out bed across from him. His busy mind was racing, and he began to feel alone and sorry for himself. He thought about that fateful day when the Legion had knocked on his front door. That morning he had awoken from a dream where he was a running from a frightening Sulgon. Then it had come again the night of his anointing. But why? And was it a vision of things to come?

Would he be prepared to face the Sulgons and defend himself when the time came? He could see now why his dad had taught him Martial Arts and the other skills. But how could his dad have known what he would face? Maybe the King and Nimue knew and had given his parents specific instructions.

Michael heard what sounded like muffled sobbing and turned to see Silvan, who was cowering on the edge of his bed and was choking back sobs as he gazed at a HoloFrame on a tiny table. The floating video showed Silvan, his dad and a beautiful woman with sandy hair and hazel eyes who must have been Lisa, Silvan's mom. The Olgath family were at what Michael recognized as the Einstein Planetarium, which is part of the Smithsonian Institute Air and Space Museum.

Michael sat up and said, "Are you ok? You thinking about your Mom?"

Silvan wiped his face and sat up straight and said, "Yeah. It's only been a month since she was taken from us. I miss her so much. It's like the cool moments we're having- she's not even here to experience them with us." He looked at Michael apologetically and said, "But, hey, I'm sorry. You shouldn't have to deal with this."

Michael felt guilty at that moment for feeling sorry for himself after seeing what Silvan was dealing with and said, "No, you shouldn't feel bad. I'm sorry for your loss. I can't even imagine what this must feel like. I mean, my dad is not with us to experience what we're learning and everything. But at least I know he's still alive. You want to talk about it? I'm happy to listen."

Silvan gave a slight head shake and said, "Nah. All good. I'll be ok. I'm sure all the pressure I'm feeling with all this Squire stuff is contributing to what I'm feeling. It's just a lot to live up to. I mean, the most powerful knight in the kingdom gave me my squire ring. How much pressure does that bring with it? Having you here has actually helped, knowing that there's another kid dealing with that pressure."

Michael nodded and said, "I feel the same way, man! I thought I was the only one expected to become this ultra-powerful knight. And the fact that you're in the same boat as far as not knowing what the future holds is very comforting. Maybe we can help each other. I think there's a reason you and your Dad are involved with my destiny."

Silvan's playful smile returned and he said, "No question. But, hey, we should probably get some sleep. I have a feeling we're going to need to be well rested for what my Dad and Uncle have planned for us tomorrow. Thanks again for being understanding and offering to help. Appreciate it. Glad you're here."

Michael smiled back and said, "No problem, Bud. I'm glad to be here too. Night." As he lay back down, he wondered what had happened to Lisa. What would he do if he lost a parent? Lost his dad? He didn't know how he would go on. He had done everything with his dad. They were like best friends. There was another video of Silvan's tall, lean figure standing next to his beaming dad. He was holding up a Certificate of Rank advancement to a Practitioner 5 in Filipino Martial Arts, which is the highest pre-black belt rank equivalent in this discipline. Peter's gray eyes were wet with tears. Michael had also received this advancement and he thought about everything he had in common with Silvan.

He thought of his dad and wondered what was happening to him at that moment. He felt so helpless. Even with all that he had learned about the power he had, what could he really do to get him back? He thought of his mission and the oath he had made and his eyes fell to his ring. The clear crystal was different from anything he had seen before. It was like some Augmented reality object, being projected like an animation onto his finger. The faint glow seemed insignificant when Michael thought of what all he was able to do with the Sullice he had learned to harness from it.

His eyes drifted over to Silvan, who was now lying peacefully in his bed, and his mind flashed back to how his dad had tucked him in like a burrito when he was young. He used to press the sides of his blanket in tight next to his body and give him a little tickle. He pushed his emotions back and he told himself to be strong like his dad had taught him. A familiar sensation came over him, and his little golden friend appeared, hovering above him.

Michael sat up, wondering why he was there, hoping that it wasn't to show him any more foreboding visions. Who was this bird, and what was his role in all that was happening to him? The beaming nightingale gazed at him with deep, knowing eyes. He landed on his arm, as he had done before, and Michael prepared himself for the worse. But instead of a vision, Michael felt a flood of calmness enter his body. As the magnificent bird hopped to his leg, Michael laid back down, his worries faded away and he slipped off to sleep.

Chapter 9

The Waicrofts

Early the following morning, after breakfast, they sat next to the two commanders on a park bench overlooking a grove of trees. Peter touched Commander Sam's arm and said, "The commander and I have been teaching you about the power of Sullice, but what do you think the main purpose of this power is?"

Silvan raised his hand. "I think it's here to help and protect all people."

Peter nodded and said, "That's true, Son. Only, there is so much more to it. Take what we have been teaching you, for instance. Sam has been instructing you on how to use the power of SullSight - to see things that are only visible through our Sullite eyes and to tap into the Sullite world around us when needed. Whereas I have been teaching you how to use the power of Sullice as a guard to protect you and the others you serve."

Sam pointed at a toppled tree. "In certain parts of my home world, Fluren, this fallen tree would never be left in that broken state. The elf inhabitants would have honored its existence by transforming it into something useful. As Elementals, we are taught that any living thing can provide assistance to us as we strive to fulfill our quests, regardless of which world we live on."

The blind commander lifted his arm in a sweeping motion and said, "The main purpose of Sullice is to save all Sullite beings and help them to return to the Realm of Trellif. It is there that we can live in harmony together with our families and King Deyan and Prince Arthur. To do this we must embrace the good in all things and rise above the evils that seek to destroy Lithegol and enslave all Sullite life forms. We must always be guarded and watchful. The seeds of corruption can be planted very subtly by feelings of greed, hostility, pride and jealousy." A kind smile formed on his narrow face. "But for now, it's time to continue our journey. You have much to ponder. Great job to both of you."

Before they hit the road for the final leg of their journey Peter sat them all down and said, "We have received new information from our Shadow Sentry operatives. It appears that the Legion is planning to send a significant number of United Legion troops to California. We believe that this could have something to do with the fact that they discovered we have a base there, and they want to be able to match our firepower. It could also be that they have figured out how to infiltrate the government facility and they're planning on going after the Gaddite ClusterSphere.

"Regardless of the reasons, this makes our little adventure that much more dangerous. They will likely dump a large group of Sulgons in our path at some point along the way. So, you must go over what you have learned and practice whenever you can. You two are definitely on the accelerated program. The good news is that Sam and I believe that you both can handle it. You have progressed much more quickly than others your age.

"As far as your dad, Michael. I have some of my Freedom Alliance operatives monitoring the area where the ultra-secret compound is located, and they have seen no activity at this point. I would be shocked if the Legion gets Spencer to say anything about it. The one thing that we have going for us is that the Legion has no idea that I know the general location of it. And we will not communicate this information to anyone. We just can't assume that every channel is secure from prying ears. When the time comes, we will assuredly need help finding the facility. It is hidden underground and nearly impossible to detect."

"At least we'll have the Doctor to help us. If anyone can find it, he can," Sam said.

"Who's the Doctor?" Michael asked.

Peter smiled. "He's the guy we've been telling you about who has invented all the gadgets, including this vehicle. Dr. Waicroft. I call him Henry. He's married to Heather. She is Lisa and Commander Sam's sister."

Sister, Michael thought. So, that was how Sam was Silvan's uncle.

"I'm sure you've been wondering what happened to Lisa. I think it's only fair that I tell you," Peter said. "Lisa was one of the brightest Elf Elementals within the Order and had been working on a ground-breaking new Renber formula that would heal a Sullite body from almost any injury or illness. The Legion wanted to get their hands on it so that they could use it for their own twisted purposes and kidnapped her. But when they were unable to get anything out of her, they killed her. They didn't want us to have anything that would help us to defeat them and that's how they saw what she was creating." He wiped a tear, his jaw clenching.

"She was the most giving, noble person I've ever known, and they just threw her life away as if she was nothing." Silvan had walked over and put his arm around his dad's shoulder. Peter straightened, composed himself and continued, "Due to the dangerous nature of our missions, Commanders are required to record a parting message for their loved ones periodically… just in case. Lisa recorded her latest one right before her abduction and I think we should listen to it now." He pushed a series of buttons on the console and a crystal clear hologram shot down from a ceiling projector port. It was Lisa. It looked like she was sitting at her desk.

She had a somber expression and looked right into the camera and said, "If you're watching this, that means that I have passed on to the next life." She gave a heavy sigh and continued, "I'm sure you both are not coping with it well and you're having a hard time. I want you to know that I'm ok. I wholeheartedly believe that I am in Trellif, working on other important projects and waiting for you to arrive *much* later. Live your lives. Be happy. Drink in the light of Sullice and grow in the order. Silvan, I am so proud of all that you are accomplishing in your preparations to enter the order. You will be an amazing knight and do much good in the fight against the Legion and the powers of Gaddin. Listen to your father and work hard and once in a while have fun."

She smiled and continued, "Piddir. I love you more than anything and I am honored to be your wife. You are the best thing that's happened to me and I will miss you. But you must move on. Find happiness and if my death was no accident, don't allow vengeance to eat away at your heart. All things happen for a reason. Life is what we make of it. Our attitude and choices determine our outcome. Choose hope. Please give my love to Sam and Heather and their families. I love you all dearly and... I'll see you soon."

Her tearful face faded away and Peter and everyone else wiped their eyes and he said, "Man, that gets me every time. She was such an incredible person. How wise and caring was this woman!" He took a deep breath and said, "I needed that. Especially the last part. I feel like my heart has been filled with anger and thoughts of revenge lately. I need to find other ways to channel the pain and grief like she said."

Silvan hugged his dad and said, "It's ok, Dad. You're a passionate guy. I think what she meant is we don't try to push back those feelings. We just need to direct them and our passion toward doing good." He smiled between sniffles and continued, "That doesn't mean we can't take out some Sulgons in our efforts to cope with our feelings though."

They all chuckled and Michael said, "I think that would be a very therapeutic solution." He patted Silvan on the back and said, "But, seriously. I'm so sorry for your loss. I can't even imagine what that must be like. She was amazing."

Silvan stifled back a sob and said, "She was, for sure. She was the best mom a kid could ever have and..." He cut off mid-sentence, as if he couldn't force the words out without it overwhelming him."

Sam hugged him and said, "But the comfort we have is that we know we can be with her again someday in the Realm of Trellif, and we must honor her life by giving our all in everything we do like she did."

Michael's mom was crying and said, "I'm sure that she would be proud of you all for your courage in dealing with this despicable tragedy."

They all gathered for a group hug and then left for Sildonia.

*   *   *

They had been driving for around two hours when Michael heard a voice from the front cry out, "Look at that. Amazing!" Commander Sam was pointing at a grouping of giant trees and smiling from ear to ear. They were obviously getting close to Sildonia, which was nestled in the heart of the Coastal Redwoods of California. Some of these trees were bigger around than a truck. At one point, they saw a massive Redwood up ahead that had a tunnel cut out of it; and cars were driving through it.

Michael pointed and said, "Silvan, check it out. That tree is gigantic!"

Sam, who still had a huge smile on his face, said, "Yes, we're entering Redwood country now. These are some of the largest and oldest trees on this world. That tree tunnel is one of the only entrances into Sildonia. We're not going into town though. We've arrived at our destination, believe it or not."

Peter pulled into a parking lot in front of a small store with a quirky wooden sign reading "The Nook;" Michael jumped out and found his way to the restroom in the back. When he came out, Commander Sam was talking to a little man with slightly pointed ears. Comparing them side by side, Michael could clearly see some common elfish features. The fast-talking man wore a half tucked in dress shirt, his hair poking out on one side. His eyes were different from Sam's though. They were an unusual dark blue color.

When Michael approached, Sam said, "We're staying here for the night. Hank has a room for us in his little motel out back." He pointed to the slender man and said, "Hank, Michael. Michael, Hank."

Hank's dark eyes fixed on him; he had a probing, curious expression on his baby smooth face. Michael shook his calloused hand and said, "Nice to meet you, Hank." He could feel the presence of someone else close by, but he couldn't figure out who it was or where they were.

The man's distinct features softened, and he said, his high voice resonating with articulation, "You too, young man. I have a good feeling about you."

Michael wondered where that came from, and as they got back in the Hummer, he asked, "So, why did he say that back there? Is he a knight also? And is he from Commander Sam's realm? They have similar facial features."

Peter looked around as if assessing whether they were alone, and said, "Well done, Michael. Yes, that is the scientist we told you about, Henry Waicroft. He is the one that developed our Sullite weapons, including this vehicle we're driving. He is a brilliant guy. Beyond brilliant, actually. He lives here and does his work in a secret lab that is more like a warehouse. He also monitors who is entering Sildonia through a special, intensive Surveillance System."

Peter started the vehicle and said, "Oh… And, No, he is not from

Commander Sam's realm, but he is from the elf triad. He is from the core world of Rellor, within the Penturi Realm. He is what we call a Cog or a Cognitive. They are the developers, doctors, engineers, scientists and such. They are also very perceptive of other's thoughts and intentions."

Michael unexpectedly felt a twinge of discomfort, as if the Legion was close by but not so close as to fully convince him that the alarm was real. What were these feelings? Why were they coming to him? And why didn't anyone else have them?

Peter drove them around the corner, where there was a little cove. The faded parking spots on the left side of the lot were overshadowed by a towering rock hill. On the right was a two-story quaint motel building, that must've been connected somehow to the little store. The backside of the motel was nestled right up against the hillside.

Peter drove up to a spot on the left in front of a trash bin. There was a 'No Parking' sign on it, which Michael was about to point out when Peter pushed a button on the dash. Nothing happened at first, and then the over-sized dumpster slid to the left. The rock wall behind it sucked in and slid quickly to the right. They launched forward, and the door and the dumpster slid back into place so quickly behind them that if you blinked you would've missed it. What was it with hidden rock doors and these people?

When they stepped out onto the concrete floor, Henry was waiting for them, and there was a hulking man standing next to him. Michael noticed that the man's armor was not engaged, which meant that this was his earthly form—impressive! He was at least six and a half feet tall and was built like an NFL lineman, with tree-trunk-size arms and legs and a thick neck.

Henry must've seen Michael staring, and said, "Oh, that's my Guardian Sentry, Senior Commander Girran. The Order sent him several days ago. He is basically my shadow and has been assigned to protect me and my family." He waved Girran off and said, "Don't worry. His bark is worse than his bite... Unless you're a Sulgon. Then – well, it won't be pleasant."

The beefy man managed a faint smile and a nod. His gruff voice said, "Nice to have you all here. Good to see you again, Commander." Peter nodded and Girran stretched his right arm out with the palm extended up to him, made a fist with it and pulled it to his chest, and bowed and stood back up. Peter did the same bowing salute to him.

Michael's mom and the others stepped out of the vehicle, and Peter motioned toward her. "This is Michael's mother, Julia. And, Julia, this is Dr. Henry Waicroft or Commander Henry or his favorite, The Mad Scientist and his Guardian Sentry, Senior Commander Girran."

Henry thrummed his fingers together, laughed maniacally, and said, "How's that for a Mad Scientist?" He turned to Michael's mom, shook her hand, bowed his head and said, "Lovely to meet you. Welcome to my home... Well, a tributary of my home."

Sam stepped forward and did the same bow Peter and Girran had done, and Henry responded in kind but in a rushed fashion. "Great to see you, my old friends. Now, if you will please excuse me, I need to run my diagnostics on the S.A.V.." He grabbed a couple of strange tools from a workbench on the wall. It appeared that they had parked in a highly specialized hidden garage. Henry leaned over, kissed the hood of the

Hummer, and said, "Thank you for taking care of my baby. It appears that you didn't encounter any trouble on the way here."

Peter's eyes narrowed, and he said, "Yes. No trouble at all, actually. It was almost too easy. I don't like it."

Henry had lifted the hood and was hooking cables into the Hummer engine. "What's not to like about not being attacked by Legion miscreants?" Before Peter could answer, he continued, "No, I know what you're talking about. We need to be very careful who we trust, even within the order. My findings tell me they're searching for ways to infiltrate our defenses in the western U.S. I think they're realizing that their whole east THEN west domination plan wasn't the best way to go."

The slight, hyperactive man had walked around and was doing some serious button pushing inside the vehicle now. He glanced up at them as if he had forgotten they were there. "Go on in. You know your way around. Make yourselves at home." He shot Peter then Sam a quick glance and pointed. "Give our new guests the grand tour. Heather is inside. I think she's working on your favorite dish, Sam—breaded salmon. Billy is building something in his room, and I think Claire is helping her mother with the food preparation."

As many things as he had spinning around in his head right now, Michael's brain had clicked into another mode altogether at the mention of two simple words—"breaded salmon." He was starving.

Sam was leading the way, which seemed odd at first because Michael remembered that he was blind. Nonetheless, Sam was far from being your average blind man. Michael thought that maybe Commander Sam's sense of smell was leading the way in this case.

As they walked, Michael almost forgot that they were walking through the middle of a hill. One would never guess that by the surroundings. The regular sheet-rocked walls were splattered with posters of cool jeeps and trucks and futuristic-looking hover vehicles. Peter pointed to the collage and said, "Yeah, Henry is a bit of a vehicle junkie. He loves working on any kind of machine, especially those that can get you from point A to point B quickly and without impossible obstacles. That is not his only area of special aptitude, as you have witnessed with his weapons. He really does have a knack for working with essence crystals."

Michael nodded and said, "So, tell me about Billy and Claire."

Commander Sam answered this time. "Well, Billy is ten and Claire is 15. They are Henry's pride and joy. As you would expect, both kids are very intelligent. Billy is already an incredible little artist, loves to build things, a gifted mathematician and speaks four languages. And Claire is a whiz on the computer and plays the piano beautifully." Then he smiled and shook his head and said, "But she loves shooting bows and practicing her martial arts most of all."

They came to a dead end, and Sam moved his ringed right hand up and down over a discreet scanner. There were the familiar clicks, and a wide, oval-shaped door slid open instantaneously like something out of a space movie.

Next, they were going down a set of stairs and back up again. At the top, Sam authenticated with a swipe over an area of the wall. A seam materialized on the wall and a swinging door opened out into a room with shelves and a desk. After stepping through, Michael studied the area and discovered that the door was actually a bookcase on a wall that had concealed the entrance to a secret passageway. As he thought about it, Michael now understood the design of the setup. The motel or Henry's house, whichever this was, had a special stairway that led down and then up into the hillside warehouse area they had just come from.

The spacious room inside contained a squared off section of couches and another area with a group of long tables surrounded by chairs. He saw more doors to other rooms, including a set of double doors at the far end that had a sign that said "Motel," with an arrow pointing up. In the corner closest to them was an enormous kitchen. There was a short woman with blond hair scurrying around, stirring this and chopping that. She was slightly heavy-set but had a beautiful, long face with high cheekbones and narrow eyes. She had braids that extended down between her shoulder blades.

There was a slight figure next to her, shucking cornhusks, her nimble hands handling the tusks with surprising ease. Michael guessed that this must be Claire. She had blonde hair that was pulled up into a complex braid and when she turned and smiled at them, Michael found himself looking into a beautiful, electric pair of hazel eyes. He could feel himself staring and managed a smile and a little wave. Had he really just waved? What a dork.

The woman, who Michael guessed was Heather, heard them enter and immediately stopped what she was doing. She wiped her hands with a dry rag from the counter and approached, her hand outstretched. From his vantage point, Michael noticed her long arms were like Sam's. Her right hand had a blue ring token on it, and he wondered how powerful she was. He was curious about matrons and their gifts and abilities. Her eyes were light blue but nowhere near as light as Sam's. The blast from the SullBomb must've made Sam's eyes much lighter. She said, "Hello, my name is Heather. It's great to have you here."

Michael could see Claire studying him out of the corner of his eye, and he felt his face flush. Hoping that his cheeks weren't too red, he said, "Hi. I'm Michael. It's nice to meet you. Thank you for having us. Peter told us about you being Lisa and Commander Sam's sister." He almost felt bad mentioning Lisa's name, as he didn't want to stir up bad memories, but she seemed unfazed. Thank goodness his brain hadn't malfunctioned during his response.

The blonde girl that Michael pegged as Claire stepped forward and said, "Hi, Michael. I'm Claire. Great to meet you." When her soft hand squeezed his, he was surprised by the strength of her grip.

Silvan stepped out from behind him, gave Heather a hug, and said, "Hi, Aunt Heather." Then he did an involved high five with Claire, almost like what Michael and Jeff did but not quite as elaborate. Silvan sniffed the air and glided into the kitchen, skimming over the pots and pans, leaning his head in to smell the delicious aromas.

Heather turned and said, half-jokingly, "Get your Herkilian head out of my pots, young man. Just be patient."

He laughed and said, "OK. I'll let you work your magic. Man, does it smell good."

Silvan was motioning as if he was going to reach down into the steaming pot when Heather smiled and said, "Out, you. Why don't you go show Michael the new *special* room?"

Silvan jerked his arm back, and his eyes lit up. "Yeah! Great idea. Let's go, Michael. You HAVE to see this. My uncle has the sweetest setup ever. He's the one that helped us put ours together, but ours doesn't even come close to what he has."

Michael's mom began introducing herself to everyone, as Michael and Silvan ran out of the room and down a hallway into a supersized door at the end of the hall.

When they walked into what Heather had called "The special room" Michael stared at it in awe. It was like a mini-theatre. There were three 3D projectors in the rear and eight in a circle around the huge projection area in the front. It was then that Michael realized that this was an immersive virtual gaming arena. He had heard of them but had always questioned their existence. The tiered rows of seating had recliner seats with cup holders and little trays off to the side of each one.

Silvan did a fist pump and said, "This is a whole different level of 'Epic Combat.' This is unreal!" He ran over to a kiosk and pushed some buttons and the projectors came to life. He reached and pulled out a thick plastic sword and a shield from a set of bins. Then he jumped into the open area, as a mounted scanner shot a beam of white light up and down his body. Glowing armor appeared on his body, and it and the sword and shield now glowed with red specks. He started walking and the entire floor turned into a track, reacting to his feet and his motion as if he were walking and leaping in a real situation.

The scene around Silvan changed as he entered what looked like a forest. 3D dragons, some the size of a dinosaur, leaped out from behind trees and rocks and attacked him. The surroundings changed to a castle with dark corridors and the young squire used his glowing sword to defend himself, weaving and dodging. He used the moves they had learned to defeat most of them without much issue, finally kneeling in front of a beautiful princess in a royal ceremony to receive his special medal.

When Silvan finished, he approached Michael and said, "Isn't that awesome? I think our training is working. That's the first time I was able to complete the mission! You want to give it a try?"

Michael thought about how pleased Silvan was with his accomplishment and didn't want to take away from his moment. He shook his head. "Maybe later. I just want to chill for a bit in these awesome chairs."

Silvan smiled and nodded, as he grabbed a remote from a side pouch on the kiosk. The muscle-bound boy plopped down in the center recliner and started pushing buttons. A 20-foot 3D hologram image of a newsfeed materialized in the open projection area. And there they were again, front and center, all their altered pictures being displayed for the world to see. The reporter was talking about how the "authorities" suspected that these fugitives, implicated in the bombing of the United Legion base in Des Moines, had entered California and all those within the Humboldt County area should keep a special eye out for them. Michael's heart dropped. Silvan paused the screen, ran out and returned with Peter and showed him the footage.

Peter's sharp features fell. "But how do they know where we are? Something's not right. We all need to go through the scanning chamber to make sure we don't have any hidden tracking devices on us. That's the only thing I can think of that explains how this could happen."

Silvan's brow furrowed, as it often did when he was concentrating, and he said, "But why wouldn't they just take us if they know where we are?"

Peter pointed at him and said, "*That* is a great question. They could be waiting for us to lead them to our base. The first thing we need to figure out is how they know where we are." He went and got Sam, and they all went into a room that was in the back section of the complex. Each of them stepped into a chamber, not unlike the ones they have at airports that have a rotating arm that scans up and down your body. The scanner found no tracking devices on anyone. Henry seemed equally unsurprised and puzzled by this fact and ran off to work on something. He was always in that mode. Michael wondered if the guy ever slowed down and took a breath.

Peter said, "Well, we know that Durrill is not part of the Legion, and we have all but confirmed that he has used a top-secret government project to hide his Gaddite ClusterSphere research activities at the hidden compound. Captain Gabriel did send in a stealth team to his home to bring him in, but he was already gone. But even Durrill doesn't know where we are. Who does, anyway?"

Before he could answer his own question, Sam said, "Besides Henry, only Senior Commander Seth from your group and Senior Commander Huni from my Shadow Sentry group know where we are. And they are both extremely trustworthy."

Henry had returned and said, "I can tell you that it wasn't me, obviously, and the only other knight or matron in my direct group that could've leaked information is Girran, but I would trust him with my life. We have a long history together." He was pointing to the corner where the hulking Secret Service type knight stood.

Michael leaned in and asked, "Does he ever talk? He seems like he's in his own world or something."

Michael's mom poked him and gave him the 'don't be disrespectful' look and Henry waved her off and said, "That is Girran's nature. He is definitely the quiet type and doesn't like large groups. But he is one of the most loyal knights I've ever known."

Henry shook his head. "What worries me is this new development in the Legion's cloaking capabilities. I have to figure out how they're doing it so that we know what we're dealing with. We need to capture one of those beasts and study their handiwork. I'm sure that this is all about capturing the western base. We may have to forego all communication to the base until we determine where the leak originated. They must have known that I am one of only a select group that knows its location. This critical stronghold must not be compromised. My hope is that they at least don't know of my secret location here. But that is probably a foolish wish, given what they have already learned. We may have to evacuate this facility sooner than later."

Chapter 10

Road Trip

After dinner Michael, Silvan and Claire were sitting, watching a movie and Billy was sitting next to his sister. Billy had a 3D holographic image floating above his mini WriP and was working on what Michael recognized as a MakRBot. The robot he designed could be created from the inside out using the latest 3D printer. This technology was amazing and impressively created moving parts and mechanisms from the designs. Once the robot was built, there were BotFights Billy could enroll it in. He was definitely a lively kid and had inherited his dad's energy.

Michael was chatting with Claire and had discovered that they had a lot in common, including a love for Martial Arts. Claire was showing Michael a new Krav Maga move. She had Michael grab her in a headlock from behind. When he did, he felt the soft skin of her cheek and smelled the lavender in her hair. Before she could show him how to escape, Peter came into the room and said, "Ok, guys. I hate to interrupt but we need to have a council. Please come join us in the main room."

Silvan glanced at Michael, shook his head, smirked and turned off the projector. He led them out through another door, and they entered a breathtakingly spacious garage area. "Little Billy" had been parked in the massive space. Michael thought it must be a secret entrance. He was shocked at the sight of a huge RV, decked out like Little Billy, and another dune-buggy-sized vehicle parked nearby. There were several rows of padded chairs set up near the wall.

Henry walked to the front and motioned for them to sit. Once they were all seated, he nodded to his wife Heather, who stood up from her spot in the front row and faced the group. He gestured toward her and said, "I want to start out by explaining why my wife, the other Dr. Waicroft, will be absent from our upcoming activities. She has been and will continue to be busy working in her lab room on our S.A.V., Martha. She is using her skills as an Elemental and a brilliant medical doctor to finish the work that her sister Lisa started. She and the others on her team are close to completing a breakthrough new cross-developed medicine that will revolutionize our ability to treat brain conditions, including Autism and Alzheimer's. I am very proud of her and excited to see her formula rolled out throughout the kingdom to help those in need."

Everyone cheered and Heather gave a slight bow and mouthed the words "thank you" before disappearing into the large S.A.V. Henry gave her a wave and turned back to the group. "Unfortunately, as I suspected, this location has been compromised and we must evacuate. The Order has been notified and we have been instructed to take all technology and our S.A.V.s to another hidden facility north of here. We have also been directed to initiate the lockdown sequence. This will secure the entire structure with impenetrable walls. The only way in or out will be a special hidden garage entrance. Please gather all your belongings and check with

Peter, Sam or me as to what we need assistance with. They have been furnished with a checklist of items that need to go." He paused, his face somber, and continued, "I *will* discover the identity of the traitor and sincerely hope that it's not one of you."

Peter stood up, his jaw clenched and lifted a fisted hand. "I'm tired of running from these tyrants. I say we wait here and crush them when they arrive."

Commander Sam, who was sitting next to him, stood up and put his hand on his shoulder. "As brave as that may seem, that is not the wise thing to do. We don't know how large a force they will send and what weapons they will be carrying. We must get ourselves and the valuable technology Commander Henry has produced to a safe place. The day to fight will come. You need not worry about that. Now, let's move quickly. We can't risk getting pinned in when they arrive."

With those stirring words and the anxious vibe in the air, everyone jumped up and ran every which direction. The RV-like S.A.V. that they had called 'Martha' was being loaded with suitcases, other gray cases and various odds and ends. The double-decker was enormous, probably close to 50 feet long, with a full upper floor and pop-out sections on the sides.

At one point, Michael was grabbing a case to load and spotted a bird cage. Inside was a parrot, with beautiful green and yellow feathers. It cocked its head at him. Then it squawked super loud and Michael jumped. It opened its beak, did the bird equivalent of a laugh, and said, "Nice one, dunderhead!" Michael laughed and peered through the cage, wondering what the story was on it.

He felt a hand on his shoulder and turned to see Silvan, a broad smile on his face. "I taught him that. Pretty hilarious, right? His name is Screech… You can guess why."

Michael smiled and said, "You taught him how to talk? That's cool. What else can he say?"

"Well, I didn't actually teach him how to talk. I just helped him expand his vocabulary. He says lots of things." He glanced around at everyone running here and there. "I'll have to show you more later."

When they were all finally done packing everything up, they stood in a half circle with their jackets on, ready to go. Henry had engaged his WriP and had a floating checklist he was swiping through in mid-air above his wrist. Michael noticed that Henry was moving through the screens faster than he thought possible and his WriP had a slicker, more professional look to it, with unique icons and lists. He was fascinated by it, even though he had seen several of them in action.

Henry had obviously added enhancements to his like he did with everything. "Ok. Thank you to everyone for your help. I have checked our extensive inventory list three times. We are packed and ready to go. Our destination coordinates have been programmed into all the vehicles, should the auto-pilot feature need to be engaged. Thank you all for your assistance. Hopefully, we can return to this wonderful location at some point. Everyone, please make sure you have all your belongings plus any essentials that need to travel with you."

Peter turned to Silvan and said, "That means you need to make sure you bring some powerful deodorant, Silvan. For our sake, mostly."

Silvan laughed and pointed at his dad. "Nice. Since when do I stink? You're the one that can clear a room."

Peter chuckled. "Hey, that was just that one time. Blame the beans for that."

Sam raised his hand and said, "Ok, enough of that. You both stink to me. Now, let's get out of here. I have a bad feeling that the Legion is on the move."

Minutes later Peter leaped up onto a bench in the garage area and raised his arms to call for their attention. Everyone stopped what they were doing to listen. "Thank you all for your efforts to get everything loaded. It is a sad day when we have to abandon this valuable safe house and Henry's home. Those who are behind this will pay for their treachery." He raised a clenched fist, then closed his eyes and took a deep breath. When his eyes opened, he pointed to an area near the vehicles. "I want to welcome two new members to our group." He pointed to a short, muscular man with a head that was disproportionately small for his stocky body and said, "Lirfta is a powerful dwarf Shadow Sentry and commander within the Order from the Irdalla Guardian Realm of the Western Triad." Lirfta waved curtly and Peter said, "Go ahead and stand up so everyone can see you."

Lirfta, who was already standing, made some gesture by slamming his index fingers together and Peter chuckled. "Oh, my mistake. I didn't notice... No, but seriously it's an honor to have you with us. Your defensive skills are legend within the Order."

At that comment, the dwarf extended his upraised palm and did the same bow Girran had performed earlier and Peter returned it likewise.

Peter pointed to the young woman and said, "And this is Aurora from right here on Prime. She is a Senior Master Matron and a Shadow

Sentry and has been working in this area for some time now. She is very familiar with the Legion activity in this part of California."

Aurora's thin lips turned up, she raised her left hand to her head in a mock salute and did the special bow. Peter bowed back. "Now that we're all here and accounted for, I want to go over our plan. We are relocating our equipment to a secret facility, which is roughly three hours from here. And then we will depart first thing in the morning for the government compound to stop the Legion from obtaining the Gaddite ClusterSphere.

"As a security precaution, everyone will be scanned again for any tracking devices and we ask that all of you turn off all phones or wireless devices until we are in the safely encrypted zone within the new facility. Aurora will be driving 'Claire,' our smallest S.A.V., and Lirfta will drive 'Little Billy.' They will be flanking the rest of us in the front and the rear all the way in."

Michael studied their new team members. Lirfta was fairly short, barely over five feet tall, and had a wide, bulky body and pokey ears. He had a gruff expression on his bearded face. But Michael was fascinated by Aurora. He hadn't seen many matrons at this point. Silvan's mother Heather was the first, and she was more of a scientist than a soldier. Aurora looked to be in her early twenties and was very beautiful, with reddish brown hair that rested in perfect waves on her slim shoulders. She had a pointed chin, high cheekbones and was about five feet eight. She was moving her eyes over everyone as if she was searching for someone or something.

A few minutes later, she and Claire were chatting, and Aurora was showing her something on her WriP. Claire was staring at the matron, her eyes wide with admiration. A few minutes later Peter walked to the center of the space, raised his arms and said, "And now in preparation for our departure Commander Sam will be leading us in the Oath of Lithegol."

Commander Sam approached slowly, deliberately. He never ran into anything, and Michael wondered what he saw with those bottomless eyes. The elf had explained it to him at one point and said that he had an echolocation capability like what he had said the dwarves and Michael had, where he could sense the vibrations bouncing off the inanimate objects around him. Sam had further explained that the animate or living objects all had an essence and these appeared as bright silhouettes to him.

As the majestic commander began the Oath, the words came flooding back to Michael's mind and he felt a closeness to the group as they recited it together:

I will show love to my King and all others who may be in need
I will stand for honor, cleanliness, freedom and justice
I will serve Lithegol and follow my knight and matron leaders always
I will fulfill my mission assignments with courage, using the power of Sullice
I will choose good over evil and heed the warnings that come to me always
I will fight for Lithegol and for the Sullite people of all worlds with all my might

As soon as they finished the oath, they all loaded up and left through a 30-foot high sliding door that opened out into a tunnel of towering Redwood trees. Michael thought about how hard it was to gauge the passage of time when they were always indoors. When he checked his watch, he was surprised to see that it was already 5:30 pm. Peter drove them expertly down the road, navigating this much larger vehicle with surprising skill and ease. Michael thought about their journey and those that were after them. What had he sensed earlier, when they entered Sildonia, and should he have told the others about it?

The first hour and a half went by very quickly. Michael enjoyed his time with Billy, Silvan and Claire and learned some cool new traveling games. They had entered an area where the green from the many branches and giant fern plants burst through the towering trees and encased the road like a tunnel. Billy's notched chin and pointed nose made it obvious that he was Henry's son. Claire was more of a mixture of both her parents; she was energetic like her dad but also easy going like her mom. She was very interested in Michael's training and his experiences with the United Legion.

On one occasion she and Michael found themselves sitting in a nook in the upper level of the S.A.V. talking about family.

"So, tell me about your dad," she asked.

"Well, he's like this former military tough guy. He taught me so much." He felt his emotions rising. "But I don't want to talk about it right now. I just want to get him back."

She placed her hand on his and said, "I'm sure we will, Michael. Especially if my uncle Peter is on the job. He has ways of making things happen."

His heart leaped at the touch. "Thanks, Claire. That helps a lot. I need to believe. It keeps me going."

The S.A.V. slowed down slightly and Michael peered out the window. The landscape had transformed from clusters of huge Redwoods to sparse patches of scrub pines, with occasional hills rolling up on either side of the narrow road.

Minutes later, he and Silvan were back in training mode with Commander Sam. He talked about extending the senses and had them do some exercises to focus their Sullite energy on the act of hearing or seeing. What was amazing was that Michael, after a few tries, was able to see an ant crawling from 60 feet away. The elf commander was shocked by this and said that if Michael kept it up it wouldn't be long before he was able to see as well as Peter could.

The commanders took turns talking about different aspects of the Order and the power of Sullice. It still seemed strange to Michael, as if it were something out of a storybook. But as strange as it was, the power he was learning to harness and control was very real. It coursed through him like a constant swarm of energy that he could push and mold and listen to.

During all of this, Claire listened intently. It was obvious that she was anxious to move forward in her development and learn for herself how to harness the power of Sullice. After a particularly intense game of the Epic Combat strategy board game in the upper loft, Silvan, Billy, Michael and Claire were chatting when the topic of the anointing came up and Michael asked, "So, Claire, when is your anointing day?"

She smiled and said, "It's coming up soon. On April 12th. But the Legion thinks it's in April next year."

Michael reached instinctively down to touch his ring and said, "I feel bad that we have squire rings and are able to learn how to use our powers, but you aren't able to yet."

"That's ok. I'll have my shot. It's just fun seeing you guys learn and discover new abilities. You're pretty amazing by the way!"

Michael blushed, and replied, "Thanks. I'm sure you'll be an incredible matron."

Silvan smirked and shook his head. "She will definitely be prepared on the combat stuff." He turned and stood up. "We should go downstairs and get back to the training."

Claire slugged Silvan in the shoulder and said, "Ok. Mr. Rambo. You're even more addicted to combat training than I am, which I didn't think was possible."

They followed him down the stairs. When they entered the main RV space, Peter was studying a hovering 3D projected image of a map of what looked like Avalon. Silvan pointed to it and said, "Hey, Dad. Is that Avalon? Tell us more about Camelot and how we can become knights."

Peter gazed out the window. "Camelot is the most amazing place I have ever seen. Like you said, it's in Avalon, where everything just seems magical. Many of the legends and books portray it as a castle, but it is much more than that. It's more like an enchanted fortress the size of a small world. The training of the elite knights and matrons takes place at Camelot within the Palace of Falindria. This huge facility has been around for as long as any of us can remember. It has undergone several facelifts over the years to accommodate new developments in science and technology, but it is and always has been way ahead of where Earth is. You're going to love it there. We have many young squires and apprentices that train there from all the different realms. Everything in Camelot is beautifully carved and ornamented, and the entire fortress is encased in a Lumithite shell."

"What is Lumithite?" Michael asked. "I remember you talking about other crystals and a LumiDoor but never Lumithite."

"Good question," Peter replied. "I did talk about a LumiDoor but never got into the role of the Lumithite powering it. Lumithite is the most powerful and rare of all the essence crystals. It gives off a dark gold aura and has lighter gold yellowish Sullite particles in it. It is normally reserved for Royal things—palaces, weapons, tokens and such."

Michael thought back to the golden bird and the gold crystal on his capsule. Should he mention them to Peter? He had been told not to speak of them. Maybe there was a reason. Michael heard typing and turned to see Henry seated in front of a massive floating 3D holographic screen. He was pounding away at a strange-looking keyboard. Something on the screen moved and Michael found himself staring at the images of people walking around. The silhouetted figures reminded him of how people appear through thermal goggles. Except that only the insides of the people glowed.

Henry noticed him staring and said, "That is a special capability of the Visithite sensors we have created. It detects and displays individuals along with their essence auras. This helps us to discern where someone is and whether they are a Sulgon or not. If any of those people were Sulgons, or in other words inhabited by a Gaddigon, we would see a dark glow instead of the white. The only challenge with this sensor system is the range. Right now, we have to be within 300 yards of the target for it to work. My main worry is that they have figured out a way to cloak themselves in a way that will hide them from these sensors."

Michael nodded and said, "That is very cool. I'm sure you'll figure out how to extend the range and see through any cloaks."

*   *   *

About 15 minutes later the RV came to a stop. Henry announced they would be making a quick pit stop to hit the restroom before the final stretch. They had explained earlier that with large groups it was easier to use other restrooms rather than try to assembly line everyone through the two onboard. Henry reminded them that Peter was to watch over the younger group and that they needed to stay with him at all times. He also said that they were near a town called Whiskeybrook.

Michael and the other younger passengers were definitely ready to get out and move around; they were the first to head for the door. Before Michael could join them though, his mother, who had been sitting reading a book, grabbed his arm and pulled him in for a big hug. She whispered in his ear, "It's so great to see you beginning to fulfill your destiny. Your father would be so proud."

Michael patted her back and said, "I know, Mom. But we can't lose hope. I truly believe that we're going to get him back. I really don't think the Legion is any match for the Order."

His mom squeezed his hand, stepped outside, and headed for the restroom building with Aurora. Michael walked by Henry's Command Center. He thought of how incredible this vehicle was and wondered about its capabilities. As he was thinking about Henry's exceptional talents and abilities, he searched around for the hulking figure of his bodyguard, Girran, but was surprised when he didn't see him in his usual spot, hovering over the doctor. As he panned the work area, he spotted a tennis

~ 144 ~

ball sized crystal sitting in an Omithite encasement and asked, "What's *that* crystal, Dr. Waicroft?"

Henry smiled and said, "Please, call me Henry, Michael." He pointed to the almost completely transparent crystal and said, "*That* is Lumithite, the crystal Peter was describing earlier. It is extremely rare and very hard to find outside of Camelot. We found this one in one of the palace rooms in Camelot, but no one can use it because it has been activated to an unknown Sullite Signature."

Henry picked it up and Michael saw its faint golden glow. It was pulsing slowly. As with the crystal on his box, he was drawn to it. He reached out and said, "May I please see it?"

When Henry handed it to him, he touched it. At that moment he heard a double-click and the crystal lit up so brightly that Michael had to squint his eyes at first to bear it. It was a beautiful, deep gold color with sun-colored specks swimming around in it. An invigorating surge shot through him. Henry's jaw dropped and he lowered his head to look closer at the crystal, as if not believing what was happening. The beaming crystal now had a steady gold glow.

Before Henry could speak, Michael heard Silvan, who had been waiting outside say, "Come on, Michael. I have to go."

Michael handed it back to Henry. As it left his hand, the Lumithite crystal dimmed and went back to flashing in a slow but steady pulse. The shocked elf was staring at him in disbelief. Michael shrugged, walked over and hopped out the door behind the other three. When he landed on the ground, he saw Peter there. The giant motioned toward the restroom and followed them there.

Michael and the other two boys were first in. When they all came out Peter's hulky figure was standing dutifully outside. He had an anxious expression and said, "Hurry and collect everyone. We need to check on something." He was looking at Michael. "Commander Waicroft just communicated regarding a new clue that may lead to your dad's whereabouts."

Michael's heart soared. Could it be true? Had they finally caught a break? Then unexpectedly the slight ill feeling that he had felt at Henry's store returned. Where did it come from and who was triggering it?

The fleet-footed Commander started toward the forest and said, "Hurry, before we miss our window. It's important we get there quickly."

Silvan was looking at his dad with a strange expression and said, "I don't know. I thought we were supposed to stay close to the S.A.V., Dad."

Peter nodded. "Yes, very good, Son. But this is an exceptional situation that has come up. Let's go."

Michael was beyond excited by the prospect of rescuing his dad. "Come on, Silvan. Let's go. You always say you want to be involved in the adventure. Besides, I'm sure your dad would never let anything bad happen to us."

Silvan nodded reluctantly, still staring ahead at his dad's jogging figure, and conceded, "Ok. But let's hurry back."

Peter shot a glance back toward the S.A.V. and said, "Our intel said that your father left something for us near a giant fallen tree at the end of this trail."

Billy's face lit up and he said, "Fallen tree! That sounds like fun.

Let's do it." He was going faster now and turned back toward Michael, his voice squeaking, "What, you can't catch a little kid?"

Michael was close on Billy's trail and wondered how a ten-year-old could run that fast. Silvan was bringing up the rear. As they entered the forest, Michael noticed that the trees around them were much smaller than the Redwoods from Sildonia and there were more of them, all right on top of each other. As soon as they got to what they guessed was the fallen tree, Silvan said, "See, there's nothing here. Let's head back. I have a bad feeling about this forest."

Michael pointed to Peter and said, "Come on. What are you afraid of? Your dad is right here. Let's just take a quick look around. Why are you all paranoid all of the sudden?"

Billy stood, admiring the leaning tree, excitement brimming in his dark blue eyes. He proclaimed, "Heck with this. I'm climbing this thing." He jumped up with lightning quickness, wrapped his tiny arms around a low-hanging branch, swung up into the air, and came down feet-first, perfectly balanced on the trunk as if he had done it a thousand times.

Michael was about to start searching the area when he felt a prick on his neck. He reached back to investigate and then everything went black.

Chapter 11

An Unexpected Event

When Michael woke up, he was being jostled around in the back of a vehicle that was speeding down the road. He was gagged and blindfolded and his hands were being held together, but they didn't feel like normal handcuffs. He did feel two bands on his wrists, but there was no actual chain between them. It was like his wrists were being forced together by some Gaddite-like power. He heard muffled cries close by and guessed that it must be Silvan and the others.

At first, he panicked and the frightening images of Sergeant Rillick and his dark dagger came to mind... but then he remembered the lessons he had learned from the commanders and the talks with his dad about staying calm in the face of danger. Commander Sam's lesson for extending his senses was fresh in his mind, and so he dug in and reached outward to listen for what the driver might be saying in the front. A dark sensation surged as he pushed to use his power, but he overcame it and heard voices, the words clear and the tone gruff.

The lower of the two voices was talking. "Do you think they knew we were there?"

The other voice, a bit higher, said, "I don't think so. Those cloaking tokens that Bamith gave us work like a charm. I can't believe how well everything is going. The full takeover of Lithegol will happen sooner than we thought. Those idiots won't even know what hit them when we unleash our new weapons. I'm so…"

His voice was cut off and the other said, "Shut your snout! You're the one being an idiot. What if they hear you?"

There was anger in the higher voice as he responded, "They can't hear us up here. Not through this wall and with all the engine noise. Besides they probably haven't even woken up yet, you buffoon."

The other growled and said, "Watch your tongue or I'll rip it out. Don't forget who's in charge here."

It was this last interaction that triggered a memory and sent a shudder through his body. He recognized the voices as Sergeant Rillick and Officer Abernat, or Serrenz and Farstus, as they had called themselves. But how did they enter the vicinity undetected? It must have something to do with the cloaking tokens they had mentioned, and it must be how Braster and the others had snuck up on Commander Sam. But who was this Bamith guy? Then it came to him and he remembered. He felt a deep chill as he recalled the two commanders talking about a particularly nasty Sulgon named Bamith. They had been talking as if he was still in the Dread Realm and hadn't come through. They had no idea he was here on Prime.

Peter was the one that had led them into the forest. But there was no way that he would allow his own boy to be kidnapped by the Legion. Even if he was a traitor. Right? And how could Michael even think for a moment that Peter was capable of being a traitor? It just didn't make sense.

Michael's head pulsed with pain. He wondered how long they had been knocked out, where they were and where they were taking them. Within what seemed like an hour his questions were answered as they came to a stop and were unloaded. As soon as Michael was outside the vehicle, he could smell forest and hear birds high up in the trees. Distant but identifiable. They were among the Redwoods. But why would they bring them back here?

Strong hands shoved he and his friends into a tight space, a door shut and then they were descending somehow. They were in an elevator. How was that possible in the middle of the forest? From the sounds he heard, he guessed that the elevator was not modern but instead used an advanced pulley system.

When they finally removed Michael's blindfold and the gag, he was shocked to find himself sitting in a luxurious room. The space was huge and filled with every amenity. The queen-sized bed had a pillow-top mattress, with a comforter on it. There was a dresser and a nightstand. In the corner of the room was a HoloTV, projecting a 3D screensaver image into mid-air, as if by magic. In the other corner was a pinball machine and an Epic Combat arcade game.

Michael noticed right away that the room had no windows, which made sense if they were truly underground. Why had he been placed in such a nice room? Just as he sat down to try to piece it together, he heard a series of locks clicking and a stocky, unfamiliar Legion soldier strutted in. Virtually all of the Legion soldiers that Michael had seen up to this point had all been like Peter and Girran. They had Herkilian characteristics. But this one looked more like Lirfta, like a dwarf. He was no more than five feet tall and was not wearing sunglasses.

The soldier's dark, foreboding eyes glared up at him as his thick hands rested on a nightstick club on his belt. It had a small Gaddite crystal embedded in its tip. The officer grinned, his narrow mouth turning up in an evil smirk. "You must be Michael. I am Sarzot. We are very pleased to have you here at our base. As you can see, we have spared no expense in making your time here pleasant and enjoyable. We hope that you choose to repay that kindness."

He was wearing the standard issue black United Legion uniform. As Michael focused in on it, he noticed something he hadn't picked up on before. It appeared to be made of an elastic material. That made sense, given how much they had to grow when they transformed into their Sulgon form. The undersized soldier swept his arm over the room and said, "You should have all that you need during your lengthy stay here."

He made the universal gesture to turn on the HoloTV, which is a rectangle, with both hands. A hologram video came to life; he created alligator jaws with his hand and closed it to mute the sound. There were projected video images of young men leaping from one building to the next, lifting outrageous amounts of weight, shooting all kinds of futuristic weapons and driving Gaddite armored hovering ATV vehicles. "Your training will begin after we get what we need from your extremely belligerent and stubborn father. I'm sure that you will use wisdom and a brain that you hopefully didn't inherit from him. You can make your time here much more enjoyable if you choose to accept that your future is with us, as a Sulgon in the most powerful army in the Universe. I know that your first thoughts are going to be to try to escape, but I must warn you now. Don't try it. There is no way for you to get away. And why would you want to? We are offering you a life where you can be all-powerful and have whatever you want. How could you possibly turn that down?"

He pointed at the black bracelets on Michael's wrists. "If you *do* decide to try anything, you'll get a not so pleasant surprise. Trust me, it's not worth it. You need to open your eyes to the opportunity you have been given here. Gaddin is the most powerful force in the Universe."

Michael could feel his emotions rising and focused on pushing away the stirrings of fear and anger.

The stout man shook his head and said, "The silent type, huh? Well, our lowly workers will bring your dinner and some appropriate clothes within the next hour. And you will have *special* visitors later. I will be right outside your door. So, don't hesitate to call for me if you *need* anything." At that moment, his eyes went from a dark brown to all yellow with a black slit. He turned, took a step toward the door, sprang up high and did a somersault in the air, then landed perfectly, almost softly, like he had glided down. He tilted his head up and laughed, his voice crackling as he stepped out and locked the heavy door behind him.

Something about that laugh jarred Michael. There was something inhuman about it. It sounded like the gravelly voice of a beast. And those menacing eyes brought back memories of Sergeant Rillick and the Sulgon from his nightmare. Michael thought of his dad. He had to be close. Maybe even just down the hall. He sat down on the bed and tried to focus on what he could do. Surges of anger and fear pulsed from the black bracelets. By concentrating and looking within himself, he was able to recall Commander Sam's words to him: 'You must quiet your fears of the unknown. These can cloud your vision and ultimately hamper your abilities as a knight.'

He knew that focusing on what he had learned and using what was around him would help him resist the evil influence of the bracelets and help get his mind off his overwhelming situation. He thought about the various lessons he and Silvan had learned. Which of those would be useful here? Even if he could unlock the many locks on the door, where would he go from there and how would he get past Sarzot? He saw flashing lights out of the corner of his eye, and his attention was drawn to the images in the corner. The young men were living it up in all the top amusement parks around the world. Among the many clips, there was one blonde youth that seemed to dominate all the others. At first, Michael thought he was Herkilian but then he noticed that his physical characteristics were slightly different. He had a wider head and small ears. If he wasn't Herkilian then what was he? He was obviously very powerful for his age. Michael guessed that he was about 16, but he towered over the others and his feats of strength were incredible. After watching the series several times, Michael did the mute gesture and forced himself to recite the Oath of Lithegol until any thoughts of fear or hopelessness were gone.

The sound of the door unlocking startled him. It opened to reveal a young, awkward looking boy carrying a plate of food. When the shy boy set the tray down Michael got a good look at his face. His expression was one of such hopelessness that Michael's heart went out to him. He approached him with his hand extended and said, "Thanks. My name is

Michael. What's yours?"

The boy cringed as if he thought he would hit him.

Michael stopped and put up his hands. "Whoa. What are you afraid of? I'm just introducing myself."

The boy shook his head, as if he had been somewhere else entirely and said, "What? Oh. My name is Isaac. Sorry. No one ever talks to me. You surprised me."

Michael extended his hand again and when he squeezed, he noticed the chubbiness of Isaac's hand. "So, how long have you been here and how did you end up working for the Legion?"

"I've been here for a year… since I was 16," he answered dryly. "I'm here because no one else wants me. My real parents abandoned me when I was a baby and no foster family would take me. Because I'm stupid and I get in trouble all the time." He shook his head and said, "At least here I have a job. I have a purpose."

Michael couldn't believe what he was hearing. "I'm sure you're not stupid. You can't possibly think that no one cares. The Legion definitely doesn't care about you. They don't care about anyone. All they care about is ruling over everyone and hurting people. I'm sure you can make a big difference out there in the real world."

Isaac jerked his head around, as if worried they were being watched, and reached for one of his black bracelets. Michael got a close look at it. They were exactly like his. The material looked like a black version of the Omithite Illuminator Band that Peter had given his mother, only with a miniature-embedded Gaddite crystal. Isaac's plump face took on a look of terror and he said, "I have to go. My time is up. Don't try to fight it. There's no way out of this place." He ran out, the door slamming behind him.

The sound of the locks and Isaac's hopeless words rang in Michael's ears. He sat on the couch, staring at the hamburger and fries that his new acquaintance had brought for him. He knew that he should eat but being held prisoner by an evil Legion of dragon men had curbed his appetite. Go figure. He finally broke down, ate it, and was surprised at how good it tasted. He was trying to get his bearings when his dad's words came back to him: 'You must use all the resources all around you to fight the enemy.' He began a search of his room to assess what he had to work with. Although there were nice things there, it was obvious that they had taken every precaution to make sure that nothing was available to use as a weapon or a tool. There was a door off to the side that led to a small restroom with a shower.

The dresser next to his bed had generic clothing in it: underwear, pants and shirts of varying sizes. This all but confirmed his suspicion that this room had been prepped for a youth occupant, maybe from the recruiting they were doing in the area. But Michael had been told that this wasn't going on in California yet.

He felt completely alone. What was he going to do? He thought of his mom and the others. Did they have any idea what had happened? He thought of how they had been abducted. The Legion had used the bait of finding a clue to his father's whereabouts to lure Michael in, and he had fallen for it without hesitation. Silvan had tried to share his concerns, but Michael hadn't listened. Maybe if he had been more in tune, he would've sensed the presence of the Legion kidnappers. How could he have fallen for what should've been an obvious trap? He knew he was smarter than that. And what about Peter's role? There had to be an explanation as to why he would've led them into the clutches of the Legion. He had to be an inside mole for them, or maybe they threatened to harm someone he cared about. If he had turned, how had he avoided turning into a Sulgon when he engaged his armor when they first met? And how could he possibly get by someone like Sam undetected?

*　　*　　*

There were two loud clicks from the door and Michael jumped off the bed as the door opened to a teenage girl. She was wearing a tight black uniform and was holding a camouflage bag. She had dark, wavy hair and a beautiful smile. Michael was taken aback at first. Where did she come from and what on earth was she doing with the United Legion?

She sauntered, her body gliding gracefully, and set the bag down next to him. When she extended her hand, Michael was lurched back into reality by her Gaddite tokens. "Hello, Michael. My name is Malina. I have been sent to deliver your new uniform." There was something so melodic and mesmerizing about her high voice. Before he realized he was doing it he picked up the bag and opened it. Inside was a dark United Legion uniform, with the emblem of a dark dragon breathing black fire embedded in the upper chest area. Part of him was disgusted by it and he almost dropped it but then another part wanted to just try it on to see how he looked. It was a cool uniform. He slipped the loose-fitting shirt on over his t-shirt and it immediately tightened to fit his body. The silky black pants were also form fitting and Michael glanced at the mirror on the wall. He did look awesome!

Malina stepped toward him, still smiling in admiration and pulled on the fabric near his shoulders to straighten it and said, "You look so handsome. I do love a boy in uniform." Then she leaned in to kiss him. An alarm inside went off and before her lips made contact Michael pulled away, his clouded mind clearing. What was he doing wearing a United Legion uniform? Had she just tried to kiss him? She seemed as shocked as he was and she lifted her right hand, her Gaddite ring glowing, as gray-speckled black mist seeped out and into Michael's chest and eyes. He felt the tug of her influence again and reached deep for the Sullice, surrendering as he had done before. The intoxicating surge disappeared and Michael stepped away from her and said, "Get away from me. I want nothing to do with your evil mist."

Malina stared at her ring, as if it was broken and back at Michael and said, "How did you do that? No squire has ever been able to resist an enticement attack." Then her eyes narrowed. "Well, regardless you better keep the uniform on or one of my dad's favorite thugs, Serrenz, will not be pleased." Then she smirked, turned and stormed out, locking the door behind her.

Michael's thoughts went to the hypnotizing power Malina had used on him. And what had she meant by her dad's thugs? Who was her dad? And could her power be what they used on Peter? His heart sank as a dreadful thought came to him. What if the others didn't know and Peter was leading them into a trap? Or, worse yet, what if he was planning on leading the Legion to the Order's Western Base? At least Michael knew that Peter didn't know where it was yet since only Dr. Waicroft and a handful of others knew its secret location. He had to get out of here and warn them before it was too late. But how?

Before he could think further on it, the same slight ill feeling he had felt outside of Sildonia came over him. The locks sounded again and in stepped Sergeant Rillick and Officer Abernat. So, that was why Malina mentioned Serrenz. Neither of them was wearing sunglasses and they had the same yellow, black-slitted eyes from his nightmare. Sergeant Rillick sneered self-righteously and planted his hands on his hips as if he thought he was Superman.

He smirked and said, "You look good in black, young Squire. I see Malina worked her magic. Our women do have the power of persuasion. That's for sure." He pointed to the bed and said, "You should get some rest. Tomorrow at dawn you will be taking a little field trip. You won't need to pack anything except maybe a jacket... and some Kleenex." He and Abernat laughed. "Everything will change for your pathetic group very soon. Be grateful we're giving you a chance to fight on the winning team."

Michael thought about the more sizeable alert he had received on the day these two had darkened his front door and he wondered how they were masking it. His heart sank when he saw Lithegol commander bands and orbs. They weren't only masking their presence; they were also showing Lithegol counterfeit tokens. He wondered how many of the knights of Herkili had fallen so that their Legion could have their precious tokens? He wanted to squash them all.

The two leering brutes vanished, and Michael was left staring at the barred tiny sliding window on the closed door. Up until that moment things had been bleak, but never had Michael felt more like they were fighting a losing battle. That night was a long and lonely event. There were so many unknowns. Would he and the others escape? Would he see his dad tomorrow? And what if Malina or one of the more powerful Gaddite women tried an attack on him again? Could they cause him to turn on his friends and the Order? Did Sam and the others know where they were? And the most chilling unknown of them all: What would Peter do next?

Had Michael's destiny been upended? He lay there, frightening images coursing through his mind, the dread growing inside him until it seemed like it might overtake him entirely. And then he recognized the presence of the golden bird, who, as usual, appeared out of nowhere and landed on his leg. He heard the soft voice in his head, "You must maintain hope and perspective, young one. Often it is difficult to foresee what good may come to pass from the challenges we face." Peace settled over him and he collapsed into a deep sleep.

The next morning Sarzot came in and put Michael's hands together behind his back. This time he saw the officer pull out his nightstick and extend it toward his restraints. Seconds later he sensed the Gaddite power pull them together, and the stronger negative pulses began again.

Sarzot blindfolded him and led him to the elevator. He was reminded how far down his room was by how long it took to reach the surface (15 seconds). When he heard the elevator doors open and they stepped outside, he smelled the forest again. This time, instead of a van, they shoved him into what Michael guessed was one of their SUVs.

He heard grunts as others were loaded into seats nearby, and he hoped they were Silvan and the Waicroft children. Michael was tempted to ask who had joined him, but he didn't know whether Legion soldiers were close by so any comparing of notes or plan making might be overheard and therefore pointless. Besides, what plan could they possibly make? They didn't know where they were or how to get back to the others.

During their long curvy drive, Michael combed his memory for lessons he had learned to find something that could help him in this situation. He thought of the extensive lessons his dad had taught him on picking locks, such as for handcuffs. But these were not ordinary handcuffs. These had a completely different locking mechanism, so those lessons wouldn't really apply. He wondered where they were taking him. Surely this wasn't all going down today with him and his dad and the government facility and the new Gaddite sphere weapon.

After what Michael estimated as 40 minutes of driving, the vehicle came to a stop. He hadn't heard any Legion soldiers during their ride, so he thought he would extend his ears out with the power of Sullice to see what he could hear. But as soon as he dug in, an extra dose of fear and rage entered his thoughts. It was as if the crystal in the bracelets could sense the power of Sullice and was able to overcome it with pulsing doses of Gaddite. He cleared his mind, the best he could and kept the wall of darkness out, but he wasn't sure how long he could keep it up.

Chapter 12

Prisoners

When the vehicle stopped, their hulking captors removed their blindfolds. Michael saw his friends and was relieved to see that they were all ok. Shaken up, but ok. They were all wearing the dark Legion uniforms. Silvan had a bruise on his cheek and Michael wondered if that had anything to do with the Legion's persuasive encouragements. What he had smelled and guessed were confirmed—they were still amongst the Redwoods. He couldn't get over how the green canopy high above seemed to block out the sky like they were in mother nature's special roofed dimension. The vehicle they had been thrown into was a black SUV, like the one that had pulled away with Jeff's neighbor, Nick and his father.

Michael thought back to the relief he had felt the night before. He hoped that his golden bird friend would return and give him some guidance and relief shortly, as he was feeling more and more overwhelmed. Another black SUV pulled in behind theirs, and a massive Legion soldier stepped out. He had to be at least six and a half feet tall, every part of him bulging with muscles. The man's puffy lips raised in a chilling smirk, causing the cleft in his chin to deepen. Rillick and Abernat stepped out from behind him.

Michael noticed that they all had their sunglasses back on and remembered Sam mentioning that they had extreme sensitivity to the Sullite rays from the Sun. He wondered why they would risk a mission like this during the daylight hours, where they wouldn't be able to fully defend themselves should the Order arrive. The gigantic man stopped in front of Silvan and said, "So, this is Piddir's boy?" He pronounced it the way Peter had when he introduced himself. "He's taller than I thought he would be."

He glared condescendingly down at Billy, his gravelly voice suddenly higher. "And you must be the famous Little Billy. You're much less threatening than the vehicle that carries your name. I wonder if you're as intelligent as your father. Time will tell." Next was Claire. She had a different expression on her face. She was normally smiling and happy, but now her eyes were down, and she was focused on a rock. Her expression resolute.

The intimidating soldier had to crane his head down to see her. "Oh, look. A girly!"

Rillick stepped toward her and said, his raspy voice raised, "Look at the Captain when he's speaking to you."

The beastly Sulgon waved him off and said, "This must be Hank's girl. What special things can you do, *sweetie*?" He had said the word "sweetie" with great sarcasm. "Oh, that's right, your anointing day hasn't happened yet. You're helpless!" He laughed, his voice cracking and Claire glowered up at him, a tear sneaking down her cheek.

Michael erupted, "You leave her alone!"

The soldier turned to him and sneered, "Oh, look. Someone has a little girlfriend. Isn't that nice?" He placed his enormous hand on Claire's head and pushed her back as she fell to the ground. Then he slid over to Michael in a lightning quick motion, a look of disgust on his broad face. "You must be the elusive Michael. I'm still not sure how you got away. But it doesn't matter now." He smirked and motioned to the somehow dwarfed Rillick and the sergeant pulled out several syringes and injected each of them in the neck. "Let's see how well you get away with a tracker embedded in your bodies. You are all ours now. The sooner you accept that and focus on being good little soldiers for the Legion the better things will be for you."

The towering man leaned his thick head down toward Michael, his massive jaw clenching. "Your father has been very uncooperative. And I think you may have inherited some of his attitude. So, know this! We'll be keeping a special eye on you. If there is any hint of rebellion maybe I decide to make life very hard for your little girlfriend.

"But where are my manners? My name is Captain Braster. I am a Captain of the Legion army, THE most powerful force in the Universe." He was pacing now like he was delivering a speech to his troops. "Now, here's how it's going to play out. You four are going to cooperate in EVERY way or you will find yourselves serving time in our filthy dungeons, until we see fit to graduate you to our custodial crew, where you will be cleaning toilets, washing dishes and mopping floors." He turned to face them, removed his sunglasses to reveal his sinister black-slitted eyes, and opened his mouth, exposing his sharp pointed teeth and long fangs. "Do I make myself perfectly clear?" he growled. When everyone nodded, he put the sunglasses back on.

He seemed to be trying to force a real smile. "What you don't realize is that the Legion is the best thing that has ever happened to this world. We're here to give those who will join us everything their heart desires. Power, money, strength, the freedom to do whatever they want- under our protective care. Doesn't that sound like a good way to live? You can have all the things that your misguided parents and leaders have always told you that you can't have." He crouched and jumped high into the air and landed on a branch, maybe 40 feet up, on one of the Redwoods. Silvan and the others gasped. Billy's face was starting to turn pale and sickly as if he might throw up at any moment.

Braster dropped straight down out of the tree, grabbed a thick branch on the way down, and broke it off as if it were a small twig. When he landed, the earth shook like there had just been a tremor. He swung the branch toward the ground, and it exploded into tiny pieces. Michael thought about how no human could do what he had just done. No human...

When Braster approached them again he was strutting like a rooster, and Michael almost chuckled when he thought of their quirky rooster back at the farm, "You see, this is the power that we are offering you. It's more than you could ever hope for. AND you get to rule the kingdom, which is a small side benefit. We're not the bad guys here. We want to use our power to make sure there is peace. To make sure that all the important people are kept... safe. The Order wants you to think that they will protect those you care for. But THAT is a lie!" Something had changed in his expression during this last statement. Michael almost saw humanity in that cold exterior- almost. He wondered who the real Braster was. What was his story? Had he lost someone, and that was what drove him into the clutches of the Legion? As if Braster could sense Michael's probing questions he glared at him and said, "But for now we have important business to take care of."

Billy's hands were shaking, and he had been staring at Braster, his mouth gaping. After struggling to speak, he finally stammered, "Yes, s...sir. Braster. Sir." It was as if he had just been waiting to respond to Braster's previous question.

Braster gave a short laugh, his voice cracking, and said, "Good, young one. Fear me. Do not doubt for a second the seriousness of what I said about your consequences should you decide to rebel."

The Captain motioned toward the SUV he had come in on. The back door opened and another Legion Soldier stepped out, followed by a smaller man. Michael's heart jumped when he recognized the familiar stout form of his dad. It took everything in him not to run and throw his arms around him. But his dad looked different. His shoulders were slumped and his head was down; he had bags under his eyes and he had lost weight. There were bruises and cuts all over his face and he had a blank expression like there was no personality behind his normally passionate eyes. Michael felt tightness in his chest as if someone had sucked the air out of him. He wondered what had happened to the guy he had always thought of as the toughest man on the planet. His dad's hands were tied behind his back with the same black Gaddite handcuffs, but in his case, there was a ghostly chain attached to one of the cuffs and to the Legion soldier's belt.

Braster had a satisfied smirk on his wide mouth, and when Michael's dad got close, he growled, "I told you we would find a way to get you to talk. If you don't give us what we want, we will make these children pay and your son will be the first. You have a choice. But think before you decide and know that I will not hesitate to follow through on my threats."

Michael's dad lifted his head as if he was just now aware of where he was and who was there. When he saw Michael, his sullen face took on new life, his brow furrowed, and his jaw clenched. "Fine. You win. But if you lay one overgrown, disgusting hand on my son you will regret it." Michael didn't know whether to cheer or cringe as he thought of the backlash that was sure to happen from that comment. Then, sure enough, Braster turned so quickly he was almost a blur. He lifted Michael's dad's frame high in the air by his neck, as his dad hung onto his massive arm, his legs kicking.

Braster smirked and brought his right hand up, and it was then that Michael saw it. The Captain's ring Token had the fisaud, which made it appear to be the ring of a Sullite commander, just like Rillick and Abernat's. A sinewy black mist with gray flakes oozed out of it and entered his dad's eyes and chest. His dad's facial expression turned to one of terror, and he cried out, "No!!"

Braster's tooth-filled grin extended. "There is strength in you, little one. We will harness that strength and make a fine Legion warrior out of you yet." He let him go and Michael's dad fell to the ground, clutching his eyes as if he wanted to gouge them out.

What had just happened? What had his dad seen? It must have

been terrifying to have him scream out like that. A pervasive feeling of hopelessness rose up in Michael's chest, and he remembered the Gaddite handcuffs he still had on.

Michael's dad had mustered the strength to stand again and was scowling up at Braster, conviction in his tired eyes. "I'll help you get into the compound. But only if you promise to let all of them go once you have what you came for. We are soldiers and all we have is our word, so you must keep yours."

Braster smiled devilishly and said, "But of course. You have my *word* that I will let them go as soon as we have the object we seek."

Michael's dad nodded, and they were all piled back into the vehicles, which drove on for another fifteen minutes. They turned off the road and down a narrow trail that led under a bridge and into an open area adjacent to a thin walkway through the trees. Michael and the other children were left in the SUV, with an unknown Legion soldier, while the others, including his dad, gathered outside to discuss something. His dad was pointing toward the opening surrounded by a cluster of trees, and the Legion soldiers were nodding.

Another mystery soldier jumped out of the other SUV. Michael and the others were led out of the vehicle, and one of the soldiers used the special nightstick they carried to free their hands. But their bracelets remained, and they were each handed a backpack. Braster said, his voice gruff, "We had these prepared for you so that you'll keep quiet and not get in the way. So, I expect no whining or sniveling. My scouts say that there is a group of stumps in a clearing up ahead where you can sit and eat something?"

"We wouldn't want our precious leverage to faint or get sick now, would we?" They walked through the corridor of trees and into a small clearing. He pointed to a group of stumps in an area about 50 feet from the corridor opening. "But don't get any ideas. We have plenty of soldiers to guard you, track you and catch you if you should try to run. And we can shut you down with your Gaddite restraints as well." With that, he walked with Michael's dad, Serrenz, Farstus and Sarzot over to the far edge of the clearing and disappeared through an opening into a large field. The other two behemoths stayed to guard them, each of them carrying Gaddite nightsticks.

The kids walked over and found a stump to sit on. Michael opened his pack and peered inside. What he saw was not at all what he expected. There was a note, written in sloppy, misspelled handwriting. He tried to calm himself and peered around to see if either of the Legion soldiers were watching. The two assigned to guard them were standing about 10 feet away on either side, but they were focused on the opening in the trees more than they were on them.

So, Michael gazed discreetly at the note, while keeping it inside the pack. It said, "Hi Michael. It's Isaac. A guy with green eyes gave me these two things for you and said that one of them was made espeshally for you. He said to keep it hiden and that you would know what to do with it when the time comes. I hope everything works out for you and your frends."

Michael's first thought was that Isaac needed some help with his spelling. And then he thought about his mention of a man with green eyes. Who could that be? He reached his hand into the pack again, dug past the snacks and was surprised when he felt like a volleyball-sized multi-sided dice. It was a SullBomb. He pulled away immediately, his heart pounding. What on earth was that doing here? He felt around again, and his hand stopped on the last thing he expected to find—a pistol. He carefully lifted the ultra-light weapon. He heard the double-clicking sound and then a familiar feeling pulsed. It was the same unique sensation he had felt when he touched Henry's Lumithite crystal. But how was that possible? It was like Henry had made this pistol with that same crystal and only he could activate it.

When he gazed down into the bag, he saw an Omithite gun with a gold-colored glow all around it. And there in the cavity reserved for the crystal was the Lumithite crystal, just as he remembered it- buzzing with tiny gold flecks. It was all so surreal.

Then he heard a slight high-pitched squealing sound. It was growing in volume. He felt Silvan's elbow, nudging him and heard his friend's panicked voice, "What's going on, Michael? Shut that off. It's so loud." Then Michael covered his ears. It sounded like it was coming from his Gaddite bracelets, and when he glanced down the dark crystals shattered and the restraints disintegrated. He turned in terror to see if the Legion soldiers had noticed the sound and he was shocked to see the two guarding them transforming. Their bodies grew and expanded and dark ghostly Gaddite wings shot out of their shoulder blades. The wings reminded him of how the hoven worked for the knights and matrons. Their dark, scaly skin resembled that of an alligator.

This felt like a nightmare. How were they able to transform during daylight hours? Was this one of their weapons? And if so, how? But that meant they probably didn't need the sunglasses. They must have been wearing them to hide this new capability. The sight of their razor-sharp teeth and menacing eyes sent chills down his spine. He had only seen this creature in his nightmares, and he had always hoped that was the only place they would ever meet. The Sulgons had the same dark gray armor, and Michael knew he had to react quickly, or they were all in big trouble.

He knew that his main weapon in this fight would be the element of surprise, as they had no idea what he had in the bag. He thought back to his hours in the shooting range and on practice courses with his dad. All of what he had learned came flooding back. He jumped up and without hesitation pointed and shot both guarding Sulgons squarely in the chest several times. They fell to the ground, as if dead. They slowly changed back into their human forms and all signs of the Gaddite aura vanished.

*   *   *

Michael rushed to the opening and peered anxiously across the field to see if the squeal had drawn the attention of anyone else. His jaw dropped at the sight of Serrenz and Farstus, who had fully transformed into Sulgons. They had Gaddite shields and enormous GaddBlades drawn and were leaping toward them now. Each of them had the gray speckled armor, with gray jagged spikes shooting out from their chests, arms and legs. Braster had also transformed. Michael stared at his sheer mass and height and couldn't help but think of The Incredible Hulk. He was at least 10 feet tall and his arms were as big around as most men's legs. He had drawn his Gaddite shield, which covered almost his entire upper torso, and he had a long Alladin shaped GaddBlade, like Commander Peter's. He had it raised and ready as if preparing to jump in if needed.

Serrenz and Farstus were now descending toward the opening, GaddBlades pointed down and Michael knew he had to act quickly. He raised his pistol, aimed and shot, targeting the unprotected area of Serrenz's right shoulder and Farstus' left knee. The shots landed, the first one sending Serrenz flying back and the second causing Farstus to do a face plant no more than 20 feet away.

They were both stunned and groggy, but they were far from unconscious. Within seconds, they leaped up. Serrenz stared at the golden pistol in Michael's hand and said, "What is that? But..." Before he could continue, the bushes and trees exploded as several figures leaped through and surrounded both of them. It was their entire party— Peter, Sam, Aurora, the squatty figure of Lirfta and two other new commanders. They each had their armor engaged, their shields drawn and were holding their unique SullSwords. The sight of Peter surprised Michael. This definitely meant that there was something else going on. Maybe Peter had been under the influence of some mind-control weapon like Malina had used. It was a huge relief to see him fighting for the good guys.

Aurora stood out because she was the only one arrayed in green armor. All the rest were commanders and thus had the familiar rich blue armor and tokens. Lirfta had a massive weapon with a hammer on one side and a spiked mace ball on the other. Sam's SullSword was long and narrow and had elegant points on the cross-guard that pointed downward. Aurora was carrying a much heftier SullSword than Michael would've expected. It was like the classic two-handed sword you would envision the medieval knights wielding. He couldn't help but notice Sam's ears. They were much more pointed now, in his natural form, and he was slightly taller by a few inches.

Michael studied the two new team members standing next to Peter. One was different from any of the others. He had elfish features but was smaller, maybe four and a half feet tall, and had narrower ears and a large, extended forehead. Michael thought back to what Peter and Sam had said about the races. This must be a faery knight. The other looked more like a grandma than a warrior but her armor was the thickest sky blue of all the commanders. She had dark skin and was holding a scepter with the illuminated Sign of Lithegol in the handle.

Before anyone could make a move, Braster leaped high in the air and came down with a crash between his two cohorts, his super-sized clawed feet digging into the grassy earth below. Michael glanced at his feet and noticed that the Captain's military-looking boots had opened up to accommodate his special four-toed foot. His legs were slightly bent, and he scowled and barred his long teeth as he stared at Commander Sam. "I see you came back for more, Commander. This time you won't get away that easily. I bet you weren't expecting us to be able to change under the light of your puny sun. Well, we can now. Courtesy of Dr. Minser's crystal extractions. And we have another little surprise for you."

The gray light of his Gaddite Orb flashed and a large group of Sulgons dropped from the sky and Legion soldiers rushed out from the trees on both sides of the field. Braster laughed, "We thought you might make an appearance. Now we're going to destroy all of you AND get the

ClusterSphere." He turned and the Gaddite crystal on his amulet flashed and Sarzot's likewise and then the smaller Sulgon nodded at him, grabbed Michael's dad and he and four massive Sulgons took off toward the other side of the field. Then Sarzot, two of the Sulgons and his dad disappeared into the forest.

Michael thought of the battle that was about to begin. What should he do next? He really should try to rescue his dad, but how could he possibly get by all of the Sulgons, including the two behemoths guarding the opening on the other side? And what about the other children?

He had been crouched at the clearing side opening to the field and glanced back and saw Claire hunched behind a stump, comforting Billy, who was sobbing quietly. Silvan crouched nearby staring at his Gaddite bracelets, a pained look on his face. Michael approached him and motioned for him to stick his arms out and he shot the bracelets. They squealed, but only for a moment, and then disintegrated like his had. He did the same for Claire and Billy. Then he and Silvan walked them back through the tree corridor, they all took off their Legion uniforms and Michael had them duck down behind one of the SUVs.

Michael thought of the scene playing out in the neighboring field. He felt drawn toward it. He turned to Silvan, who was comforting Billy, and said, "I need to go help the others."

Silvan's eyes went wide and he said, "But we need to stay here and watch over these two."

Michael nodded and said, "I know. I need you to stay and do that. But I have to go. Please do this. I can't explain how. I just know I'm supposed to go. Stay hidden, keep an eye out and be careful."

Michael was about to surge his hoven and leap when Claire grabbed his hand. "Thank you so much for standing up to Braster before. Please don't go. It's too dangerous. I don't want anything to happen to you. Just stay here with us. They can handle them."

Michael squeezed her hand and said, "It's ok. I'll be ok. Just stay here. I'm sure you can take care of yourself and besides you'll have Rambo here with you." He let go of her hand and smiled at them both. Then, without waiting for a response, he surged his hoven and jumped, soaring high above the trees and landing in the clearing near the opening to the field. He decided to close his eyes and calm his mind before joining in on the battle.

When he opened his eyes, Aurora was standing next to him. She hugged him and said, "It's great to see you're ok. Commander Sam sent me to check on you guys. Where are the others?"

Michael pointed back toward the path through the trees and said, "They're back, hiding behind the SUVs. Silvan is watching over them."

Then she nodded, her eyes wide, and jerked her head toward the sky above them. When Michael followed her gaze, he saw a Golden Eagle descending toward them. His heart leaped and the familiar golden glow lit up all around the bird as it landed on a tree branch in front of him.

It took a minute for Aurora to collect herself, and she said, "Umm, Michael, how are you not startled? Have you seen this before? Do you even know who that bird is?"

Michael heard the familiar voice in his head. *Tis fine. You can inform her about me.*

He nodded. "Aurora, this golden bird has guided me and helped me several times. But it was always in a much smaller form."

Aurora gazed in awe at the magnificent bird again and stammered, "Michael... *that* is Merlin, the Royal Overseer. He is one of the Royal Guards."

Michael stared at the perched figure, who appeared to be smiling again. How did it do that? "What? As in Merlin the wizard that fought alongside King Arthur?"

"Except that we don't call them wizards. That's just how humans chose to explain the power of Sullice. But if he is here and helping you..." She gasped. "You ARE the High Sentinel. I didn't believe Henry when he told me." With that statement, she fell to one knee in front of him and extended her right arm forward with the palm up. It was the same bow the others had done.

When she stood, her eyes lit up. "Wait. If you truly are the High Sentinel, then you have all the powers of the Order at your disposal. Which means that you can invoke a Stealth Cloak."

Michael didn't know what to make of what she said, but it was starting to make sense. That is why he was as strong as Silvan and so gifted in so many different areas. This talk of cloaks triggered a memory and Michael blurted out, "That reminds me. I overheard Serrenz and Farstus talking before and they mentioned that Bamith is here and helped them to cloak themselves."

Aurora's eyes widened. "Bamith! Really? How do they keep sneaking these nasties through? I'd better let the others know. Bamith is the only senior commander from the Faery Triad to fall to the Legion. He is beyond evil and is very good at hiding."

Her orb flashed and Michael asked, "How do you communicate like that?

"It's easy," she responded. "Just engage your Sullice and focus your thoughts outward at the knight or matron you want to communicate with, and your ring or orb will do all the work to get it to them."

Michael decided to try it and sent a thought to her in the form of a question, "What do you mean- Bamith is good at hiding?"

Aurora smiled and said, "Very good, Michael. I got it." Then her expression was serious again. "Faeries have the ability to shapeshift into anyone. Their main limitation is that they can't hold the shapeshifted form when they engage their armor... well, except for Derrilin, of course. He's amazing... That's it! Bamith must have been pretending to be Girran for these last several days. But that means that Girran is probably... Oh. Poor Henry. He will be devastated. Bamith must have transformed into Peter to draw you kids away." She had a look of shock on her face. Her orb flashed and she said, "He may have stolen the plans to the western base. Unbelievable."

Michael looked around, hoping Bamith didn't jump out from behind a nearby bush, and said, "That's crazy. But that makes sense. He must've been the one that I sensed but I could never tell for sure if it was a Sulgon. His special cloak was getting in the way. Speaking of cloaks, what is the Stealth Cloak you were talking about?"

"The Stealth Cloak is what Merlin has been using to hide himself from others. You basically change the way the Sullite armor works, and it makes you invisible, not only to those who can't see through essence materials but also to everyone else. Well, everyone except those that are cloaked at the same time. Normally elves are the only ones that can do it. I can do it too because my mother is an elf."

"Your mom's an elf? That's cool. Does she look like Commander Sam?"

"Well, they all have similar features. She's actually a Cognitive from the Penturi Realm, a senior commander in the Order and the Head Matron at the Haven of Gareth. It's in Europe. My little brother, Percival, is a 17-year-old apprentice. He is in training at Camelot. You may get to meet both of them soon."

Michael nodded and said, "Cool. I look forward to it. Now as far as this cloak thing goes, I'm only a squire. How am I supposed to do that? It sounds like something you would have to be at a much higher level to do."

Aurora said, "You can already do things that only a master should be able to do. You just don't realize it yet. The way you use SullSight and your hoven is way beyond any of the apprentices that I have seen. Don't limit yourself. You have the potential to become the most powerful knight to ever live, except for Arthur." She pointed at the pistol and said, "How many squires have a Lumithite Sullera pistol? None!" Then she noticed something on it and turned it to the side and said, "We need to set this to ten before you go in there, by the way. I don't think five will cut it." She twisted the knob on the side of the barrel. This triggered a memory from when Peter had been describing the rifles. Michael wondered how many level ten shots remained in his Lumithite chamber.

Aurora was now sitting with her legs crossed, her hands on her knees and her eyes closed. "Do as I do, please. Just let your whole body relax. Then engage your armor, grab hold of it and follow my instructions."

Michael tried it but was obviously struggling. "How do I grab the armor if I don't know what it feels like?"

Aurora shook her head and said, "Don't think of it so literally, Michael. There will be pockets of concentrated Sullice surrounding you that you can sense. That is your armor. Send it out from you while commanding it to hide you. Sullice knows what you need it to do, but you have to guide it and believe in it. That part is very important."

At first, Michael didn't feel the pockets of Sullice, but then he stopped searching, just called for them and there they were. Each one felt like a mini version of what he had experienced when he touched the Lumithite crystal. When he pushed them out away from him, he felt a strange sensation and said, "That feels weird. I feel so light."

Aurora exclaimed, "That's it, Michael. Unbelievable. You know how long it took me to figure that part out? Days!"

When Michael opened his eyes, he was shocked to see a faded, transparent version of Aurora standing inside a green speckled shell that was more like a bubble and less like the normal Sullite outline.

She shook her head. "That is just crazy. A squire with a Stealth Cloak. You really are the one…"

A voice from behind them said, "Can it be?" and Michael turned with a start, his cloak falling from his break in concentration. Aurora had her armor up and her SullSword drawn, but as soon as she saw their tall visitor, who was floating down to the ground on a giant white and gold hoven, she pulled her SullSword back in and disengaged her armor.

Their mysterious visitor was arrayed in a brilliant white aura with radiant yellowish-gold armor and when Michael saw his green eyes, he thought of the note from Isaac and the items in his backpack. Aurora ran over to the beaming figure and hugged him. When she pulled away, she put her hands on her hips and said, "Nice of you to finally show up, Dad."

Michael's mind was reeling. Dad? So, the powerful knight with the green eyes was Aurora's dad? But if he had golden armor that meant that...

Aurora pointed toward the trees and said, "Dad, a Legion troop has attacked. They are hoping to use Michael's dad to get into the lab and steal the Gaddite ClusterSphere."

The man nodded, an unmistakable confidence in his sharp features, closed his bright green eyes for a moment, and said, "I am aware of their activities and it is most unfortunate. But they will not accomplish their goal. Commanders Piddir and Lirfta are intercepting them and will rescue Spencer." He gazed fondly at the majestic bird perched in front of them, "Is it really you, my old friend?"

The bird nodded, but this time kept its head in a lowered position for several seconds. Gabriel answered by performing the same crouching bow, his arm extended and then pulled into his chest. He stood and smiled at Michael and said, "The answer to the question in your mind is yes, Michael. I am Captain Gabriel. It's nice to finally meet you." He was gazing at Michael lovingly. It was as if he knew him already. What was it with people recognizing him when he had no recollection of ever meeting them?

Michael noticed that the Captain towered over him, and from this, he guessed him to be around 6' 5." There was something elegant and majestic about him. Maybe it was the calm wisdom in those unusual green eyes or the way he gracefully moved toward him to shake his hand. And just as Michael had imagined, he had a perfect English accent. Gabriel pulled him in and hugged him, which caught Michael off guard, but he went ahead and hugged him back.

Gabriel said, "You cannot fathom how long we have all been waiting for your arrival."

Chapter 13

The Reunion

The elegant leader was wearing the same soft illuminated outfit that all the knights and matrons wore. His white aura and golden speckled Sullite uniform and cape made him appear that much more magnificent.

Michael noticed the orb on his chest. He remembered how Peter's had also had all the compass points lit up. But Gabriel's had the star and the moon lit up, too. Gabriel put his hand on Michael's shoulder and said, "Because I am an overseer, all of the signs, including the sun, moon and star, are illuminated on my orb. Also, the Captain is always stationed on Prime and has jurisdiction over all realms; that is why all of the four compass points are likewise lit up."

This was the second time it had happened and Michael had to ask, "Are you able to read my mind? How did you know what I was going to ask?"

Gabriel replied, "I know it must seem like that, but it is actually a special insight that is broadcast through the power of Sullice. Remember, who we are and what we think is all inter-related to our essence core. It's a bit like how certain dogs are able to smell very slight odors. Your essence gives off a vibe or an inclination and because I have mastered listening for all things related to the essence I can pick up on these unspoken inclinations."

The Captain lifted his closed hand and extended his palm, to reveal a large metallic pill. "Dr. Waicroft said that you need to swallow this to be rid of the Legion tracker they injected."

Michael gave it a hesitant glance and then grabbed it, took some water from his backpack and choked it down.

Aurora chimed in and said, "Speaking of Dr. Waicroft, he just sent me a message that Commander Sam needs me to cloak and assist him with a particularly nasty Sulgon. I'll see you soon." Then she leaped over the trees and Michael wondered why she hadn't just gone through the opening. All this leaping... I guess if you can do it, why not? With those thoughts of Aurora, he thought back to what she had said and asked, "So, what is the High Sentinel that Aurora was talking about?"

"There is a prophecy that Prince Arthur will send one of his most powerful knights, The High Sentinel, in the last days, and that he will lead the armies of Lithegol in the End of Days War against the Legion and the forces of evil. The prophecy also states that Merlin, who was transformed into a Golden Eagle at the time of Arthur's departure from Prime, and the rest of the Royal Guard will fight by his side and teach him the ways of the Order and the power of Sullice."

Michael's mind was overloaded. "And what is that special bow that everyone does- with the palm out?"

The Captain said, "That is called a Revin. Normally we, as knights and matrons, only perform that bow for someone we have the utmost respect for. There is a form of it where both open hands are placed up. But that is very rare."

"Thank you for explaining that," Michael said. "I don't know about all those formalities, but what I do know is that the Legion is evil and they need to be stopped." He pulled out the SullBomb from the backpack and said, "And I believe that you gave me this so that I can blow up the Gaddite sphere."

Gabriel smiled knowingly and said, "Yes. Very well said indeed, young Squire. As soon as we help the others and defeat this group of Sulgons, your father can lead us to the government compound's secret entrance, and you will be able to use that SullBomb to destroy the ClusterSphere. Lead the way."

Michael cloaked and was preparing to leap, when three large figures landed between them and the opening, causing the ground to shake. Michael gazed in terror at the towering figures of Braster, Serrenz and Farstus. Braster smirked at the Captain and said, "I thought I sensed your arrogant vibe close by. It's time for you to pay for the murderous acts of your followers! I will avenge Bethany's senseless murder." He leaped high into the air, his GaddBlade swiping down, as Gabriel dodged it effortlessly. A speckled golden hammer shot out of Gabriel's ring and knocked Braster back.

While the towering Sulgon regained his composure, Gabriel said, "What happened to your wife was an accident and those who did it were banished from the Order and imprisoned immediately after it happened."

Michael wondered what had happened. It sounded like that was the event in 1865 that had caused Braster to leave the order. Michael saw

Farstus staring at Braster and knew he had to attack right away. He did a somersault to get a better position, took careful aim at the Sulgon's amulet, and fired two shots from his pistol. The stunned Sulgon didn't even know what hit him and fell to the forest floor, unconscious. Michael turned and saw Serrenz joining Braster in the fight against Gabriel. One would think that this was completely not fair but the Captain swatted Serrenz off with a six-foot golden hand like he was more of an annoying mosquito.

Michael decided to even the score and aimed his pistol at the recovering Sulgon's chest. But Serrenz raised his shield at just the right time and it was deflected. The angry hybrid turned, his sharp teeth barred.

He jumped high into the air toward Michael, his wide GaddBlade raised. Michael jumped, engaged his cloak, and using his hoven changed trajectory to land behind Serrenz. But Serrenz was ready for him, so as soon as Michael pulled in his armor, which removed the cloak, Serrenz sailed through the air to attack, his spectral wings flapping.

They exchanged blows for several minutes, navigating through the air. Michael thought of how grateful he was that Peter and Sam had made them do the hoven attack exercises or he may not have done as well against the agile Sulgon. Serrenz was very good at countering Michael's moves and never left himself open or vulnerable to attack. Then Serrenz touched his amulet and a thick Gaddite mist slithered out and entered Michael's chest. His echolocation ability seemed to be muffled and Serrenz seized this moment of vulnerability and swung his dark blade at Michael, striking his chest and sending him flying through the air. He landed near the tree line and Michael was trying to gain his bearings when

Rillick leaped over to him. The towering Sulgon was standing in a pose straight out of a Sulgon Brute Squad magazine, a condescending sneer on his dragon snout.

Michael felt like some of his Sullite power had been removed or pushed back and a panicked feeling rose up within him. He pushed it away and focused on his surroundings. He thought of how Sam had always talked about using living things around us, including the trees. Surely, he didn't have enough power to do anything like that yet. Before he could try to reach out, Serrenz raised his SullSword to strike and Michael jumped up and raised a shield, prepping for the blow.

A flurry of blue baseball-sized Sullite bursts hit the hybrid's exposed shoulder and head, sending him flying to the ground. When Michael looked to see where it had come from, his mouth dropped. His mother was standing there, awkwardly hoisting a giant Sullera rifle. She glared at the groggy dragon figure and said, "Don't you dare try to hurt my boy!" Michael smiled and reached out with all the Sullice he could summon and directed it to an overhanging tree nearby.

He felt the tree respond with crawling branches that wrapped themselves around the dazed Sulgon and squeezed him tight. Michael jumped up, pushed the Sullice from deep within into his SullSword, and stabbed directly into the helpless Legion soldier's amulet. A high-pitched screeching sound followed.

Serrenz was now in his human form but Michael felt the Gaddite pushing back on him and a burst of gray specks exploded out of Rillick's amulet and threw Michael back. The tree branches were darkening and then they crumbled and fell to the ground, like dust. The partially revived hybrid was transforming back into his Sulgon form as he stood up, still a little shaky. Michael's mom was wrestling with the bulky rifle and kept looking back and forth between the gun and the recovering Sulgon.

Right then, a blue flurry of mace ball shots struck the Sulgon's amulet and he fell back to the ground, reverting to his Rillick form. Michael turned to see the ATV-sized S.A.V. called Claire racing toward them, a large cannon protruding from the top. It came skidding to a stop and Michael was shocked to see Claire jump out and approach them. She was holding a glowing Sullera rifle. It was smaller than the beast of a gun his mom was carrying. She smiled warmly at Michael, and said, "I couldn't let you guys have ALL the fun." She put up her index finger and said, "Excuse me." Then she approached the near unconscious Sulgon and said, "Prepare to be ended, you ugly lizard-head." She knelt down and said, "Look at me when I'm talking to you." The incoherent sergeant managed to lift his head, a deep scowl showing through. She smirked and lifted her rifle, and said, "There you are. I just wanted to say one word… Goodbye." She pulled her trigger and three rapid-fire softball-sized mace balls from the rifle struck Serrenz's amulet.

The Gaddite crystal on the Sulgon's chest disintegrated and Serrenz the Gaddigon exploded out and passed through Claire and then Michael, his sharp teeth gnashing. When the floating menace made impact, Michael felt a wave of fear and despair crash over him and he fell to his knees like his breath had been sucked out of him.

Aurora descended out of nowhere, landing close by and a thick green speckled beam of white light burst forth from her orb and encircled the snarling Gaddigon, but a blast of black, gray speckled matter exploded from the retreating figure and Michael watched as the dark dragon ghost disappeared into the trees. Why hadn't he helped Aurora capture him? Something about the sinister creature's attack had caused him to go into a hazy stupor for a minute. Who would this evil creature inhabit next and when would they meet again?

The dark haze left him, and he got up and said, "Sorry, Aurora. I would've helped you but Serrenz attacked me and I was in some kind of a funk. By the way, are they all that gnarly looking?"

Aurora smiled slightly and said, "Don't worry about it. He won't do any damage. Not for a while at least. As far as their charming looks, unfortunately, yes. But believe it or not some Gaddigons are even uglier." She reached into her pack for an RP. Aurora handed a vial to Michael, and said, "It looks like you may need a little of this, buddy. How did you even last that long against him, anyway? From what I've heard, that cocky jerk can handle a blade!"

Michael shrugged and said, "It was really my mom and Claire that saved me. I would've been toast if they hadn't shown up." When Michael lifted the vial to his lips and took a sip, the liquid that poured out was creamy and tasted like a mixture of cinnamon and apple. He could feel it lifting his energy and the power inside immediately and he stared at the bottle in wonder and handed it back to Aurora.

Michael gazed at Claire and smiled. The young blonde had an eager smile and was looking around like she hoped for more Sulgon visitors. Aurora high fived Claire and his mom and said, "Alright! I'm impressed. Way to represent, you two."

Michael's mom searched the area, as if the danger could be lurking around them, and said, "Thanks. I just couldn't sit there anymore, while my son was out here facing this on his own."

An anti-gravity drone, that Michael recognized as one of Henry's, zipped up to the group and a projected visage of Henry appeared and he did not look pleased. "Claire Elise Waicroft, you get back in that vehicle and return to the safe house. Now! It is way too dangerous for you out there." His expression softened and he said, "Your time will come, Peanut. You've had your moment. Now, get back here. The drone will escort you so that I can be sure you return safely and aren't followed."

Claire looked like she might object and then she shook her head and grabbed Michael and his mom's hands. She gazed pleadingly into Michael's eyes, and said, "Please be careful out there. I care about you... all very much." Right before she got back into the small S.A.V., she said, "Hopefully next time I can fight *with* you. Apparently, daddy's not ready to let his little girl join the fun yet." Then she pulled away, and both Claires and the drone disappeared into the corridor.

Aurora looked toward the battlefield and said, "Henry is right to be concerned. Julia, you must stay away from the action out there. It's way too dangerous. At least you're wearing an undershield. That will protect you from their Grobel daggers." Aurora's orb flashed and within seconds Commander Sam alighted next to her.

He stared at Michael's mom incredulously, and said, "Julia? Why did you come? This is far too dangerous for you to be here." Then he gazed in the direction of the fallen Rillick and said, "But, perhaps I have underestimated you. Well done."

She smiled sheepishly and said, "Thank you. But I had help. Claire made an appearance and finished him off."

Sam gave Aurora a questioning look, and the young matron said, "She borrowed the smallest S.A.V., but apparently forgot to ask permission and had to go back."

Sam smiled and shook his head. "She definitely has the fighting spirit. Henry has his work cut out for him with that one."

*   *   *

There was a loud crack, that sounded like a tree snapping in two, and Michael turned to see what was going on with Gabriel. He and Braster were flying and doing twists through the air, hurling nasty-looking essence weapons at each other, including mace balls, flurries of blades, spinning axes and comet-like fireballs. Michael could see their spectral helmets occasionally shooting out from the speckled discs behind their heads to block incoming enemy fire. The huge dragon figure towered over the Captain, but it was clear who was winning this fight.

At one point, Braster's GaddBlade quickly extended into a spiked lance and he used it to try to stab the overseer. But the agile knight just dodged and used a shield that wrapped itself around the blade, slowing it way down.

Then Gabriel performed a move that Michael never would've guessed was possible. He lifted his SullSword high above his head and started spinning at a crazy fast rate, the blade acting like a spinning propeller, slicing at varying angles on each rotation. When he moved toward Braster, the Sulgon put up an ultra-thick Gaddite dome of protection. But it had little to no effect on the Captain's lacerating tornado. Braster tried to dodge and evade but the spinning vortex just zipped here and there, slicing through him at every turn. There was a screeching sound as the Legion Captain's shield broke down and disappeared.

As the lashes from the spinning SullSword swiped through the dodging Sulgon, he started to fade. His dragon jaw opened wide and he yelled out. Braster's body went limp and he fell to the ground, now in his human form. Gabriel was breathing heavily as if what he had done had taken a lot out of him. He glanced at the fallen Captain, shook his head, and reached over his shoulder as a golden lasso and special bands flew into his hand from his sleek shoulder pack. He secured Braster's hands with the bands and used the glowing rope to fasten him to a nearby tree.

Commander Sam smiled and said, "Now THAT is the sweep. When performed by a true master like that it is just unbeatable. But now it will take him a bit to replenish his Sullice reserves." He pointed to his shoulder pack and said, "Take him an RP from my reserves, please."

Gabriel accepted the two items and said, "Are you all ok? I saw Serrenz escape. He is a powerful one. I was watching Michael closely and would've intervened. But it looks like between his amazing natural skills and his assistance from Claire and Julia he is ok."

His daughter smiled and said, "Yes, they had everything under control when I arrived."

Commander Sam stared down at the fallen United Legion soldier and pointed to a strange baton with a Gaddite crystal embedded in the tip and said, "That looks like their net baton. But that is definitely a more powerful Gaddite crystal. We have to be careful. They must have used some of the ClusterSphere extractions to make it." He turned to Michael. "I still can't believe you three defeated Serrenz. It's too bad I wasn't here to witness it and capture him."

Michael smiled and said, "It was my mom that saved the day. I'll never forget the shocked look on that cocky Sulgon's face."

Sam shook his head. "It is true then. What Overseer Zaldar has said: 'A mother's love is the most powerful force in the four kingdoms.'"

Michael's mom shrugged. "We do what we have to do to protect our babies." She lifted the rifle and said, "I just have one question, though. Am I even using this crazy thing correctly?"

Captain Gabriel pointed to the fallen Legion Sergeant and said, "It looks like you used it masterfully, young lady. I'm honored to have you join us. But as Commander Sam said, you must stay close to him or me at all times. What we just experienced is only the beginning of what we must face." He looked at Captain Braster's unconscious body, tied to the tree. "But first things first. It is time for Veeral and Captain Braster to end their reign of terror."

Sam nodded and pointed to his backpack as Gabriel removed a mini-SSB from the top pouch. "This may not provide the blast necessary to extract him. I need all of you to help. He's not going to come easy. If Veeral has utterly taken over his essence core and his life is in danger from our efforts, I will let you all know. Michael, how about you and your mother fire a shot directly at his amulet right after the bomb detonates. Commander, you place the bomb and fire an extraction shot from your Sullera rifle at him when the time is right and I will prepare to capture

Veeral when he is forced out. Hopefully, it's not too late."

Sam placed the bomb right next to the unconscious Sulgon and pushed the 15-second button. He then hurried back to crouch with the others roughly 30 feet away, his rifle aimed and ready. Michael, Sam and his mom timed it perfectly. Right after the bomb went off, they fired shots directly into Braster's chest. Sam's spiked mace ball extraction shot dug in, the blue particles attacking the Gaddite Amulet. Aurora was also shooting a green ray of Sullice into the Sulgon's chest. Gabriel flew up and landed close to the trapped prisoner as the Gaddite crystal disappeared. The ravenous Gaddigon called Veeral shot out so quickly that he was nothing more than a blur. Immediately a beam of gold speckled white light burst forth from Gabriel's orb and he used more Sullice from his ring to strengthen it, as the squealing and snarling dragon ghost struggled and then finally disappeared into his orb crystal.

Michael jumped up from his crouched position and exclaimed, "Wow! AMAZING! That thing was nasty!"

Commander Sam stood up and patted Michael on the back. "You are correct on that. Anyone but an overseer would've had a hard time capturing him. Nice shot, by the way. How did that feel?"

"It felt good," Michael answered. "I just wish Peter could've been here to see Braster go down." A thought came to him and he asked, "So, who are the new team members, by the way? Is the small commander guy a faery? He looks different than the others."

Sam smiled and said, "Peter would have enjoyed helping take down his old nemesis, to be sure. And, yes, Senior Commander Derrilin is a faery. And Senior Commander Eileen is from here on Prime. She is the Head Matron of the Haven at the Portacon of Galahad."

Michael nodded, his eyes moving to the unconscious body of Sergeant Rillick. He shuddered at the remembrance and said, "It was weird when Serrenz came out of Rillick's body. When he flew through me, I felt an overwhelming evil feeling and I was out of it for a minute."

Sam patted him on the shoulder and said, "The evil feeling you describe is part of how Gaddigons attack embodied beings. They try to break the host down and then force the broken individual to invite them in. The good news is that Gaddite Essence Beings are no match for most knights and matrons. Most of their power comes from the corrupted Sullite tokens and the captured essence core of the embodied host they take over."

Michael shook his head and said, "They are so despicable. I can't wait to squash them all."

Gabriel stared at the lifeless form of Braster on the grass, shook his head and said, "Me too, Michael. Commander, you and Julia need to stay and guard the children and the prisoners. Please bind and harness them and then the rest of us must go. The others need us to join them in the battle."

Commander Sam handcuffed Braster, Rillick and Abernat. Then he put an over the shoulder harness on each of them. As Michael watched closely, it was clear that the harnesses were for transporting prisoners. The center section had a tiny Sullite crystal strategically placed over their chests. The radiant lasso extended from it to a heavy-duty pulley style latch on Commander Sam's backpack. The soldiers, other than Braster, who seemed completely out of it, struggled and growled and barked at their captor right up until the harness was installed and then it was like they were in a trance. Their faces became expressionless, and Sam said, "There, that's better."

At that moment, there was a loud squealing sound, that sounded like an extraction and Michael exclaimed, "Sounds like there's one less Sulgon now. Hopefully, the others are kicking some butt out there."

Michael's mom gave him a hug, her voice quivering, "Please be careful and stay close to Gabriel and the others. Don't take any unnecessary risks."

Michael patted her back and said, "I will, Mom. I promise. I'll be fine. Don't worry. I'm with Captain Gabriel."

She nodded and forced a smile as Michael joined Gabriel and Aurora. The Captain smiled at her and said, "Do not fret, Julia. His Mentor Sentry won't let anything happen to him. But know this, he can certainly take care of himself." Gabriel's orb flashed and seconds later Peter descended on a massive hoven, the blue Sullice flecks dancing around it furiously.

When Peter saw Gabriel, he did a fist pump and ran over to him, like a little boy whose parents had just returned from a long trip. He grabbed him and effortlessly lifted him up, and exclaimed, "I knew you couldn't stay away." The Captain patted him on the back and Peter put him down, bowed low, in the Revin, and said, "Now let's obliterate some Sulgons."

Gabriel smiled at him and said, "It's great to see you, Commander. Remember, nobility and reverence."

Peter shrugged. "Oh, yes. Sorry, Captain. I'm just so excited to see you again." He smiled at Michael. "And I'm so relieved to see that you're ok. We rescued your father and he's with Aurora. She will keep him safe and hidden until we are ready to proceed to the lab."

Michael was so overwhelmed by this good news that he rushed forward and hugged the towering giant, who hugged him back and gave him a few pats. "I told you we would get him back." Peter looked at the harnessed Sulgons and said, "I heard that you've been keeping busy. I can't believe I missed the fall of Blister, I mean Braster."

Sam smiled, and said, "You should have seen Gabriel take him down with The Sweep. It was incredible. He couldn't do anything to defend himself."

Peter did a celebratory fist clench and proclaimed, "Yes! That's crazy. That guy can take almost anyone out. I've seen him take on like three commanders."

Gabriel gave a humble smile and said, "I think you and the others must have weakened him before I faced him." He winked. "Are we ready for the next battle?"

Peter patted Michael's back and said, "Let's do it. Looks like you and I are going to be together on this one."

Gabriel motioned for everyone to lean in and whispered, "This is going to be very dangerous and we have to be extremely attentive and aware of the Sulgons and their whereabouts at all times. Peter, you two must stay together and I want Michael to stay cloaked as long as possible. And remember we can use the S.S.B.s when it is safe for the others to do so. May the King and the light of Sullice empower you."

Gabriel put his finger to his lips, a look of urgency sharpening the soft features of his face. "We must make haste, I sense the presence of Erubamir." He motioned for them to follow him as they set off quickly through the opening.

Gabriel was the real deal and even spoke like a medieval knight. Michael wondered again what his full story was. He thought about what he was about to walk into. Was he ready? Then he remembered how he had handled Serrenz and the fact that Peter was by his side and he felt better about his chances.

Chapter 14

The Battle

As they entered the open field, they could hear major battling going on with shrieks and clashes. Michael heard cheers and saw Commander Lirfta mowing down two United Legion soldiers, who weren't in their Sulgon form. Captain Gabriel already had three soldiers wrapped up with a special extendo mace, with a long glowing chain. It had them pulled in tight against each other around their chests and three Sullite blades shot out from the chain, puncturing their amulet crystals. A high-pitched sound pierced the air, the crystals exploded into thin air, and they all collapsed.

Michael still had his cloak up but had been separated from Peter as they entered the fight when Peter was attacked by a pair of massive lumbering Sulgons. There were others fighting soldiers who had a Gaddite violin bow baton weapon. And the thought came to him that maybe the Legion had created something to take the place of the GaddBlade for those without special tokens who were unable to transform. From the battles underway Michael could see that the Sulgons were losing ground now that Gabriel had arrived.

The tiny faery knight they had called Derrilin and also Eileen were taking on Erubamir, and Michael stared in awe at how quickly the faery commander dodged and attacked, timing his assaults perfectly. His movements were different from the elves. He would move slow, then explode in a flurry of quick attacks, instead of swift graceful elf style attacks. The Legion leader was beyond anything Michael could've imagined. He had to be over twelve feet tall and he had a white scar that extended from his left pointed ear to his dragon jaw. Michael wondered when Gabriel would square off with him and how well he would do against him.

Peter had taken out one of the attacking Sulgons and Michael positioned himself behind the other. He communicated using Sullice to him and Peter did a risky but effective uppercut move that knocked the soldier back just as Michael called down his armor, releasing his cloak. He extended his SullSword through the startled Sulgon's chest and Peter followed likewise with his. After the Sulgon fell, Peter captured the extracted Gaddigon and said, "Nice one, Michael. Good timing. Let's see who needs our help."

Gabriel and the 13-foot mammoth that was Erubamir were squaring off for what promised to be a fierce battle. Michael could see that the Sulgon leader's spiked armor was much thicker than anyone else's, the gray speckles creating a blur of frenzied chaos. Michael spotted the squatty figure of Commander Lirfta, who had just taken out a soldier with his massive hammer mace weapon. Aurora had a Sullite green arm with a pincher on the end of it that extended from her SullSword. She wrapped it around a soldier's neck, lifted the flailing man and slammed him to the ground.

There were a handful of knights taking on multiple Legion soldiers. Michael gazed out at them and a vision of an obstacle course came to his mind, each one of the soldiers forming an obstacle. He turned to Peter and said, "I'll be right back." Before Peter could respond, he summoned the Sullice from deep within and jumped. Everything happened in a blur. He moved faster than he ever had, slicing and upending each one before they knew what hit them. When he stopped, he looked back and saw the others staring in awe as three more soldiers lay prostrate and unconscious.

Within moments everyone was back to fighting as if someone had pushed a pause button and then hit play again. Peter was taking on two more Sulgon attackers. It seemed like when a Sulgon was taken out two more were popping up. Where were they coming from? Michael saw Lirfta dodging and smashing, his hammer jarring all those unfortunate enough to be smashed by it. The dwarf was exceptionally light on his feet for someone so thick.

Lirfta had noticed Michael and was looking over in his direction as if checking to see that he was ok. From out of nowhere another two attackers, one of them in his Sulgon form jumped the dwarf from behind and the Sulgon stabbed him in the chest with his GaddBlade, a dark gray speckled surge attacking his orb. Lirfta cried out, his eyes went blank and he fell to the ground.

Michael felt his heart race, as panic set in. He had to act quickly. He surged his hoven and zipped over to them, his SullSword pointed at one attacker and his pistol at the other. They hadn't been expecting this and when he came down, he stabbed and fired simultaneously. The soldier fell to the ground from the pistol shot but the other more allusive Sulgon dodged, causing Michael's SullSword to only puncture his shoulder. Before the dragon hybrid could recover from the blow, a familiar towering figure descended from high up in the air, landing right on top of the startled Sulgon. Silvan's massive seven-foot form thrust his wide SullSword into the dazed Sulgon's chest and he yelled out, "Yahoo! Time for a double team." They both surged and thrust their blades deep into the fallen dragon figure's chest and then did the same to the soldier that he had shot; the Gaddigons flew away before Michael even got a good look at them.

Michael couldn't help but smile and said, "Nice one. Where did you come from?"

"I told Commander Sam that it was my mission to come and protect you and he gave me a funny look and then told me I could come join the party." He pointed up to a floating drone and continued, "He had Uncle Henry drop me a rifle with one of his cool drones. Of course, he had it stay around to keep an eye on me. I couldn't let you have all the fun. That was crazy what you did with those three soldiers, by the way. What was that?"

Michael shrugged and said, "I don't know. Just call it an obstacle course."

"Well, you definitely shredded those obstacles. That was amazing."

Commander Lirfta wasn't moving and the only evidence that he was alive was his slowly rising chest. Michael thought about his Herkilian partner and called up his Sullice and sent a thought message to him about Lirfta. Before any response came back, Silvan's head jerked around and he raised his SullSword. "Watch out!"

When Michael looked up, he saw a Legion soldier leaping toward them. But it appeared that he had jumped too hard, causing him to fly over their heads. As Michael followed his trajectory, he noticed another Legion soldier directly behind them with one of those nasty Gaddite batons drawn. He pointed it and a dark net fired out at them.

Before Michael could react, a thick ribbon of red Sullice from Silvan's ring surrounded them in a protective dome. Michael could see the Gaddite crystals pulsing on the net above them. Silvan's jaw was clenched and his eyes were closed. Peter landed close by and after a few blows from his SullSword and a few shots from Michael's pistol the GaddNet dissolved and disappeared.

The leaping Sulgon had come down right next to Mr. GaddNet. And he transformed into Commander Derrilin and took out the attacker with a plunge of his SullSword before the shocked soldier even realized what had happened. Once he had captured the resulting Gaddigon, the tiny commander turned and said, "Welcome to the fun. That shield dome was remarkable, Silvan. I've never seen one that powerful from a squire before."

Silvan sighed and said, "I'm not sure where it came from. I've never done that before. I didn't know I had it in me."

Michael shook his head and said, "That was awesome. But, Senior Commander, you seriously scared me on that one. I had no idea it was you."

Derrilin shrugged, his sparkling eyes squinting, and said, "Sorry about that. It comes with the territory where I'm concerned." Then he sprang over and crouched to look at the motionless form of Lirfta on the forest floor.

It was interesting to see Derrilin up close in his natural form and to note the differences between the faeries and the elves. His ears had a longer and narrower point on top and a larger earlobe on the bottom. And the extended forehead, which in this natural form had barely noticeable ridges down the middle. It was amazing to think that a person the size of a child could be that powerful.

Michael did a quick count and noted that the number of Sulgons was down to eight. Those that remained were losing ground fast as others from the Order teamed up against them. Michael spotted Senior Commander Eileen. She was squaring off against a small but fast Sulgon, with pointed ears. Michael realized that he was looking at the only elf hybrid he had seen.

Derrilin frowned and shook his head. "*That* is Rangstrum. He is a senior commander elf Sulgon. Several elves from Briffta, the Guardian Realm of the Eastern Triad, have fallen and joined the Legion, like their Herkilian clansmen. Eileen can handle him though."

The old matron floated up on her massive blue hoven to meet the nimble Sulgon, whose dark gray spectral wings were flapping rapidly. Her face and demeanor were surprisingly calm. She fought him without moving quickly but there was a grace and fluidity to her strikes and counters. Like Michael, she seemed to be able to predict the attacks that Rangstrum was going to make before he made them. It was an incredible sight. While maneuvering through the air and dodging effortlessly, she conjured whipping lassos, strangling nets and what looked like floating Sullite quicksand, that slowed the speedy elf down and allowed her to strike him with greater ease.

Before Eileen had fought for long, Peter sent a thought message to Michael that he was going to get her and flew up high in the air. He hovered in front of her and motioned for her to stay back, and said, "You're doing great, but I can handle this tiny wimp. Lirfta needs you." She nodded and rushed away as Peter turned to face the scowling dragon figure.

Peter dodged a blow and shot forward, his hoven surging as he swung his thick SullSword directly at the Sulgon's chest. Rangstrum's dark shield shot up, barely blocking the blow and he yelled out, his raspy voice screeching. Then with lightning-quickness, he hurled a spinning vortex of Gaddite daggers at him. It smashed into the giant's large shield, catching him off guard and sending him flying across the field, where he came to a skidding stop. Michael was surprised by the possibility that this Sulgon might give Peter a good fight.

Senior Commander Eileen had sailed down and was leaning over the fallen dwarf Commander's lifeless form, as a radiant Sullite scepter appeared in her left hand. Michael noticed the frenzied particles of her thick blue armor. Her right hand, which had a strange circular Sullite instrument in it, glided just above his body, stopping near his chest and she shook her head.

Michael's jaw dropped and he felt dizzy, as the words he never wanted to speak came out, "Is he… dead?"

Eileen placed her aged hand on Michael's shoulder and said, "I'm afraid he is in a deep Gaddite coma. We need to get him to the Haven right away for more extensive care." Blue speckles surged to the device in her hand and then flowed out, forming a cocoon around Lirfta.

Derrilin gazed at the cocooned form and shook his head, his expressive face somber. His orb flashed and he jerked his head toward the action and said, "If anyone can bring him back, it's you, Eileen. Come, young Herkilian. I need you to help me with some supersized pests. Have you ever been a decoy?" Silvan pointed at Michael and started to protest and then conceded and he and the small commander flew away, the drone following close behind.

Then, all of a sudden Michael felt the familiar draw on his mind and his Merlin-based SullSight took his vision away and he could see a frightening scene unfolding. It involved Sarzot and another Sulgon with an extended forehead. Bamith! They had an enormous black sea urchin crystal mass. Bamith was preparing to insert it into what Michael guessed was a large Gaddite cannon. Michael had to stop them. But, how did they get the sphere without his dad? Eileen was busy using her scepter to levitate the cocooned dwarf and had begun walking back toward the clearing. She turned to talk to him, but right then Merlin sent him an image of Bamith's location.

He turned to her quickly and blurted, "Sorry, I have to go. Get Lirfta to the Haven. Bye." He surged to his hoven and sailed up in the air. As he gazed down on the field at all the mini battles, his attention was drawn to a glint of green armor and he immediately descended to a hidden area off to the side, that was concealed by a large patch of thick bushes.

His dad was standing with Aurora and she was tending to his wounds and had given him an illuminator band.

Michael dropped the cloak and ran to him and squeezed him, forcing a grunt. He remembered how strong he was and loosened his grip. His dad patted his back and as Michael stepped back his dad said, "What are you doing here? You should be somewhere safe. And how did I not see you before?" He had a frantic expression and for the first time, Michael saw legitimate fear in his dad's eyes. "What have I brought you into? I'm so sorry. I can get us out of here." He peeked around a hedge toward the field and said, "Let's make a break for it. I can take you back to the SUVs."

He gazed at the SullBomb in Michael's hand and said, "What is that thing. And how did you get that sparkling red armor?"

Michael hugged him, his emotions rising and said, "I'm so glad you're ok, Dad. I have to blow up a cluster weapon with this special bomb. I've been continuing my training with Peter and the knights of Lithegol. It's a long story. What you should know though is that you did everything that you were supposed to and what you taught me is helping me to be a better soldier."

His dad smiled, genuinely and said, "That's great. I'm so glad. Now, find me a gun so I can shoot some overgrown lizards?"

Aurora looked questioningly at Michael and asked, "What do you mean? We can't blow up the cluster until your dad lets us into the facility-right?"

Michael shook his head, and responded, "No. Bamith and Sarzot have it somehow and I have to destroy it before they weaponize it."

Michael felt Merlin's urgent call and turned to his dad and said, "Aurora can set you up. Just be careful, Dad. I have to go. I'll be right back." He turned and jumped, feeling the hoven surge as it lifted him high above the treetops.

He could see Bamith's location in his mind, so as soon as he spotted the large knobby tree in the distance he glided down, engaging his cloak. When he saw the many twigs and potential noisemakers he made a decision and hovered just above the ground, floating from one tree to the next to get in closer. He thought of the vision he had seen and what he had witnessed Senior Commander Derrilin do and wondered how powerful the fallen faery commander was. When the beachball-sized Gaddite crystal came into view, it was as he had seen it. Bamith and Sarzot were trying to place it into an opening in the cannon.

There was a strange Gaddite funnel extending from the opening into the massive front barrel. This must be how they channeled the Gaddite. He wondered how they recharged it. The cannon appeared to be made out of the same Gaddite equivalent to Omithite and had a small control panel on the side of it and was mounted on a tripod. The tripod was floating steadily about three inches off the ground and Michael wondered if it had the same anti-gravity mechanisms as the Legion drones. Bamith was much smaller than the other Sulgons—probably about five feet tall. He was even shorter than Sarzot's dwarfish hybrid figure by probably three inches. Bamith was yelling at him to turn it the other way, as it needed to fit in the cannon chamber a certain way.

Michael knew that he didn't have much time. He bounded toward them, his cloak still engaged. About halfway there what felt like an invisible cloud of evil swept over him and he jerkily glided down, almost falling on his face. He regained his composure and right as he was about to leap the last 15 feet, he heard a Sullite communication and he saw Aurora's cloaked figure sneaking through the trees, his dad close behind.

Bamith stopped in the middle of a tirade and turned toward them, a cocky smirk on his wide mouth. "Well, well. It feels like we have some unwanted visitors who are here to *save the day*." He cackled. Then he transformed into Peter, "How about now? You can't attack your old friend, Peter." Then he was a Sulgon again and he laughed and turned to Sarzot and said, "Why don't you give them a proper welcome?" Aurora was almost to where Michael had just been when she launched, de-cloaked and a green Sullite crossbow appeared in her hands.

Sarzot jumped toward them, his wicked-looking hammer mace drawn. Before he could attack, a barrage of Sullite arrows from Aurora's crossbow pelted him across his head and shoulders and he fell to the ground, reverting to his unconscious dwarf form. Aurora landed about twenty feet away from Bamith and was preparing to attack when there was a yell from above the trees and the towering 8-and-a-half-foot figure of Peter came gliding down beside her.

Peter patted her on the back and said, "You weren't going to start without me, were you?"

She smiled, but her response was cut off as the sound of a child crying out pierced the silence and Billy's small form came running out from the trees nearby. He looked like he was running from someone or something. Peter jumped over to him and as he was preparing to pick him up the small figure transformed into the largest Sulgon Michael had seen, probably close to 20 feet tall, and his first thought was that it had to be a Paranin. But how did it transform like that? Could they do what faeries in Lithegol could do?

The Paranin had super small dragon ears, a wide head and a beefy snout filled with razor-sharp teeth. In a motion that seemed too quick to be coming from a creature of that size, the gigantic monster swung a double-bladed Gaddite battle-ax that had to be at least six feet long. The dark edge hit the shocked commander and he flew back, banging his back on a tree. He stumbled forward and then regained his composure and growled, "Hurrall. I should've smelled your foul stench from a mile away. What, your lizard-head leaders gave you a break from terrorizing my people?"

He lunged toward the hulking soldier. Michael noticed that in his fully transformed Sulgon form Hurrall had some distinct physical characteristics. The outside edge of his dragon ears resembled a miniature mountain range that came to a point. He had disproportionately short thick arms and his legs were long and skinnier than Michael would've guessed they would be.

Peter dodged a blow and swung his thick SullSword directly at the Paranin's chest. Hurrall eluded the attack, as the commander's blade missed his chest by less than an inch. The towering Sulgon yelled out and swung his battle axe, catching the giant off guard and sending him flying across the field. The Herkilian knight extended a double-headed Sullite mace from his ring. Both spiked balls spun on glowing chains, like a propeller, pelting the massive Gaddite shield of his opponent with such power that he was knocked back several feet with each blow.

Catching Aurora looking at the fight, Bamith scowled and reached down to his belt and drew a baton net weapon and fired it at her in one blurred motion. It was the same one Commander Sam had identified on Serrenz. She saw it coming and expanded her shield into a downward facing dome, but shortly after she landed the net broke through and began squeezing her until she cried out. The dark gray specks seemed to be attacking her as she struggled to fight them off. Bamith waved his curved blade as the net responded, flinging her farther away near a tree. Michael was torn. If he helped her it may compromise his mission.

His heart sank as the stealthy image of his dad shot out from behind a tree and jumped in front of Aurora. He had a large Sullera rifle, and it was trained on the darkly uniformed Bamith. He got off a few shots that the nimble Sulgon easily deflected with his shield. After several desperate swipes with her SullSword and a few shots from Peter's rifle that he managed to get off, the net finally disintegrated, but Aurora was blinking as if she was having trouble remaining conscious.

Michael communicated a desperate plea to Peter, who was locked in fierce combat with the massive dragon creature. Peter responded that he was trying to break free and that Aurora would have to help him and that he needed to move quickly to destroy the sphere. This communication jarred him. Why hadn't he pushed the timer yet? He reached down to push it, but movements from his dad distracted him.

His dad had positioned himself directly in front of Aurora and said, "Don't move or I will blow you away. I don't know who you are, you ugly freak, but you have chosen the wrong side on this one."

Michael knew that his dad was in danger, but he also knew that if he blew his cover, he might not be able to sneak the SullBomb in and destroy the cluster. He had to stay hidden. He pushed the 30-second timer and prepared to leap. He thought about how he couldn't bring the bomb to the cannon and reveal its presence until the timer had ticked down to almost nothing. Why hadn't he pressed the 15-second button? The next several seconds felt like they happened in slow motion. Michael froze, gazing at his dad helplessly, unsure what he could do to protect him without blowing his cover. Right as he was sending a thought message to Aurora, Bamith's clawed hand moved in a blur to his belt, and Michael's dad got off two shots. One ricocheted off the Sulgon's shield and the other hit his shoulder. But it wasn't enough. His dad's shoulders slumped, and he fell back to the forest floor, a dark dagger sticking out of his chest.

At first, it didn't seem real. It was like a terrible nightmare and despair and pain rose up in Michael's chest. Bamith got up, after recovering from the shot, smirked and said, "Your services are no longer needed here puny one. We found another way to obtain the sphere. Who chose the wrong side now?" He shrugged and said, "Oh, that's right. You can't hear me anymore. You're dead!" And he laughed, his voice cracking.

With those despicable words, something inside of Michael snapped. He aimed his pistol and lunged at him, shooting continuously until he had drained the chamber with what he counted as four level 10 shots. Although not every shot had hit its mark, the impact of the barrage sent the shrieking Bamith flying through the air and he came crashing down at least 15 feet away. He was moaning incoherently and was reaching for something in his uniform pocket. A feeling of panic rose up and Michael wondered if the Legion had the Gaddite equivalent of the

Replenishment Pack.

As Michael neared the rough black prickly mass, he felt a sickening, all-consuming wave of hate and fear flood over him. He dug in using his Sullice to try to push it away. He did feel some relief but all it did was take a slight edge off.

Michael felt the bomb in his other hand. The timer was now at 7 seconds. He stared at his dad's lifeless body lying there. Aurora had just finished off a Replenishment pack. She was trying to revive his dad as tears rolled down her cheeks.

A sense of urgency was growing inside of him and he placed the bowling ball sized bomb next to the tripod. When he did his heart sank— the red light on the bomb was flashing. The flashing meant that the timer couldn't be stopped. There were enumerable gray flecks swarming the dark prickly sphere and he wondered if the bomb would be enough to destroy it.

Bamith had struggled to his feet and must've seen the flashing button because he scowled in Michael's direction, and growled, weakly. Michael was afraid to leave the bomb there for fear that Bamith may throw it away and ruin their plan or worse take the sphere and escape. He pointed the pistol at Bamith, counting on the fact that the Sulgon didn't know his Lumithite Sullera crystal was drained. Bamith scowled at him and shrieked, his amulet flashing as his spectral wings launched him upward and he and Hurrall flew off together.

Michael was surging his hoven to leap out of range when everything went blurry. An overwhelming flood of light and energy overtook him, and he slipped into a dizzying stupor. He kept expecting to fall down on the forest floor, but he never felt himself land. This was the feeling from his anointing night multiplied by 100. He saw why they had talked about too much being a bad thing. He felt like he was drowning in the depths of a warm ocean and all the water was pushing in hard all around him. But the difference was he could feel the pressure also growing from inside of him.

He was pushing on it, trying to control it and harness it, using every ounce of strength he had. He knew he couldn't last very long like this. He remembered what he had learned about surrendering to it, and he focused on giving in to the Sullice. As a feeling of intoxicating peace overcame him, he lost consciousness. But instead of everything being black and dark as you would imagine it would be while being unconscious, everything was blindingly bright.

When he came to, he was sprawled out on the ground and the all-encompassing bright light and the overwhelming pressure were gone. The first thing Michael noticed was the Gaddite cluster and the cannon. They had disappeared. The power of the oversized Sullite explosion had destroyed them completely. Now he understood why Bamith took off like he did. Having been around Henry and the others for a few weeks and learning about the destructive power of these larger SullBombs firsthand, he must've known that he needed to get as far away from it as possible.

The realization hit Michael. He had done it. He had accomplished their mission. But why hadn't he died when the bomb exploded? He had only been a few feet away from it. He noticed something different about his hand, and when he looked closer, he gasped. The crystal in his squire ring was now glowing green. How was this possible?

Michael remembered his dad and ran over to him. Aurora had pulled out the dagger and was tending to his wound. Her face had an expression of shock and she was trudging around like she was in a trance. Peter was shooting a massive beam of blue speckled light into his dad's chest and shaking him. He was trying to pour what looked like a vial of thick Renber juice into his mouth, only to have much of it drain out the side and down his neck. The giant was growing more and more frantic with each passing moment. Then he fell on Spencer's chest, "I'm so sorry, my friend. I should've protected you." His eyes filled with anger and he clenched both fists and yelled, "Bamith!" Then he looked longingly at Spencer again, "Please come back."

Michael's dad wasn't moving and his chest was not rising or falling. Michael knew from his First Aid training that this meant he was dead. He fell to his knees and said, "Isn't there anything we can do? We have to get him to Gabriel? He has to be able to bring him back!"

Peter's orb was flashing rapidly and he reached down and picked Spencer up, like his body was a feather and said, "I'll do all I can, Michael. Now, come with me, you two and stay close." Aurora's face was white as a sheet and she was staring at Spencer's lifeless body. Then she engaged her hoven and she and Michael glided up and followed Peter, trying to keep up as he sped through the air.

Michael saw the battle up ahead and felt his strength fading. He surrendered to the remaining Sullite essence within and shot forward. He spotted Eileen at the edge of the field and they all landed, Peter rushing up to her. Peter set his friend's body down on the ground, his gray eyes pleading with the powerful matron.

Eileen leaned over him and waved the same round Sullite instrument from before over his body and then placed her hand on Michael's shoulder, and said, "It is as I suspected. Unfortunately, as soon as the Grobel penetrated his heart he was out of our reach. Even Gabriel would be unable to bring him back. I'm so sorry, Michael. What I can tell you is that his Sullite Essence lives on, and you will see him again. That much I can promise you." She extended her right hand as a stream of thick blue Sullice flowed from the circular instrument, forming a cocoon around his dad, as it had for Lirfta. She turned and touched the green glowing crystal on Michael's squire ring and bowed low on one knee in the Revin salute, a look of admiration crossing her transparent features, "Amazing. It really is you."

Michael pulled his hand away. "I don't care about any of that right now. I would give it all away to bring him back." As reassuring as the whole thing about his dad's essence and seeing him again sounded, he was still looking at the lifeless body of the man that had been like a best friend and protector to him all his life. His thoughts immediately went to his mom. "Where's my mom? She will be destroyed by this."

Before anyone could answer, Peter's orb flashed and his head shot up. "It looks like we have a new party crasher. Bamith has arrived. He must have recharged. Good. I want to be the one to crush him for this! Stay with Eileen, Michael. I promise you that I will avenge your father's death." With that, he turned and he was gone.

Aurora handed Michael an RP and said, "Peter is right. You need to stay here with Senior Commander Eileen. I, on the other hand, need to rejoin the fight and inflict some hurt on some lizard-heads."

Michael's teeth clenched. "I don't want to stay here. I need to help Peter take out that monster!" He finished off the RP and before Aurora could object, he engaged his green armor and cloak and moved quickly toward the opening in the trees that led to the battle zone.

As Michael's cloaked figure entered the field, he spotted Peter right away. He was squaring off against Bamith. Michael's heart raced and he felt his deep anger swelling in his chest.

Bamith was very agile and seemed to be holding his own. At one point he created a Gaddite essence chain with like a dozen jagged Gaddite blades on the end of it and was swinging it like a helicopter blade above his head. Peter dodged most of the swipes but one of them landed and sent him careening to the ground. Michael wasn't going to waste any time this time.

He sailed high in the air and as he came down next to Peter, he de-cloaked and aimed his SullSword directly at the menacing Sulgon's chest. He pushed every particle of Sullice he could summon as a radiant beam of green speckled light shot out and penetrated Bamith's amulet. Bamith froze, a look of shock showing through in his dragon features. The small dragon hybrid fell back and Peter, who had since recovered, formed a giant blue Sullite fist in the air. It extended from his ring and then he surged, as the fist punched the reeling Sulgon continuously in a barrage of hits. A thought came to Michael that this must be another one of Peter's elite moves. Bamith cried out in a guttural scream. Aurora joined in from behind, firing a massive green net, which encased the Sulgon and squeezed in on him. She leaned into it and yelled, "How does it feel, Slimeball? Your murdering days are over!"

He thrashed to escape but he seemed to be losing strength as the combined barrage of Sullice drained his power.

Finally, Bamith let out a desperate screech, his amulet flashing rapidly. Erubamir turned away from his battle with Gabriel and jumped high in the air, his roar sending shivers down Michael's spine. As the oversized beast descended, he shot a Gaddite comet at Aurora and she fell to the ground, unconscious. The dinosaur-sized leader landed right next to the fading Sulgon and lifted his massive Gaddite Shield, blocking their attack. He moved to support his fellow Sulgon. Gabriel had landed slightly in front of Michael and motioned for him to stay back. Bamith's slight form was leaning heavily on Erubamir, his eyes half closed and his expression blank.

All the knights and matrons had gathered behind Gabriel. All of the Legion soldiers had gathered around their leader and several had their GaddNet batons focused on the Lithegol group. Michael could see the enormous Paranin poised toward the rear of their group but the elf Sulgon was nowhere to be found and Michael wondered if Peter had defeated him. Erubamir, who was holding Bamith up with one of his tree-trunk-sized arms, focused his evil slitted eyes at Gabriel and growled, "This is far from over, Gabriel. You have witnessed our new tokens and our weapons. This is just the beginning. We will find Drakkir's cluster horde and conquer this world and all of Lithegol."

Michael heard a whirring sound approaching off in the distance. As it grew louder, the others put up their defenses. Erubamir sneered, his wide mouth seeming to disappear into the sides of his head. He lifted his snout and laughed maniacally. The low crackling laughter gave Michael the chills. A black, futuristic-looking helicopter flew out from behind the trees, hovering no more than 100 feet away. It had more guns and bombs mounted on it than any Michael had ever seen.

Erubamir continued, "But it won't matter for any of you, as you will all be dead, and the world will praise ME for ridding it of some of the most despicable terrorist leaders from your pathetic Freedom Alliance." He laughed again. But before he could give the order to fire, a golden dome of Sullice encircled the helicopter, the propeller stopped twirling and it crashed to the earth.

Erubamir stopped mid-laugh and stared in disbelief at the smoking rubble that was once his prized weapon. Several soldiers stumbled out and joined Erubamir's group, still looking back as if to ascertain what had brought them down. The Legion leader and the other soldiers stared, their eyes wide, at something above Michael's head. When Michael looked up, he saw Merlin, in his full glowing Golden Eagle form, descending onto his shoulder.

Gabriel turned to Erubamir and said, with deep conviction in his sharp resonant voice, "You have failed again, Therok. You will never take our world or our kingdom. There will always be good people prepared to stand and fight for Lithegol and all that is right. And now we are joined by the greatest of them all. The one the Legion hoped would never come, The High Sentinel and his mentor, The Royal Overseer, Merlin himself."

Erubamir snarled and snapped at them. It was like a warning from a cornered animal. The Gargoyle-looking behemoth yelled, "I am Erubamir, High Captain of the most powerful army in the Universe. And soon you will ALL bow at my feet." He opened his long snout, raised it to the sky, and a flame of black Gaddite billowed out. It reminded Michael of the image on the Legion crest and he felt the hairs on his neck stand on end.

Captain Gabriel pointed his SullSword directly at him, as it surged with magnificent speckled gold energy. "You don't deserve a bow from anyone. Now I will finish this war and put you where you belong, in a dungeon with the other Legion traitors." Erubamir's amulet flashed, followed by the others in his group. Then abruptly GaddNets shot out from the batons aimed at them and several protective domes formed as various knights and matrons deployed shields above the group. Then there was an explosion as rays of Gaddite, filled with a swarm of dark grey flecks, surrounded them from what Michael guessed was a GaddBomb. When did they make one of those? Henry had not expected them to have one.

Michael felt a pervasive cloud of darkness and despair all around him. Then the feeling, the nets and the GaddBomb were gone. And so were Erubamir and the others. Michael noticed that Merlin was also no longer on his shoulder and he heard his distinctly articulate voice in his head say, *I am scouting the area to assure that the Legion is not preparing to attack again. Well done out there, young Sentinel. I will rejoin you shortly.*

Chapter 15

The Aftermath

Michael gazed around to assess the damage and saw Gabriel leaning down over Aurora, where she had fallen. He was stroking her hair, white and gold Sullice flowing from his orb into her eyes and chest. Michael rushed over to them and stood, frozen in shock. Silvan had made his way over and was standing next to him. Aurora's pale cheeks were sunken in and she wasn't moving. Then Eileen landed close by and joined in, thickly speckled Sullice extending into the fallen matron from her scepter. Aurora's color began to return and her cheeks filled in. She sat up, a startled look on her face.

Michael sighed with relief and then a rush of dizziness swept over him. He hadn't realized how hard he had pushed his limits during the battle. He reached up and placed his hand on Silvan's towering left shoulder to steady himself. His friend said, "You look spent, buddy. You were really letting Bamith have it, weren't you? I think you almost finished him off – between you, Aurora and my dad." He handed Michael an RP. "Can you believe how savage that battle was? That was crazy."

Michael downed the vial and the Braiz bar and said, "Yeah. It just seemed like they kept sending more and more bad guys."

Commander Sam walked through the opening to the clearing, a line of trancers plodding behind him, followed by Michael's mother. He was so overjoyed to see her unharmed. It was still weird to see her carrying a Sullera rifle. Sam had a thick stick that he was using as a cane to prop himself up and his left leg was dangling. Michael wondered what had happened and how bad his injury was. Michael ran to his mom and hugged her. "Are you ok? What happened to Commander Sam? And where are Claire and Billy?"

His mom hugged him tight and stroked the back of his head like she had done when he was a child and said, "Dr. Waicroft came and picked them up and brought them to the S.A.V. As far as Sam, the commander fought so bravely. He must've taken down at least eight soldiers who tried to free the prisoners. He was injured protecting me. I think I need some more practice with this thing."

Commander Sam forced a smile and said, "You are far too modest, young lady. You held your own fairly well. There were just too many. I also had much help from my SullSight friends of the forest. What is important is that we didn't lose any prisoners."

Michael's mouth trembled as he thought of what came next and he said, "Something terrible has happened, mom."

Peter stepped to the side, revealing Michael's dad's lifeless cocooned body on the ground, and she gasped and let out a chilling "Noooooo!"

Peter approached, his head down. "He was trying to protect Michael and I was attacked and unable to help him. I failed your family and I'm so sorry." He seemed more downtrodden than Michael had ever seen him, and Michael's heart went out to him.

He put his hand on Peter's shoulder and said, "It's not his fault, Mom. It's…"

Aurora interrupted, "It's my fault. I was right there, but I let Bamith get the upper hand on me. I should've been more careful. I didn't realize their new GaddNets were so powerful." She was sobbing. "When he was killed, Spencer was actually protecting me. I feel terrible. I hope you can forgive me."

Michael patted Aurora on the back and said, "It wasn't her fault. She risked her life to protect us. It's mine. I should've done something to stop him. But I froze. I was torn between helping Dad and blowing up the cluster. I should have shot Bamith with my Sullera pistol BEFORE he threw the knife."

Julia pulled Michael in, and said, "Don't you dare do that. Your father made a choice to be there and protect you. That was his way. It's no one's fault."

Peter growled and said, "You're wrong about one thing, Julia. It is someone's fault. It's that traitor Bamith's fault, and I will finish him off next time and make sure he pays for this. He has disgraced the clan of the Guardians for the last time! I wish I could be there when he finds out his precious mentor, Braster has been captured." He swung his fist hard, leveling a small tree. He rubbed his forehead and said, "Sorry about that. I just feel so angry right now."

Commander Sam put his hand on Peter's fisted hand. "That's because you care deeply for Spencer. Don't worry, we will all make

Bamith pay for this. But as Captain Gabriel has said, allowing anger to overcome us will only keep us from performing our best as knights in the Order. Remember our Oath. We fight to protect out of a love for those we serve, not out of a hate for those we fight against." He gazed Michael's direction and smiled. "Besides, we have so much to rejoice about." He fell to a knee, his palm outstretched and said, "The High Sentinel has finally arrived."

Peter was staring down at the green crystal of Michael's ring. He bowed his head and also knelt in front of him in a Revin salute, and the others joined in. Commander Sam spoke again, a tear trickling out of his ultra-light eyes. "Your identity has been confirmed. Now it all makes sense. I often wondered how that part of the prophecy would be fulfilled and now I see it."

"What are you talking about, Commander?" Michael asked. "Everyone just stand up. I don't deserve all this bowing."

Commander Sam said, "You had better get used to it. All who meet you from the Order from now on will respond this way. Especially when they notice that you have the power of a master but the ring of a squire. As far as the prophecy question—part of what has been foretold is that the High Sentinel will enter the Order of Lithegol as a master. But we were never able to understand how this is possible since the only way we all knew to gain the power of a master was for someone already within the Order to do so by advancement." He was shaking his head in disbelief and said, "What we all underestimated was the High Sentinel's capacity to absorb and increase his Sullite power. Where most squires would've been overcome and killed by the SullBomb blast, you drank in the Sullice and it only made you more powerful."

Michael glanced from them to his dad. Overwhelming sadness rose within him, and he whimpered, "But my dad is dead. How can I go on without him?" Feelings of emptiness and loss returned as he sobbed and fell down onto his dad's chest. He closed his eyes and tried to visualize a time in the future when he would see his dad again, be with him again. At that moment a Sullite communication came into his mind and he recognized Sam's reassuring voice, *"Remember, Michael...choose hope."*

He could hear that everyone else was crying with him. He thought of what Sam had said and what his dad had taught him about being a strong leader. He knew he had to rise up and continue on. He owed him that. He wiped his eyes and forced himself to stand and face everyone. His first thought was about his mission. He had at least fulfilled his mission. The Legion now had to find another way to create new weapons. But the bad news was they knew the location of the Lithegol base.

"I'm ok. Thank you all." He tried to focus on the mission. "I just feel bad that they got away. And they know the location of the western base. And how did they get the sphere? And if they had another way, why did they need my dad?"

Captain Gabriel had been standing close by, observing with his usual kind expression, and chimed in, "You shouldn't feel bad at all. You need to better understand the power and potential of what you destroyed. A ClusterSphere is part of the core cluster that powers a core world. In the case of a Gaddite ClusterSphere, it's part of the cluster for a core world within a Dread Realm. This one was likely from what we call the lost spheres, which were taken from the fallen Siock Northern Dread Realm core world, Jorik. If the Legion had been able to weaponize that sphere, it would've had the firepower to enslave thousands of people. You saved them all, Michael. The fact that they were able to hide the presence of that powerful item concerns me greatly."

Gabriel shook his head and gestured out to the others, "It was up to the rest of us to defeat the Legion leaders. The other way you speak of that they used to get the sphere is Dr. Robert Gidwell, the head of research for Senior Commander Durrill's rogue operation. And, he just barely turned on us. As of earlier today, he was not their ally. He has resisted and I'm not sure how they got him to help them. He has been the main one keeping them from getting the cluster since he and Durrill were the only ones who knew the codes to release it. The Legion's plan was to use their captive, your dad, to have him try to hack into the security system and bypass the code restrictions all along."

Gabriel gazed into the trees, a disappointed look on his regal face. "Dr. Minser is the one that hurt us the most. He was a part of Dr. Gidwell's team and allowed himself to be seduced by the Legion. We believe that when Durrill discovered that Minser had been sneaking cluster extracts to the Legion, he made him mysteriously disappear. We think that the way the Legion learned about Spencer's knowledge of the facility was through Durrill. He may have slipped and accidentally revealed this information in a private conversation with Minser."

Peter shook his head, and said, "It very well could've happened that way. And knowing Durrill it was most likely after he had downed a few drinks,"

Gabriel put his hand on Peter's shoulder, and said, "Unfortunately,

Durrill paid for it with his life when the Legion arrived."

"I can't believe my friend is gone," Peter said. His head was down and his lips pursed. Then he breathed in deeply and shook his head. "What you young Squires should learn from this is that you're always better off to honor your oath."

The Captain nodded and gave Peter a sympathetic look. Then he turned to Michael and said, "The good news is: when they kidnapped you, they didn't realize that I had started watching over you and I ended up following them. So, they led us straight to their western stronghold. We have what we need to take down their base now."

"That's great news," Michael said. "When do we leave?"

The Captain smiled, patted his back, and said, "Not yet, young Sentinel. There are other things we need to do. Important things."

Peter, who had been staring at Michael's eerily lifeless father, put his hand on Michael's shoulder, and said, "All of my years of experience and I don't know what to say." He wiped his cheek. "I failed my good friend." Then his head shot around like he sensed something and he said, "But we should get out of here before they come back with more dragon psychos."

Everyone ran around gathering supplies as Michael stared in disbelief at his mother's sobbing form, prostrated over his lifeless father.

Someone moved off to the side and Michael turned to see Eileen. The aged commander was adding Legion soldiers from the field to the group of trancers (this is what Peter called them) when one of them yelled out, "You will pay for killing my family. How could you just murder innocent children?" His face had a look of anger and disbelief on it.

Eileen gazed kindly at him, and said, "Do you really think that that was us? Search your thoughts. You know who really murdered your loved ones and why. And you have been fighting for them. Is that what those precious family members would want you to continue to do?"

"But... I," he stammered, recognition soaking through as his expression went from one of rage to one filled with sorrow and guilt.

Eileen approached him and put her hand on his shoulder, and said, "I believe your name is Bradley. Or is it Brad? It's never too late to make the right choice for your future. I can help you with that choice and the changes that must come."

The man nodded, a tear streaking his dirty cheek. "I think I'm ready for that. The Legion must pay for what they've done. But how long will it take to get rid of this poison inside?" He extended a hand and said, "It's Brad, by the way."

She shook his outstretched hand, smiled that Grandma-still-loves-you smile and said, "Well, Brad. I'm Eileen. Nice to meet you. In answer to your question, it depends. Mostly it depends on you and the work you're willing to put in to rid yourself of the lingering evil. But my team and I will be there to help you, and you are on the right track. Now you need to sleep for a while. All will be well, friend."

He managed a faint smile and said, "Thank you."

She nodded as she placed the harness over his chest, and he slipped into a trance.

Michael stood there, in awe of what had just happened and stared as she did her work, smiling and humming as she went. What was her story? She reminded him of his mom in many ways. What an extraordinary woman.

She must've sensed that he was staring and said, "Hello, Michael. How are you? This must all seem overwhelming for you. I'm so very sorry for your loss. It is always so hard to see loved ones pass from this life." Then she smiled encouragingly and said, "You handled yourself so well out there. I've never seen someone so young harness the power of Sullice like you did." She bowed low in a Revin salute and said, "I just can't believe I lived to see the fulfilling of the great prophecy. It truly is an honor to meet you. I am your grateful servant."

Michael said, "Thank you. I'm still trying to get a handle on everything. That means a lot coming from you, Senior Commander. I can't even imagine harnessing the power you were unleashing out there... And what was up with that prisoner, Brad? What did that mean when you said . . . work with him?"

"Please call me Eileen. I don't need all that senior commander stuff. The thing that you need to remember, and this relates to Brad, is that we are all in the same situation. We are all trying to do the best we can and sometimes we make mistakes. In Brad's case, his mistakes led to him tragically losing his family at the hands of those he had chosen to trust. My assignment as Head Matron at the Haven of Galahad is to help prisoners like Brad to rediscover their true essence, the goodness within themselves, and work their way back to a place of good standing within the Order. There is nothing more rewarding."

Michael was taking in everything she was saying. "That makes sense to me. Everyone should have a second chance."

She pointed her bony finger and said, "Exactly. Brad has had a rough life and we don't know what conditions led him to the choices he made. He needs to be with people that love him, encourage him and believe in him. That is what my team and I do." She shook her head, patted him on the back, and said, "You're a remarkable young man, Michael, and I look forward to learning more from you in the years to come."

After Eileen had them all assembled and harnessed, she said, "Now let's get them to Galahad."

*   *   *

Henry had parked the oversized S.A.V. in their destination safe house around four miles away. When Gabriel and Aurora arrived back from the S.A.V. with the others, they, along with Henry, were each seated on thin floating platforms. Each platform had what appeared to be several hovens under it. Each driver was controlling the fascinating crafts with their WriPs from Omithite chairs. They each used a floating joystick as the platforms slowed, and the crafts floated gently downward, closer to the ground. Henry smiled, slid an image to the side on his WriP and said, "Hurry, everyone. Climb aboard. Next stop, the Portacon of Galahad."

Heather was seated on Henry's platform next to Claire and Billy. Claire was staring at Michael, a look of relief in her deep hazel eyes. Seated next to them were two people Michael was not expecting to see—Isaac and Malina from the Legion base. Omithite stairs unfolded from the side of the strange hovering vehicle and Claire bolted down them and hugged Michael. Squeezing him tightly. Then she collected herself, her face flushed. "I'm sorry. I was just so worried about you." She looked at Silvan, who was smiling down at her. "All of you, I mean. It sounded like it was a dangerous battle."

Michael smiled at her, gave Silvan a side hug and said, "It was pretty crazy out there. It was a good thing I had my double-team partner to watch over me."

Silvan high-fived him and said, "That's right! They didn't know what hit em', especially that Sulgon I plowed to the ground."

Michael followed Claire aboard and gave Heather and Billy a hug, and gestured at the other two and said, "It's great to see we have some new recruits. How did you guys escape? Did Gabriel spring you?"

Isaac nodded and smiled and said, "He was amazing. He used some kind of a cloak thing to sneak us out."

Malina, whose head had been turned to face the prisoners, jerked toward him, her stunningly beautiful face solemn. "I'm just along for the ride. The Legion and my jerk of a father burned me one too many times and I'm done with them." She turned her head back toward the prisoners one more time and Michael thought he saw her wipe a tear from her cheek.

Michael was going to ask more about what she meant but his instincts told him otherwise and he settled with, "Well, it doesn't matter at this point. We're happy you're both with us and free from the Legion."

Silvan filed on with Michael's mom and they introduced themselves to Isaac and Malina. Heather jumped up and hugged Silvan, tears trickling down her cheeks. The hovering rafts elevated to a height just above the tree line and then zipped quickly through the sky. It was odd. It felt like they were going extremely fast but there wasn't a sensation like they would fall off. It was almost like something in the floor of this futuristic magic carpet secured them to its surface.

They all sat in awkward silence until Silvan blurted out, "So, tell us what it was like to face off with Bamith in the forest! I can't believe I missed out on that. Don't let that happen again."

Michael lowered his head and said, "It was crazy. I did have lots of help, though or I would've been toast."

Michael's mom wiped a tear from her cheek and Silvan's expression fell. "I'm so sorry, Mrs. B," he said. "I remember when my mom got killed. It was very hard on me, but it did get easier."

Michael's mom forced a smile and said, "I'll be fine. I just need time. Time heals all wounds, right?"

Claire had been staring at Michael's ring and finally stammered, "So, you really are the one? Look at his ring, Silvan." She caught herself and her cheeks flushed, "Oh, I'm sorry. I didn't acknowledge your loss. My deepest condolences. It's just that my parents have been telling me stories about the High Sentinel since I was tiny and to be sitting next to him is so surreal."

Silvan reached over and lifted Michael's hand and moved in closer to get a better look at it. "That is amazing! I couldn't believe it when you showed up with green armor. You HAVE to tell us how that played out!"

Michael proceeded to catch his mom up on the details of the past few days that she hadn't already heard from Silvan and the others regarding their abduction. After that Michael told the group about his adventures with Aurora and the cannon confrontation. When he got to the part where his dad saved Aurora and threatened Bamith, he tried to move through it quickly and no one asked any questions.

But when Michael spoke about the SullBomb exploding, Silvan nearly jumped out of his seat. "You were right next to it when it went off? What? That's insane! Commander Sam was like 15 feet away when his went off. How did you survive that?"

Michael shrugged and said, "I don't know. It felt like I was drowning in the ocean and there was like pressure all around me from both the outside and the inside. I didn't think I was going to make it."

"Wow!" Billy chimed. He clapped his hands excitedly. "Ok. Now tell us about the Sulgons. About Erubamir and Bamith."

"Well..." Michael began, thinking about it. "Erubamir has this crazy white scar down the side of his head, and he's like 12 feet tall. He was holding his own against the Captain, but I don't think he could've lasted much longer." As Michael thought about Bamith he felt anger rising up in his chest. He tried to push it down, his jaw clenching. "Bamith is pure evil. We weren't expecting him and no one knew what form he would take when he showed himself. He is different from any of the others. He is smaller and has a big forehead, like Senior Commander Derrilin. He transformed into Peter when he sensed our presence. It was like he was rubbing it in."

Michael noticed his mom's blank expression. Then his eyes wandered over to Isaac. "But we have been neglecting our newest friends, Isaac and Malina. Tell us your stories. By the way, thanks for helping us out, Isaac. That pistol came in very handy."

Isaac's full cheeks went red and he lowered his head. "Thanks. But it wasn't really me. Gabriel gave me those to give you. He's a super nice guy. I didn't know it was him at first though because he changed himself to look like one of the guards. I couldn't believe it when he said he was taking me with him." Isaac's eyes teared up. "I didn't think anyone wanted me around anymore after my last foster family threw me out."

Michael's mom stood up and bent down to give him a big hug. "People do care about you, Isaac. You have us now. I can't believe you've had to live this way."

Isaac was really crying as if he had been holding it in, and Michael's mom held him tight, his shoulders quivering. Everyone but Malina joined in on the hug. Michael thought about how good it felt. This was what it was all about—caring for people, lifting them up, and working together for a good cause. It's what his parents had always taught him to focus on. The thought reminded him of his dad and a sting of sadness crept in.

When Isaac finished crying, he told them about his life living with foster families. It was obvious he was leaving out details, but it was clear that he had been abused and mistreated. "The Legion found me and took me in," Isaac said, "at a time when I didn't think anyone cared . . ."

Michael thought how much he had taken for granted in his life. He had been raised by loving parents who cared deeply for him. They had done everything in their power to teach him, protect him and ensure his happiness. Then an idea came to him, and he jumped in, not even realizing he had cut Isaac off in mid-sentence.

"Hey! That gives me an idea!" Michael shouted. "Sorry for interrupting you, Isaac, but why don't you come and live with us?" But then a realization came over him. "If we are able to get our house back, I mean."

Shortly after that comment, they arrived at a clearing near a large mountain. They all stepped off and the pilots touched their WriPs. The platforms folded in on themselves. Each one resembled a SullBomb due to the Sullite crystals throughout its surface. They picked them up and put them in their backpacks as if it was no big deal.

They all set out together on a path through the forest. Michael wondered to himself how many squires and other knights and matrons had walked this trail to the portacon. As they came around a grove of trees Michael saw a golden speckled wall of light extending from high in the sky to the ground no more than 100 feet from where they stood. His mom was holding his hand as they walked like she had when he was a small boy. On her other side was Isaac, and Michael wondered how their living situation was going to play out. Where would they call home now?

So many questions were still unanswered. And what was this ceremony that the Captain had mentioned where he would take his place as the High Sentinel? Would he know what to do with all the steps involved? Michael was pulled out of his overwhelming stupor by the sight of Isaac tripping on a tree root and nearly doing a face plant. Silvan caught him right before he fell, his muscled arm lifting him back up like he was a feather. "Hmm," he said, pointing, "there's a root right there you may want to watch out for, bud." He grinned and jabbed him lightly on the shoulder.

Isaac forced a smile, his chubby cheeks flushing, and said, "Yeah. I didn't see that. I was too busy looking at that golden force field. How do they generate that thing?"

Chapter 16

The Portacon

Commander Sam, who was walking close by with the assistance of his makeshift crutch and Peter on his other shoulder, said, "That, young Isaac, is generated using a flowing river of Sullice, called a Saren. The Lumithite particles from the Saren form a dome with a Lumithite ClusterSphere at its center in the heart of the mountain. As we saw from Michael's Sullera pistol, Lumithite is extremely powerful. This is why a majority of the fortresses, strongholds and portacons are secured with Lumithite spheres and crystals. It provides a much more impenetrable barrier against the Legion and their attacks.

"In fact, no one with a Gaddite token can pass through a LumiDoor or Dome. It is a very unpleasant experience for them if they try and not one that they normally care to repeat. A LumiDome like the one you see here is not set to authenticate those who pass through it, but the actual door into the portacon will require it. This is another aspect of how the Legion has been and continues to sneak Sulgons through. They are using special Dread Realm entrances, designed to transport Gaddigon prisoners. But a senior commander knight or matron must still authenticate at the designated checkpoints in order to bring them through. We have to figure out who is helping them, or they will continue to bring through these unwanted visitors."

Michael thought of Malina and her Gaddite tokens. When he searched for the ring on her hand, it was gone and he wondered what had happened. What was her story? He thought back to her words about her father's thugs. Who was her father? Was it Braster? Was that why she was staring at the prisoners earlier? If so, could she even be trusted?

As they approached the dome it became immediately clear who had walked through one before. Those who had, walked right through, as the hyperactive swimming flecks gathered around them and absorbed them into the field. They then reappeared as silhouettes on the other side. Michael and several others, including his mom, Isaac, Silvan and the others, stood and stared at the spectacle in awe. Malina's expression had some shock and fear in it also.

Heather had stayed back with them and was holding Silvan and Claire's hands, with Billy holding tightly onto his sister's hand. "Ok, you three, it's important for you to continue to hold onto my hands. Those with orbs will automatically enter the dome, but those without them need to be touching someone wearing them directly or through another's grip in order to come through. Then she winked at Michael. "Unless you're the High Sentinel, of course. Now, if no tokens are present then your average person would have no idea any of this was even here." With that comment, Michael reached out and offered Malina his hand and she grabbed it, reluctantly, unable to make eye contact. Her soft touch made him blush and he focused on the glowing wall, his mind racing with thoughts of what crossing through it would feel like. Malina squeezed his hand and managed a faint smile.

Heather smiled at her anxious children, and said, "Yeah, I had the same reaction. It is a little odd. But you get used to it. Just take a deep breath and do it. It feels good." She looked at Michael and said, "You should know how it feels, Michael. Since you have your own Lumithite crystal." She took a step toward it, and said, "Come on. We'll all do it together. It's fun."

Isaac had Michael's mother's hand and was staring up at the dome. Michael decided to be the first from his foursome to make a move and stepped forward to follow her. He, Malina, his mom and Isaac stepped through, as a rush of positive energy shot through him. He heard multiple gasps as the others came through, and when Michael's vision cleared, he saw the first group, standing and pointing, smiling at all of them like they were enjoying seeing them experience it for the first time. Behind the onlooking group were several breathtaking and unique Lumithite waterfalls. The speckled golden torrents, spaced about 20 feet apart on the face of the mountain, flowed in streams into the dome perimeter. Gabriel motioned for all of them to follow, and they walked together toward a rocky area near the base.

The Captain waved his ring in front of a hole in one of the elephant-sized boulders and an authenticator, like the ones Michael had seen before, slid out. This one had a tiny keyboard and monitor that folded out, and Gabriel used his ringed hand as an audible double-click sounded. He typed in something, a mechanism sucked it back into the boulder, and the whole rock slid to the right. Behind it was a Lumidoor that looked to be at least 20 feet tall.

Michael flashed back to his nightmare. This was the golden door by the mountain, and the battle they had just fought must represent the close encounter with the dragon-man. But how had he, or his subconscious self or whatever power gave him the dream, predicted this exact moment?

He stared up at the enormous door. "I keep seeing all these gigantic doors. Is that to accommodate like those Paranins or whatever they're called?"

Peter smiled and said, "Exactly, Michael. And for other large creatures from the other two kingdoms. Also, believe it or not, I'm considered small compared to other Herkilians. And like you said, some of the Paranins actually have to duck to get through doors like this."

"So, are there many Paranin knights and matrons on Earth?" Michael asked.

Peter's brow furrowed, and he said, "Yes, not all of them have betrayed the Order and joined the Legion traitors." He gazed up at the glowing door, his expression suddenly distant. "I'm sure you'll meet some of them when we get to Camelot."

Michael noticed that Eileen was smiling at the door and then she gazed back at her tethered group of trancers. They were still staring ahead, expressionless, like well-behaved zombies. He saw the man from before... Brad ... and he wondered what would become of him. Michael remembered Peter talking about the Haven. He had said that it was like a prison but had a remarkable rehabilitation program. He noticed Braster, Rillick and Abernat. They looked so strange in their dazed stupor. Michael didn't want to second-guess anything regarding Eileen's program but for it to have any positive impact on these three it would have to involve some kind of a miracle or a brain transplant.

Gabriel had explained that any of them with tokens needed to authenticate before walking through. Michael placed his fist into the special hole, not knowing what to expect, and there was a sharp double-click. Gabriel motioned for him to continue and he tentatively walked through the buzzing door.

This sensation was different from what he had felt before, entering the LumiDome. Michael felt dizziness at first, followed by a strange out-of-body sensation. It was like the feeling he had experienced when Merlin had teleported them but definitely more pronounced. Finally, a blanket of comfort and peace settled over him. After the overwhelming feeling of contentment subsided and his eyes came into focus, he gasped. They were in an enormous futuristic looking room.

It had car-sized Radiathite chandeliers, each with hundreds of the glowing cones, and the whole room was super bright. In the center of the room, there were knights and matrons gathered around an area where long Lumithite plumes of light shot down from a ceiling that was barely visible high above them. People were in lines, interacting with talking holograms and calling up screens on their WriPs. Elsewhere, knights and matrons appeared to be conversing with life-sized 3D projections of other individuals. Each group was inside a dome of white light, which must have allowed them privacy because they couldn't be heard.

Captain Gabriel glanced around, his expression one of contentment and said, "Welcome to Avalon and to the grand Portacon of Galahad."

*   *   *

People from all the different realms were gathered in groups and moving toward the Lumithite pillars as guards monitored their activities and helped them authenticate. Michael noticed a group step into one of the tractor beams and a floating console appeared on one of the walls of the pillar. Each individual approached, authenticated, and pushed different buttons. What followed was an incredible spectacle. The swimming gold light around them grew and encased each of them in a thin cocoon. After that, they faded and disappeared. Michael gasped and turned to Silvan, who was staring in awe. Silvan turned to him and they high-fived. "That is so sick! How did they do that?"

Peter patted Silvan on the back and said, "Those are called corridors and that is one of the ways that we get around within the Order. Think of it as a limitless elevator or teleportation mechanism. That area over there with all the Lumithite corridors is called a local station since it is only for transporting within this Portacon. The corridors to Camelot and to other realms within Lithegol and the three kingdoms are elsewhere, in a secure area within Galahad. Are you guys ready for it? It's a fun experience."

Claire had been listening and said, "I know I'm ready. I'm so excited to see Camelot. I've heard so much about it."

Michael was still watching all the people around him and then it occurred to him that everyone there was in their radiant uniforms, like entering through the LumiDoor had somehow engaged them. It didn't take long before people noticed their group and a wave of silence swept through the space, many staring in awe. Knights and matrons at all levels were doing the Revin all around them, and some were pointing at Gabriel and at Braster, their jaws dropping.

Captain Gabriel smiled and extended his hand, palm up and waved it over the entire group. He then pulled it into a fist over his heart and bowed slightly as they walked forward toward the station. Someone on the side closest to Michael was staring at his ring, pointed at him and whispered something to the person next to him. More people were noticing, and he heard one person say, "Is it really him?" And another said, "He only has a squire ring but he's a master. It has to be."

Michael's mom was beaming and patted him on the back. "I'm so proud to be your mother."

"Thanks, Mom." He felt overwhelmed by it all and didn't know how to respond to the escalating wave of dialogue and admirers, so he just smiled sheepishly and waved as if he was on a float in a parade. He didn't feel comfortable doing the full Revin salute because he didn't know if he was officially supposed to do what Gabriel had done.

They all approached the admittance area where the Station Guards were talking to the Captain and checking everything over. Gabriel turned and said, "Okay. All of the knights and matrons that have Gaddigon prisoners to incarcerate need to come with me. Senior Commander Eileen and Commander Sam will be taking the group of embodied prisoners to The Haven in a separate corridor. Commander Heather will be reporting her research findings to the Providential Council and Claire has chosen to escort her."

Michael glanced at Claire and she shrugged and mouthed the words, "I have to go."

Gabriel lightly patted Malina on the back and said, "Malina, you will need to go spend some time with Senior Commander Eileen at the Haven where she can help you."

Malina shrugged and said, "Whatever. If she can."

Gabriel smiled at her and said, "We know she can. You're on the path to happiness now, young Matron. It's up to you to stay on it. But know this, we all believe in you." Then he motioned toward the man Peter had aptly called a Mad Scientist and said, "Commander Henry will take the rest of you to a waiting area where we will meet up before we go to Camelot. For those that can, you will need to authenticate once you enter the corridor. The commander will help you. I'll see you all soon."

With that, he and the other commanders and Aurora entered one of the brilliant pillars and within seconds, they were cocooned and disappeared into thin air. Michael's heart was racing. Even though they had just traveled through a portal via the LumiDoor to this dimension, it still frightened him to think about his body dematerializing and then materializing in some other location. What if he left like a hand behind? Or his bellybutton ended up on his cheek? He chuckled at that thought and his mom said, "What? What were you thinking about, little man?"

"Oh, nothing. Just kind of freaking out on the whole teleportation thing. I guess I shouldn't be though, given all the other weird stuff I've seen lately."

Billy was anxiously watching Henry, as he talked to the Guards and punched Michael's shoulder lightly and said, "Are you serious? I'm excited to do it. It looks like a blast. It's gotta be like a fun amusement park ride or something. Aren't you supposed to be like super powerful? What are YOU afraid of?"

Michael tousled his hair and said, "You're such a thrill-seeking little kid. Nothing frightens you, does it?"

Billy's smile faded and a look of dread replaced it. "I don't like Sulgons. They scare me. Especially Braster. That guy was a monster." He tilted his head and continued, "But that's really the only thing. And I think someday after I become a knight, I won't be as afraid of them anymore."

Henry was approaching now. Michael took a deep breath as he motioned for them to follow and they all stepped into one of the pillars. The feeling that rushed over him was like what he had felt when stepping through the LumiDome, only it was continuous. The same panel popped up on the wall, floating in mid-air like something projected from a WriP, and Henry motioned for him to step forward. He extended his right hand and there was a familiar double-click and a floating 3D rendering of his face appeared with his name underneath and it said: Rank: Squire. Under the Advancement field, it said: Master. Approver: Captain Gabriel Prinder. The word Approver had a box next to it with a glowing green check mark inside.

Michael backed away and Silvan stepped forward to do the same thing. When would the big ceremony take place? What was he supposed to do for it? Was he really ready for this step? His thoughts were cut short by a growing sensation of peace and warmth, as he was surrounded by gold speckled light. Then the same out-of-sorts feeling washed over him, like it had when they stepped through the LumiDoor, but not as deeply this time.

When Michael's vision cleared, he could see that they had landed in a lobby. But this little mini-station was much smaller and only had two corridor pillars. There were Guards blocking the way to a giant double door and one other master knight sat at a terminal. He had multiple floating hologram screens in front of him, and he was sliding things this way and that. Henry smiled, his deep blue eyes gleaming, and said, "I think you'll like the *new* version of "Epic Combat" I helped create in our waiting area. He motioned for them to follow and he authenticated on a floating kiosk as he left the transport area. The guard nodded at him and motioned toward the over-sized door.

Michael was expecting the door to lead to a hallway but when he stepped through, he was shocked to see an enormous room with a round couch in the center, like those he had seen at the other locations. There was light pouring in from the windows, which seemed to surround the entire space. Silvan's voice rang out, "Whoaa! Do you see that, Michael? Look at that huge virtual training arena! That must be the new 'Epic Combat' version Uncle Henry was talking about. Let's check it out. You owe me a round, remember?"

When they entered the space, Michael was amazed at what he saw. There were dozens of Visithite crystals mounted all around the gymnasium-sized space and multiple individual tracks, like the one at Henry's. Each track was like 15 square feet and there was a main larger kiosk in the center of the room. They all stepped onto tracks and as soon as Silvan engaged the kiosk the overhead lights in the room dimmed and they each saw a floating 3D prompt. They were able to pick their map, weapons and armor. Michael decided to try something different and picked a large sword, with the Herkilian notched blade.

They played as a team and took on an assortment of different Sulgons of varying sizes, shapes and abilities. It was good to put their training into practice. As he moved on in the game and watched what the others were facing, it was clear that the game was able to detect their respective abilities. Isaac's Sulgons were small and slow and he was doing his best to swing at them, sometimes falling and stumbling in the process. But he kept getting back up, a determined look on his round sweaty face. Michael smiled and wondered what his future with his new brother would hold.

Michael's dragon hybrids increased in size, power and ability. A particularly nasty one nearly bested him by using advanced fencing techniques toward the end of their quest. The ferocious figure had backed Michael into the corner of his track when he flipped high in the air and landed behind his opponent. He dealt the finishing blow as his glowing blade sliced through the back and out the chest of the dark creature.

Off in the corner were several more familiar games, including Air Hockey, Ping-Pong and a basketball game with side-by-side hoops.

After taking on several quests and trying multiple weapons, they graduated to the game area and had been playing for about 30 minutes when Michael saw something out of the corner of his eye and looked up from his fifth game in a row of beating Silvan at Air Hockey to see Peter in the doorway. Silvan capitalized on Michael's momentary lapse and scored the winning goal. When Michael turned back, his ecstatic friend had started an elaborate victory dance. Something about it triggered a flashback to that day at Jeff's house when the crow screeching from Nick's house had distracted him and Jeff had taken him out in the VRT-Pod version of "Epic Combat." Had that really only been several days ago? So much had happened in that short time.

Here he was in another dimension, about to receive a special advancement that would set him on a course to become a leader of a mysterious kingdom that encompassed 13 realms. Michael noticed that Silvan had moved over to the basketball game and he and Isaac were battling it out. He chuckled as one of Isaac's balls flew completely off to the side and smacked Billy on the side of the head. Isaac stopped to apologize and then resumed hurling balls at the tiny hoops. When Michael turned back to check on Peter, he was startled to see him standing right next to him and blurted out, "Whoa. What are you? A Ninja?"

Peter chuckled and said, "Something like that." The bulky commander looked at him with concern in his eyes. "How are you holding up, bud?"

"I'm ok," Michael answered, trying to sound convincing. "Just thinking about the ceremony. What's it going to be like?"

Peter patted his shoulder and said, "Well, I can tell you how most advancement ceremonies go, but I'm afraid that won't really cut it since there's never been one like this in the Order. What I can tell you is that the figure of Vivienne, the Royal Matron holds the Hallowed Sphere above the Lake of Tranquility. The Royal Tokens are locked inside and have been for over a thousand years. The prophecy states that when the High Sentinel comes, he will approach the sphere, reach inside and claim the

Royal Tokens for himself. Excalibur will be brought forth and the End of Days will begin."

"So, who is this Vivienne and why is she called the Royal Matron?"

Peter smiled, as Silvan won his game and did a fist pump. "She was a powerful ally to Prince Arthur and helped him defeat Drakkir. She also masterminded the building of the Havens that we have today and is held in high regard by all matrons throughout the kingdom. It is said that she has a key role in the ushering in of the End of Days."

Michael was trying to envision the Hallowed Sphere. "But how can someone reach inside a sphere?" Michael asked. "Aren't they solid?"

Peter said, "That's a great question. You see, this sphere is actually a LumiDome, like the one we passed through that protects the Portacon of Galahad, but this one is much smaller and has been activated with the signature of the High Sentinel."

"But wait. How, if I'm the one, did I activate it? Didn't you say that it has been there for over a thousand years?"

Peter nodded and said, "Yes, it has. That is a mystery and there is no one alive who has the answer to that question. But think about the aspect of the prophecy that spoke of the High Sentinel entering the Order as a master. That was inconceivable to all who heard it until today. There are many things that have happened and will happen that are outside the scope of our understanding. That doesn't make them impossible."

Michael thought about what Peter had said. He nodded slowly and said, "That makes sense. When I think about how little I knew before I learned about Lithegol, it's mind-blowing. I'm sure there are a ton of other things like that still out there."

"Bingo, Michael. The learning never ends."

Chapter 17

Camelot

Minutes later Michael was sitting at an ancient-looking table in a nook toward the back when Claire walked up and sat down. She had a concerned expression on her face. She touched his arm and said, "I just got back. Are you ok? I'm so sorry about your dad. I wish I knew what to say to help you feel better."

"I'm ok, Claire. Thanks for asking. It just doesn't seem real. Is my dad really gone? Am I really the High Sentinel? It's all so unbelievable."

She was shaking her head and Michael noticed her flowing flaxen hair. She was strikingly pretty. But in a real sort of way. He didn't know what it was about her that made his heart race. "I seriously don't know how you do it," she said. "You're only 16 and you're being asked to take on so much. I'm not that much younger than you and there's no way I could take on half of what you're facing." Then a tear formed in her eye and she said, "I can't really explain it but when I was forced to leave you there on that field, it was all I could do to not rush back and follow you into battle. I was so relieved you were ok."

Michael felt her deep concern and affection for him, and he leaned toward her and they kissed. When their lips touched, he felt a surge of exhilaration and he extended his hand to her face and she did the same to him. When they pulled away, they were both smiling and Michael said, "Wow. Ok. Not sure where that came from… but it felt right."

She nodded shyly and said, "I agree. But I hope it doesn't seem like I'm taking advantage of you in your time of tragedy. It's really not like that at all."

At the mention of tragedy Michael's thoughts drifted to his dad and Claire must've sensed it because she squeezed his hand and said, "Just know that if you ever need someone to talk to, I'm here. And you need to remember that we all believe in you."

Michael nodded and forced a smile. "Thanks, Claire. I appreciate that. I'm glad you dropped by."

She smiled, her face turning red, and said, "Oh, me too. Definitely glad we had this little *chat*." She paused, then disappeared around the corner.

Michael thought about what had just happened. Was Claire his girlfriend now? He thought about her and everyone and was reminded how lucky he was to have so many new friends to support him. He saw the guilty looks of Aurora and Peter in his mind and an image popped into his head of his dad lying there motionless. His guilt returned and he thought of how he had frozen. Why did he do that? He had had the pistol right there. And why had he pressed the wrong button? How would things have played out if he had pushed the 15-second one instead?

As that thought sank in, he heard a familiar voice ask, "How are you doing, Michael?"

It was Gabriel, and he sat down across from him, his unusual green eyes seeming to drill into his soul.

Michael felt raw. Like he could cry at the least mention of his dad or of what had happened. "I just keep seeing my dad lying there. Why did it have to happen? And if I'm supposedly so powerful and such a great leader, why did I freeze up like that?"

Gabriel paused and said thoughtfully, "Your father's death is not your fault. You did exactly what you were supposed to do. I've often asked myself that same question when something bad happens to someone I care about. The answer that I have come to is that everyone has their freedoms. This is one of the greatest gifts that we have been given and one that the Legion seeks to take away. Your father chose to stand in front of Aurora, to protect her. Bamith chose to throw that dagger. The choices you made led to the destruction of a weapon that would've enslaved and destroyed many lives. You should be very proud of what you accomplished.

"I know that you feel angry and alone and it hurts right now. I have felt those feelings many times over my long lifetime. It's ok to have those feelings. It's ok to cry. It doesn't make you weak. It makes you strong, actually. Because you feel. You feel love. You care about others. You fight for others and you believe in a cause greater than any of us. That is what matters. And as I mentioned before, you will see your dad again, sooner than you might guess. It reminds me of what I went through when I lost my dear friend, Abraham Lincoln."

Michael jumped. "You knew Abraham Lincoln? Was he a knight in Lithegol?"

"Yes, he was a senior commander from Prime and an incredibly honorable man. He did so much good for the Order. He was assassinated by a coward of a man, John Wilkes Booth, a commander and a Shadow Sentry who was seduced by the Legion. The night after he killed Lincoln, Booth became a Sulgon, which completed his utter betrayal. At the time, I felt the same way Commander Piddir felt. I wanted to hunt him down and make him pay. Unfortunately, others, including Senior Commander Braster followed through on this desire and kidnapped the assassin and left a decoy in his stead. Braster and Senior Commander Raithbine, Lincoln's Sentry Guardian, or as you know him, Bamith tortured Booth for details of the Legion before savagely killing him. They were banished from the order and you have seen where these choices have led them. Unfortunately, when knights were sent to arrest them and strip them of their knighthood, Braster and Bamith were gone and the knights accidentally killed Braster's wife, Bethany… thus why his rage is so deep."

"I learned from that whole horrific experience that anger and bitterness just destroy us and limit our abilities. I felt very guilty afterward. I kept getting overwhelmed with thoughts of what if. What if I had been there? What if I had delayed my mission, at the time, to be with him? I could've stopped it. But it wasn't meant to be. This is one of many such experiences that I have had. And each one is still painful.

"What helps me is to remember that this life is but a fleeting moment in the timeline of our existence. You must look forward to your future and not dwell on the injustices or tragedies of the past." He stopped and placed his hand on Michael's shoulder and continued, "It doesn't mean we forget the ones we love, Michael. We use that love to make us better, to drive us to accomplish more, to fight harder, to serve more completely, to show love more often, to train that much harder. You have boundless potential and a great destiny ahead of you, and I know that your father will be by your side the entire way, whether you see him there or not."

Michael stared into the probing eyes of the majestic leader and wondered to himself what those unusual green irises had seen through the course of all those years. "Thank you for the reassuring words." He paused, his head reeling. Who knew that there was so much involved with Lincoln's assassination? "I can't believe you knew Abraham Lincoln and that he was a senior commander. Although, it does make total sense, given all the great things I've read about him. You will have to tell me more about some of your adventures together."

A feeling of warmth began to seep in, slowly replacing the bitter sting of guilt and grief. He was surprised to feel excitement beginning to well up. He was energized at the thought of training and advancing in the Order. Everything in him looked forward to eventually invading the Legion base and taking out their army of vile monsters. He thrilled at the thought of Bamith and Erubamir behind bars and jumped up and said, "Well, what are we waiting for? When do we get to blow up that base?"

Gabriel said, "All in good time, young Sentinel. We must be sure that we are as prepared as we can be before we set out on that mission. For now, we need to make our way to the long-awaited ceremony." He stood, then floated several feet away, his graceful movements making him seem more like a ghost than an embodied person. We will be meeting in 15 minutes in the main area to go over what happens next." Then Gabriel smiled, nodded and floated around the corner.

As Michael sat there, thinking about what Gabriel had said about his boundless potential, he couldn't help but be overwhelmed by it all. It just felt so odd. Was this really who he was? They were all expecting him to be their leader and take out the Legion. How could he even begin to imagine doing that? Just seeing Erubamir and the power he had made Michael doubt that he could ever be that powerful. He thought about how long Gabriel had been around and even he wasn't able to easily take out the gargantuan Legion leader.

*   *   *

Michael entered the main room and all the others who had since returned greeted him warmly. When Eileen hugged him, Michael leaned in and said, "How is Brad doing?"

She patted his shoulder and smiled warmly. "You are very perceptive and concerned for someone so young. That's no big surprise to me. Brad is doing well. Most of his issues now stem from his deep-seated anger for the Legion. I believe that his stay at The Haven will be a short one." She turned her head thoughtfully and said, "Maybe you can pay us a visit and talk to him sometime. I'm sure that would mean a lot to someone like Brad."

Michael nodded emphatically and said, "I would love that. I'm also very curious to see what you do there."

"I look forward to that, young Sentinel. Please know that I and all within my circle of influence are behind you and believe in who you are and what you can do for Lithegol."

Michael did the Revin salute and said, "Thank you. That means a lot to me, Senior Commander."

She bowed gracefully in return and glided over to Commander Sam. Senior Commander Derrilin spoke briefly to him and mentioned that he was looking forward to teaching Michael and the other Masters during the upcoming Training Cycle. Michael still couldn't get over how small he was.

They all sat around the couch waiting anxiously for Gabriel to speak. His mom placed her hand on his knee and said, "What are you thinking about? You have that look."

"I was just thinking about what the Captain said. Everyone is going to be there and all of their eyes will be on me. What if I trip and fall on my face on my way up to the sphere? What if I'm not the one and I'm not able to reach in and retrieve the Royal Tokens?"

She squeezed his leg and said, "How can you say that, Michael? How can you have any doubts at this point? Everyone here knows that you're the one. Think about Gabriel's vast experience and knowledge, and he's sure of it. You're just getting anxious, that's all. You need to relax and focus on the wonderful things that you're going to do in your new role."

She stopped and he could tell that she was holding back her emotions when she said, "And I know that your father will be there watching you with proud eyes. You won't trip because you're going to remember the things he taught you about confidence and leadership and poise and you're going to take your time and take deep breaths and walk

~ 254 ~

carefully forward. I believe in you and all of the people here believe in you. All of the knights and matrons there today will be excited that you have arrived."

A peaceful feeling settled over Michael, and he said, "How do you always know what to say to make people feel better? You have a gift, Mom. When I learned what Eileen does at The Haven, it reminded me of you, and I'm excited to see you become a matron and make a difference in the Order like she does."

"Thank you, Son," she said. "Yes, I spoke with Eileen. She was very supportive and encouraging. She said that I can begin my training with the new set of squires in the upcoming Training Cycle. They have a special group for adult squires. I'm excited and a bit nervous like you are."

Gabriel glided in and stopped near the golden chair in the center. He was as regal as ever, his glowing cape shimmering from the rays of what Michael now noticed was a massive sun through the wide panoramic window. It was hanging in the sky much closer than the one on Earth. There was much smaller second sun next to it. The windows and the entire wall were curved as if they were in a round tower room. He searched around for a clock, wondering what time it was there.

The Captain extended his hand to Michael and said, "We are all a part of one of the most important moments in the history of Lithegol. I want to thank you all for your bravery and courage against what played out to be immense odds. Each of you has fought valiantly to protect our greatest asset, The High Sentinel of Lithegol. I have informed the leaders of the Order of his arrival. We need to arrive early, as they have set aside special seating arrangements for our group. The Tintagel arena will be beyond full for this. I thought you all might also be interested in how our brave dwarf comrade, Lirfta is doing. I just received a report that he is making progress and they have high hopes that they will be able to revive him and that he will make a full recovery."

Everyone clapped and cheered. Gabriel smiled and motioned for them to be quiet and gazed at Michael and said, "Because of the prophecy regarding the High Sentinel joining the Order as a master there is a special event at every Master Advancement Ceremony. Those who are moving on to the master level are brought to the Lake of Tranquility, where they must see if their Sullite Signature is the one that will unlock the Royal Tokens trapped deep within the Hallowed Sphere."

Hearing Gabriel utter this phrase gave Michael goosebumps. An excited energy was building inside of him at the thought of the magical click sounding out when he reached in.

Gabriel smiled, as his deep dimples lit up his face. "I am so excited to see Michael take his place. I have seen thousands of apprentice graduates anxiously walk down the platform of destiny, only to find out that they weren't the one. But I know in my heart that the outcome will be different tonight."

Everyone was looking at Michael and started clapping and cheering.

His face flushed and he said, "Thank you."

Gabriel motioned to an apprentice knight who had been standing quietly in the corner. The boy approached carrying a covered platter and handed it to him. He looked to be about 17 or 18 and had a quiet confidence about him. The Captain took the platter, nodded and said,

"Thank you, young Apprentice. You may be dismissed." The tall brown-haired boy, who had slightly pointed ears, nodded and did the Revin. After sneaking a few glances at Michael, he exited through the door to the lobby.

Gabriel held up the platter, smiled and said, "No, Commander Piddir, this is not food, as I'm sure you had hoped." He removed the lid and said, "I have had special WriP units made for each of you. Dr. Waicroft and the other engineers have designed them brilliantly to make them secure and useful to our forces, and I feel that you all deserve to capitalize on our developments. As you learn to interface with the WriP you will learn how to manage and control your abilities from it." He engaged his WriP as several screens shot out above his arm and he said, "One of the basic things that will be useful, since time is reckoned altogether differently here in Avalon, is this clock." He pointed to a set of hovering digital numbers that read 6:30 pm. Michael checked his regular watch and was shocked to see that it said it was 10:00 pm. He wondered, if time doesn't change on Earth, what time it would actually be if he were to go back now. It made his brain hurt.

Gabriel's orb flashed and Aurora nodded, stood, and began passing the WriPs out to everyone. As Michael studied it, he saw bb-sized Sullite crystals next to each projection lens.

Gabriel continued, "To activate your specialized WriP you'll need to touch at least one of the Sullite crystals, and then once again to authenticate it. If you have any questions, Commander Henry, Master Aurora or I can help you." Next Gabriel removed a tiny magnetic dot from the WriP strap, and said, "This is a headphone and a microphone combined, which will temporarily adhere to the skin when placed just inside the ear. As much as I'm sure you all want to play with them, unfortunately, we have a date with destiny and need to leave right away for Camelot. There is a record-breaking crowd arriving there. Now, everyone, quickly gather up your things. We will be departing in ten minutes."

As Michael finished fastening the WriP to his arm, Gabriel approached, Julia and Isaac at his side, and motioned for them to follow him. He led them into a side room. The first thing Michael saw was a beautiful elf woman, with wavy reddish-brown hair. She was wearing an elegant, flowing red dress with intricately embroidered designs adorning the skirt and blouse. The boy standing next to her Michael recognized as the apprentice from earlier. His thin lips were turned up in a knowing smile. He was wearing a red and black outfit that reminded Michael of something out of a Robin Hood movie. Gabriel motioned toward them and said, "This is my wife, Raylynn. She is a Cognitive from the Penturi Realm in the Eastern Triad. Aurora would be here but is helping the others with their new WriPs."

Raylynn extended her hand, Michael shook it and stared into her hazel eyes. She seemed to be looking right through him, but in a kind way. Michael smiled nervously. "Nice to meet you, Raylynn. Your husband is amazing."

"Yes, I would tend to agree with you on that point, Michael," she replied, smiling. "So great to finally meet you. We are excited that you're here." She pointed at the boy and said, "Michael, this is Percival. Percival, Michael. He is 17-years-old."

The eager youth shot his hand out and said, in a sharp voice, "I'm actually almost 18. Nice to meet you. I heard that you're the High Sentinel. That's so awesome!"

RayLynn gave him a stern look, and said, "Percy, we told you not to say anything."

Michael said, "It's ok." He turned to him, and said, "That's what they say. But we're going to find out soon. It's all pretty crazy."

Gabriel introduced Michael's mother and Isaac. Michael's mom just stared at Raylynn's super pointy ears and beautiful Cinderella-looking dress. After a few moments, she managed a smile and a "nice to meet you." This was all foreign to her. Isaac managed to look Raylynn in the eyes but right away his head went down and his cheeks flushed. The poor guy had no self-confidence.

"Come with me, Michael. I have a special gift for you," Gabriel said, as he walked by Percival, playfully poking him in the stomach. When the Captain opened the closet door, there was an outfit hanging there, straight from medieval times. It had a long-sleeved top made of some dark brown silky material. The shoulders had an upturned lip that made it look very elegant, and on the front, was a gold embroidered design of the Crest of Lithegol.

There were dark pants and some soft black boots on the floor. Michael asked Gabriel, "What is this for? Is that for me? Where did you get it?"

Gabriel replied, "That is the outfit I wore when I was made an apprentice knight many years ago. I only wore it for that event and Percival wore it for his apprentice ceremony. And now you will wear it for your special ceremony. Although my ceremony was nowhere near as magnificent as yours will be."

Michael's mother said, "Thank you so much, Captain. You and the others have been so good to us."

He patted her on the back and said, "It is my pleasure, Julia. You don't know how long I have been waiting for this day to arrive. It would truly be an honor if he would wear it."

Michael bowed, extending his palm anxiously, and said, "Are you kidding? The honor is mine. I'll go try it on. How old were you when you became an apprentice?"

"I was barely 16 and the youngest to ever advance to that level, until today. You are skipping that altogether and will be our first 16-year-old Master Knight." He smiled, his dimples showing through, and pointed to a door in the back of the room. "Hurry and put it on though, please. We need to go."

The clothes fit fairly well, although they were a little loose and Michael wondered how big the Captain was at 16. When Michael walked out into the main area, everyone stared at him in awe and several bowed in a Revin. Except for Isaac, who walked beside him, oblivious to everything going on around him. He had some holographic image up on his WriP, was shaking his rear and stepping to the beat. Michael realized he was watching music videos and stifled a chuckle.

Within a few minutes, Gabriel gathered everyone together and motioned for them to follow him. They all walked, or more like hopped with excitement, out to the Lumithite transport station. Gabriel pointed at the corridor areas, with gold illuminated circles on a clear glass floor.

Everyone had authenticated and it was Gabriel's turn. When he approached the console, he placed his orb in a special custom space, in the exact shape of the Sign of Lithegol, and there was a high trumpeting sound. Within seconds, the gold-flecked light gathered around each of them and they were off.

Chapter 18

The Ceremony

When his eyes came into focus, Michael stood and stared at the palace below. The corridor had brought them to an overlook and he could see elegant spires, towers and courtyards that seemed to extend for miles. Everything had a golden Lumithite glow to it. His eyes rested on the arena. Only a massive courtyard separated them from it. There was a beautifully ornamented archway leading into the towering stadium.

Michael's heart was racing. This was it. There, no more than 300 yards away, was where it would all happen. The platform by the lake that Gabriel had talked about was the path to his future. He just wanted it to be over and done with. He was tired of waiting to confirm whether he was really the one. Gabriel led them down some stairs and they came out into a magnificent courtyard. There were elaborately carved glowing fountains, statues and light displays with hovering holograms of knights and matrons that were talking and sharing biographical details about themselves and their families. Some of the people were interacting with the holograms, almost like it was a conversation. Exotic plants, similar to those from Sam's garden, some even more breathtaking, lined every orifice along what appeared to be a Lumithite walkway.

In the center of the yard was an intricately carved solid gold statue. It was of a noble looking man with a simple but stately crown and an intimidating bird carved onto his shoulder. As they approached, Michael noticed Sullfloras surrounding it on either side. They were different from those he had seen in Sam's garden. These had tiny Lumithite crystals packed into them, which were shining brightly. Gabriel took in a deep breath and said, "Ahhh, you can never get too many scents from a Sullflora. It is so regenerating. These are extremely rare Lumithite Sullflora and are amazingly powerful."

Michael took in a long and deep breath and it was as if he was sniffing in a waft of happiness. Any worries he may have had disappeared from his mind. He felt a hand on his shoulder and he turned to see Commander Sam. "That is a statue of Prince Arthur, and I think you know which bird is on his shoulder. It was carved, based on a painting that was completed right before the final battle of the Meridian War. Merlin was added to it later." He motioned toward it and said, "Go ahead, take a closer look."

As Michael approached the ancient-looking statue, he studied the eyes of Arthur. His face was kind but strong, like Gabriel's, but he had more of a square jaw and a cleft chin and a short beard. He had the kind of expression a parent would have if they were watching their child doing something remarkable. Michael wondered who he really was and whether he would ever meet him. As his eyes moved down, he saw an engraving on the base platform. It read, "He fought for Lithegol and his King and saved us all from a plague of evil. The Prince lived each day as if that day was his only day. Long live Arthur and long live Lithegol."

Michael thought about those words. How profound a statement was that? 'He lived each day as if that day was his only day.' How great a man must he have been to live that way? Not an easy task at all. Something stirred within him and he felt a growing warmth as he thought about Arthur and what was about to happen. He reached out with his thoughts to Arthur and recited the Oath of Lithegol to himself. He made a silent vow to always strive to live the same way that this great leader had.

He felt his emotions building up and a distinct feeling fell over him. It felt like his dad was there giving him a hug. Tears fell down his cheeks and he closed his eyes, hoping he would somehow see his dad or a vision of him—anything. But nothing came. Then all of the Sullfloras lit up and he was blinded by the flood of bright yellowish lights. What did it mean? He stood up and turned around; everyone was staring at the flowers, a look of awe on their faces. Most of them were wiping their cheeks and smiling.

The towering Captain gestured toward the flowers and said, "They recognize you, young Sentinel. Are you ready for what comes next?"

Michael nodded, and said, "I really feel like I am now. I can't explain what just happened but those words really sank in deep. I want to live my life the same way he did."

Peter stared at the engraved words, as if discovering them for the first time, and said, "What 16-year-old has that as their goal? You continue to amaze me."

Michael gazed out at their little group and said, "Regardless of what happens tonight I want you all to know how much I value our friendship. I look forward to working with each of you and I'm grateful for all that you've done for me." They all nodded and dropped to one knee in the Revin, but instead of pulling their hand in, they kept both of them extended, palms up. Michael gasped, thinking back to how he had heard about this rare form of the bow, and he did the same thing back to them.

As they approached the other side of the courtyard, Michael's eyes stopped on the tall archway that led into the arena. At the archway's center was a gold illuminated Crest of Lithegol. There were words etched in calligraphy on the left that read, "May love and honor enlighten you." On the right, it said, "True power is gained by protecting and serving."

He felt a small hand grab his and he looked down to see Claire gazing up at him. She smiled warmly, and said, "This is your moment, Michael. Just stay calm and enjoy it. We're here for you. The whole kingdom is here for you."

Michael squeezed her hand and said, "Thank you. That helps. It's just a lot to take in." She nodded, reassuringly and let go of his hand and joined the others behind him.

As Michael crossed into the open area on the other side of the arch, his ears were overwhelmed with a wave of voices all around. The stadium was the size of a professional sports stadium and it was filled with people. Instead of a playing field, there was a lake in the center and immaculate thrones with various glowing colors assembled in sections around the lake. Each amazing throne seat had intricate carvings and designs. It was truly a remarkable sight. There were even people standing shoulder to shoulder in the aisles and front area of the stands.

All around, above the highest level of people's heads, were 11 massive Visithite 3D projections where you could see others watching live. As Michael thought about it, it came to him. They were watching from the other 11 realms throughout the kingdom. Which meant that the Herkili Realm truly had been taken over and wasn't able to attend. He instinctively looked at Peter, but his friend seemed too involved with catching up with old friends to notice at that moment. The enormity of it all seemed to crash down on him and Michael froze in his tracks. He saw people pointing at him and whispering to each other. The arena became suddenly quiet and he saw an ultra-clear 3D rendering of himself projected high above the lake. It felt like everyone was staring at him.

Michael glanced down at his hands. He was wringing them together nervously. It was then that he noticed the glow all around him. It was the brightest green aura he had seen yet as if the light was exploding off him. Why was that happening? Maybe it had something to do with the lake. There was a group of distinguished-looking knights and matrons seated in white throne-looking chairs directly surrounding the lake on the far side, facing him.

As he studied them closer, he realized that these individuals were all glowing with a white aura and gold Sullice. These were all Overseers and Grand Matrons. He thought about the incredible Sullite power contained in that group. Four of the white thrones were taller than the others and one of them was empty. Then it hit him. This was the Herkili Guardian Overseer chair vacated by Therok the traitor.

Directly ahead of him, to the right of the lake, was an elevated platform with a glass table and a padded, blue throne. Further away from Michael, but closer to the lake was a white throne, but this one was bigger than the others. Farther down from it was an ornate open mini-tower with two levels. The entire structure was gold in color. The top level had the largest of the gold thrones and there were three more, slightly smaller golden thrones on the lower level.

As his eyes scanned the motionless, clear lake, he locked in on the dock at the far-right end of the lake, which extended over it like a bridge. The statue of the woman Peter had called Vivienne extended up from the water, the body half submerged. She had long straight hair, her kind face was calm, and her eyes fixed on the Lumithite sphere that she was holding in both hands above her head. He wondered why her statue had been chosen to hold the sphere.

He felt a hand on his shoulder and Gabriel walked past him. The uniformed Captain pointed to the front of the audience seats near the dock where there was a row of blue padded chairs and he said, "These seats have been reserved for this group. All except for Michael." He walked over to the neighboring section of chairs and pointed to the last one in the row.

These scaled down thrones, with Green padded backs, had the Crest of Lithegol embroidered on the back cushion. The workmanship looked very old and had unusual markings throughout. All of the red glowing soon-to-be master knights that were waiting to be a part of the ceremony appeared to be in their early 20s, except for the one sitting next to the empty seat on the end of the row, who looked closer to 19 or 20. When Michael sat down the knight smiled at him and introduced himself as Jude. He had thin lips and bushy dark eyebrows, framing in narrow blue eyes. He had his own unique look with his dark pompadour and beak-shaped nose. Jude was dressed in an outfit right out of Party City for a medieval knight, with a vest that had an embroidered lion on it and dark pants and boots.

The knight studied him closely and said, "Well, I WAS the youngest knight to graduate to the master level until you showed up. You are some kind of anomaly. What's your story anyway?"

Michael shrugged and said, "I'm Michael Brenlan. Nice to meet you, Jude. I'm just a simple farm boy. This is all crazy for me, actually." He shook Jude's hand firmly and said, "There's definitely a big crowd out there."

Jude forced a smile and said, "Don't worry. You'll get used to it after you've been here as many times as I have. That's the way it is in Camelot."

Gabriel was standing in front of the largest of the white chairs, located on the right side of the platform. He raised his hands, all eyes turned to him, and he touched his orb. His voice rang out loudly as if it was being piped through powerful speakers overhead. "You are all gathered here today for a special Advancement Ceremony. As is the case after every Training Cycle, we allow advancing apprentice knights to approach the Hallowed Sphere to find out if they are the High Sentinel. The High Sentinel is the one that was prophesied would come, to lead the knights and matrons of Lithegol in the End of Days War."

Gabriel pointed to the other smaller blue chair to his left and said, "Each knight must kneel at the feet of the Master of the Ceremony and repeat the Oath of Lithegol. Then he must place his current tokens on the Token table and proceed to the platform. If he is the chosen one, he will be able to reach into the Hallowed Sphere and the Royal Tokens will fasten themselves upon him. Then the prophecy will be fulfilled and the great SullSword Excalibur will be reborn." He motioned toward the tiered platform with the gold thrones on it and continued, "Then the Royal Overseer will be summoned to advance the High Sentinel master. And the High Sentinel will take his place atop the Royal Spire and the Royal Overseer likewise as the first member of the Royal Guard."

Michael's heart was racing. He thought about what this meant. Merlin was the Royal Overseer. Was he going to be changed back into his human form and take his place? So much was riding on Michael being the one. He felt dizzy. He peered over at his mom, who gave the ASL sign for *I love you,* by raising her thumb, index and pinky fingers. Michael saw that Isaac, Silvan, Claire and the others were giving him a discreet thumbs-up.

Gabriel motioned to his left, toward the ancient wooden token table filled with carvings, and said, "For those that are unable to reach into the sphere please make your way back to the Token table and reclaim your original tokens, kneel at the feet of the Master of Ceremonies and repeat the Pledge of the Master to receive your advancement. Then take your place with the other new masters."

Gabriel gestured toward the blue thrones and Commander Sam stood up and made his way over to him, as the audience cheered loudly. "This is the Master of Ceremonies, as chosen from our nominated commanders by the Overseers of the Round. He is one of the most distinguished knights in the Order and we are privileged to have him in our midst. Please join me in welcoming Commander Samas Perren."

The elf commander stepped, no longer limping, meekly on to the advancement platform as everyone stood up and cheered loudly. He looked like a small child out in the middle of this huge forum, but his dignified air still somehow commanded authority. Gabriel touched his chest again and sat down.

Sam touched his blue glowing orb and said, "Thank you very much. I am honored to have been chosen as Master of Ceremonies for this event. Captain Gabriel has explained well these proceedings so let's get right to today's ceremony." His soft, lyrical voice filled the arena and Michael wondered again how the orb speaker magnification system worked.

*   *   *

As the commander proceeded to call up knight after knight, only to have them unable to reach into the sphere, Michael's nerves heightened. The time came for Jude and he stood up, his face filled with anxiety, and sauntered over to the commander. When he approached the sphere, nothing happened and he hung his head. He retrieved his tokens and Sam issued him his advancement. When the lanky master walked back to his seat, his lips were pursed and he was wiping his eyes. Michael felt bad for him and said, "Congratulations, Jude. You're a master knight. That's awesome." He gave him his best smile and Jude just glowered at him, sadness in his eyes, and forced a smile. Commander Sam's voice sounded again and Michael turned to watch.

"Our next master candidate is the youngest we've ever had at just 16 years old. He has the highest capacity for Sullite power that I have ever seen, and he comes to us miraculously as a squire with the power of a master. We are excited to have him here and I can't wait to see him traverse the path to the Hallowed Sphere. Please welcome to the platform, Michael Brenlan, son of Spencer and Julia Brenlan."

Everyone around the lake stood up and cheered, as did everyone on all the projections. Michael could see his friends waving their arms in the air and yelling his name. His eyes scanned the crowd and rested on the petite figure standing next to Silvan. Claire was clapping high, near her head. As she lowered her hands their eyes met and she blushed and smiled, her deep dimples showing. Michael smiled back, as he felt his face flush. He was now on the platform and Sam motioned for him to kneel. As Michael got down on one knee, his mind traveled back to when he had assumed this position, just days before, when he became a squire. So much had happened in that short period of time. He almost felt like a completely different person from that naive boy.

He raised his arm, as he had before, and repeated the Oath with the commander. He felt the anxiety and excitement rising in his chest:

I, Michael Brenlan promise to continue to live by the Oath of Lithegol:

I will show love to my King and all others who may be in need
I will stand for honor, cleanliness, freedom and justice
I will serve Lithegol and follow my knight and matron leaders always
I will fulfill my mission assignments with courage, using the power of Sullice
I will choose good over evil and will heed the warnings that come to me always
I will fight for Lithegol and for the Sullite people of all worlds with all my might

Then Commander Sam said, "Now, please stand and make your way to the Hallowed Sphere."

Michael thought he would faint, but he focused on staying calm and stood slowly. The gentle commander put his hand on his arm and sent a thought transmission to him. "You are the one, my young friend."

Michael smiled and mouthed the words, "Thank you," before he made his way over to the token table. The dark wood reminded him of his special box and he wondered what the significance of it was. The table, like most of the furniture he had seen in Camelot, appeared to be hundreds, if not thousands of years old and had intricately carved designs on it. Michael recognized the crossed swords of Herkili within the tabletop of carvings and realized that these engravings must be the signs for each of the realms. He had seen knights and matrons in the stands waving flags with some of these striped and ornamented designs. He carefully placed his squire ring on the table and turned to face the ominous pier of destiny. The golden walkway seemed to float above the water. This was it. This was the moment he and the others had been waiting for. He hesitated as some doubt snuck in. He thought about Gabriel and how sure he was and the words his mom had said. He took a deep breath and stepped out onto the crystalized dock.

As he approached the sphere, he could see the tokens inside more clearly. Instead of the gray Omithite material, these were white. The crystals were larger and they each had a faint golden glow. And like the other tokens, there was something carved in immaculate detail on either side of the crystal. It was a magnificent sword with a simple crown surrounding the blade.

Everything was completely silent like all sound had been sucked out of the massive arena.

Michael timidly extended his hands until they rested on the Sphere. It felt solid and pushed his hands back at first like you would expect a force field to do. Within a few seconds, he could hear it, a whizzing sound, like the one generated by the SullSwords when they were swung swiftly through the air. It was building in volume. The vibrant hum reached a climax and two notes, from low to high, like the trumpet sounds from Gabriel's authentication rang out.

Michael's hands fell through the Sphere and he was overcome by a surge of happiness. He could feel the Royal Tokens on his chest, hand and wrist. He turned his right hand and felt a burst of energy shoot out into the handle of a sword. The SullSword was golden and magnificent, the blade curving in slightly on both sides right before the handle. The pommel had the same radiant sword in the crown insignia, as was the case with all of his tokens. His green speckled figure now had a rich gold aura, instead of a white one.

A shield materialized out of his band and into his left hand and he turned and raised the SullSword high into the air. A gold fleck-filled sheen formed on the surface of the lake. The noise from the thousands of people all around and the cheers coming through the projections erupted like that of a crowd at a Pro Football game. Michael focused on the crowd and there, floating over the lake, were hundreds more people. But these cheering people were ghosts, with vaporous bodies and various shades of glow around them.

Michael heard an unexpected voice call his name and when he turned toward it, there was his dad. He was hovering in a section of the lake closest to him and there were others from his family that had passed away standing with him. Michael's eyes teared up. He wanted so badly to run out on the water and hug him, just one more time. But deep down he knew he couldn't. His dad mouthed the words, "I love you so much." He signed, using ASL, "I'm so proud of you. I will always be watching over you, my son."

Michael felt tears falling and he tried to pull it together. His eyes scanned over to his mom. She was staring at the floating figure and crying and his dad was now looking at her and they were conversing in ASL. Peter, Silvan, Sam and the Waicroft family were also staring at who Michael recognized as Lisa, who was there with others as well. Many people in the audience were waving at figures, crying, embracing each other and cheering.

There was so much happening that Michael didn't even notice the glowing form behind him that had materialized. When the figure moved into view, Michael was startled to see that the Royal Sphere and the statue had disappeared and in its place was a woman, directly resembling the statue.

The gentle-looking beauty had extremely light brown eyes and her golden Sullite form, with yellowish flecks, was floating above the water beside the dock. She motioned for all to sit, and just like that the crowd was silent and everyone sat back down. Looking out at the vast throng Michael couldn't help but notice a group sitting in an upper tier that towered over the rest. These had to be the Paranins. He wondered about their kingdom and the other races in it. They were three times the height of most men and he noticed that they had wider heads and small ears. He hadn't put it together on the battlefield when he had seen Hurral. The realization hit and an ominous thought crossed his mind. The boy from the recruiting video was a Paranin. But what did that mean?

The woman gazed at Michael, bowed in a low Revin and said, her voice resonating through the arena, "I am Vivienne, Royal Matron of Lithegol and the Lady of the Lake, and I have been waiting patiently for your arrival, young one. You have a glorious future ahead of you. I was there, just after the War of the Meridian times, when Arthur departed for the Realm of Trellif and you, I, and the Royal Guard were set aside for another day. And I am honored to be here now as you take your place as the High Sentinel of Lithegol." Her high voice was soothing and she spoke with a British accent.

She started singing. It was the same tune Merlin had sung—the one Gabriel had called "The Liberty Anthem." Her voice was soothing and melodious. The lyrics spoke of Lithegol and the quest for peace and happiness and knights and matrons and principles from the Oath and Camelot and the power of Sullice. Michael got goosebumps at the end as she soared to an extremely high note and the audience roared and clapped.

After the cheering subsided, Michael heard a gasp from the crowd and he gazed up as the familiar beaming figure of Merlin glided down in his Golden Eagle form. He landed on Michael's shoulder as the audience exploded again. Vivienne gave a gentle downward gesture and they quieted. "It is now time for the Royal Overseer to take his place again, as the first member of the Royal Guard. This time on the right hand of the

High Sentinel of Lithegol."

She was smiling and gazing at Merlin as if he was a long-lost friend. A tear snuck down her cheek and she reached forward, a beautifully ornate golden scepter appearing in her right hand. Merlin flew out in front of her, she pointed it at him, and a mist of golden Sullice floated out and the lighter colored flecks surrounded the bird. There was a blinding flash of light and there standing in the bird's place was a man. He had the same yellow flecked uniform as Gabriel but instead of a white aura, his was a rich gold color like Vivienne's. He was about five feet ten inches tall with a short beard and blue eyes, which were full of kindness. Michael guessed he was in his late 40s.

He had slightly pointed ears and Michael wondered if he had some elf in him. In the place of a SullSword, he had a tall staff, with a Lumithite crystal embedded in it. The very first thing he did was to hug Vivienne and he kissed her passionately on the lips, which made Michael wonder what their story was. Then Merlin turned to Michael and said, in a kindly high voice that Michael recognized, "I am so proud of you, Michael. You don't know how long I and your King and his son, Arthur have waited for this day to come. How long your mother and I have been waiting for this day to come."

Michael's heart leaped. What was he talking about? Merlin and Vivienne opened their arms and took him in for a big hug.

Vivienne held up Michael's face in her hands and said, "Look at you. You made it. It was so hard for both of us to give you up, knowing that we wouldn't see you or be with you until this event occurred. But we each had our part to play. Everything changes now." Then she extended her hand toward Michael's mom and the essence figure of his dad out on the lake and said, "Thank you so much for taking such good care of our son. And for all the sacrifices you made. We can now all be part of the same family. You have done well."

Merlin placed his hand on his shoulder and said, "You don't know how many times I wanted to step in and intervene along the way, but I couldn't. I was bound unless you were in mortal danger. It did feel good to take down that helicopter though. The look on Erubamir's face was a pleasure to behold."

Merlin glanced out at the crowd and said, "Julia, Spencer? Would it be agreeable if I used Michael's given surname for the remaining parts of the ceremony?" They both nodded their agreement and Merlin continued, "Thank you. Michael Emrys, you have fulfilled your destiny and now I will do my part. Please descend to one knee."

Michael did as he was asked. His mind felt foggy from everything happening all at once.

Then Merlin said, "Now, please repeat the Pledge of a Master after me..."

I, Michael Emrys, promise to serve as a Master in the Order of Lithegol

I will serve others with courage, wisdom and kindness

I will follow the counsel of my knight and matron leaders and will step in to lead in their stead when needed

I will love all Sullite beings unconditionally and will strive to protect them and lead them to happiness always

I will use my Sullite powers wisely and only when it is absolutely necessary for the good of Lithegol

The overseer placed a hand on his chest and said, "By the power given to me as the Royal Overseer of Lithegol I dub thee, Michael Emrys, a Master Knight and bestow on thee all the powers, wisdom and judgment needed to govern the Order alongside Captain Gabriel, the Royal Matron and the Royal Guard as a delegate of the King. There will be another ceremony when you become an overseer and you will take your place, officially, as the High Sentinel and leader and the most powerful knight in all of the living realms of Lithegol. May you live by the Oath and Pledge you have made and grow in the ways of goodness and courage with that goal in mind."

Vivienne raised her hands high in the air and proclaimed, "The King's High Sentinel has finally arrived to lead his army to victory. Long live Lithegol!"

With that, Michael stood up and Merlin grabbed his right hand and they raised their arms in the air as the crowd erupted. Michael felt deep pulses of happiness and power coursing through his body, and he wondered what came next in the adventure that was his life. Merlin let go of his hand and sent him a thought message to raise up his SullSword. When Michael raised Excalibur up high in the air, a rumble sounded from all around the fortress. Ribbons of gold Sullice at least 10 feet in diameter burst forth out of the 11 projected screens and came together in the tip of the mammoth sword. Michael felt an explosion of Sullite energy ten times that of what he had felt earlier. A gold hoven exploding with green speckles appeared under his feet, with images of the crown encircled sword on either side, and he floated high into the air.

All of those he loved were all around him and he had found his biological parents and they were powerful and ancient leaders of Lithegol. And he finally had the Royal Tokens and the power to really do something against the Legion and to protect his fellow Sullites in the world. The tears were flowing, but this time they were tears of joy. His heart filled with excitement and he extended the mighty Excalibur high in the air again as the crowd cheered and chanted, "Li-the-gol," over and over. It was a surreal moment and as Michael floated down to the beautiful throne on the second tier of the Royal Spire he hoped this feeling could last forever. But he knew better.

About the Author

Josh Oelrich was born and raised in Alaska. He attended: Brigham Young University – Idaho and Utah State University, where he studied Music, English and Secondary Education. He has four grown boys and lives with his wife and sons in Utah. This is Josh's first published work. You can support Josh's growth as a self-published author by writing a review for Lithegol on Amazon or at his website and by spreading the word to others. Keep your eye out for Book 2 in the series: "Lithegol: The Legion Uprising."

To learn more about Josh, visit: https://www.joshoelrich.com/author or https://www.facebook.com/JoshOelrichAuthor